Flyover Fiction

Series editor: Ron Hansen

Stolen Horses

Dan O'Brien

UNIVERSITY OF NEBRASKA PRESS

LINCOLN AND LONDON

© 2010 by Dan O'Brien
All rights reserved
Manufactured in the
United States of America
(∞)
Library of Congress
Cataloging-in-Publication Data

O'Brien, Dan, 1947–
Stolen horses / Dan O'Brien.
   p.   cm. — (Flyover fiction)
ISBN 978-0-8032-3108-5 (pbk. : alk. paper)
I. Title.
PS3565.B665S76 2010
813'.54—dc22
2009049569

Designed and set in
Bitstream's Iowan
Old Style by R. W. Boeche.

Acknowledgments

I'd like to thank my siblings Scott and Mike for teaching me about brothers, Barbra and Bob Bonner for reading and commenting on an early draft, Jill for her love and patience, and Bill Harlan for lending me the flying Vietnamese cat story.

1

❧ 1 ❧

Since Erwin Benson was a young man he has been an early riser. Belief that the darkness would cease and that the sun was on its way made him hopeful and was as close to religion as he ever managed. From time to time he wished he could believe in more. He always knew that such a leap would have made life easier, but he could never take that leap and had to settle for the predawn. His early morning ritual has served him well enough. He was eighty-five years old and still working. Already this morning he made his way in the dark from his house on Calvert Street to his office in the Lakota County courthouse. He moved through the inky air like a blind man in his own home, navigated by the scent of waning lilac and columbine. By feel he found the office key on a ring of many. Without switching on the light, he puttered with the coffeepot and wandered the three rooms of the county prosecutor's office waiting for it to perk. He glanced out the window and was pleased to find the darkness still exhilarating. There was still the sense of risk. There was a chance that today was the day the sun would not rise. Rising early was an act of faith.

When he finally turned on the light, the rooms illuminated dimly, as if by candlelight. Erwin stood in the yellow glow of the overhead and stared at the small statue of the town's founder, Henry McDermot. The statue had been on his bookshelf for a very long time. Long enough that he couldn't remember how it had come to him or who had sculpted it. The bronze had taken on a rich, green patina, but Henry McDermot was still middle-aged and he still sat a rangy cowpony like the ones Erwin could remember. The horse and rider appeared to be looking out over what Erwin had always figured was the valley of the Pawnee River. The legend was that Henry McDermot and his cowboys were bringing a herd of longhorns up from Texas in the late nineteenth century and found the fertile valley full of Indian horses. There was a smile on McDermot's face as if he was just then seeing the valley and the horses for the first time. There was a fight, a dozen dead Lakota warriors, and McDermot ended up with the valley, the horses, and the naming rights for the town that came soon after. Erwin Benson ran his long, liver spotted fingers over the cold bronze. He looked hard at the statue of Henry McDermot and considered the irony of having a bronze of the country's first felon in the office of the county prosecutor.

He let his old hand settle to the surface of his oak desk, touched the piles of papers, and sniffed the air for coffee, but all he detected was the ancient trace of cigar smoke. He used to love a good cigar but had to quit. He wasn't sure why he quit. What were doctor's orders to a man old enough to remember horses? He glanced back at the statue of McDermot, and horses filled his mind. Personally, he never liked them much, but he was aware that they ran in the blood of human beings and that Lakota County had had a special relationship with horses since before the county was organized. When Erwin was a boy, even though most of the country was running on gasoline, Lakota County still ran on horsepower. Interspersed with the Model A's, horses lined the streets of McDermot on Saturday nights: thin little cow ponies, long-legged saddle horses, bucket-footed plow horses pulling family wagons. Horses were there from the beginning. They were there with the Lakota before white settlement. They were the first sign of power and status, and at once the last gasp of mobile wealth and the first sign of stationary empire. He knew full well that everything, even the big things, changed in cycles, and that there was a good chance that horses would return. He had lived through most of the great orgy of cheap gasoline and never had to deal with horses. That suited him just fine, but he knew there were others who would be happy when the cars ran out of fuel. Erwin thought about this as the coffee began to perk. He supposed there were genes for loving horses and that most of the old-time citizens of Lakota County inherited those genes from their forebears. The genes would be intact when they were needed again.

That got him thinking about what else had been passed down from Lakota County forebears—an insuppressible work ethic, honesty, faithfulness, racism, cruelty, greed. Of all people, perhaps Erwin Benson best knew that the inheritance of his fellow citizens was a mixed bag. Since he began his career, his job had been to keep a lid on four generations of Lakota County men and women. He was the oldest serving prosecuting attorney in the state of Nebraska by ten years. He'd been in office for nearly sixty years, but until recently there was no one who really wanted the job. He ran unchallenged nine times. Even when there was a Republican governor he managed to win reelection. Of course things were changing and he expected to be opposed vigorously next time around. There was a new attorney in town, John Tully. Nice young fellow, Erwin supposed. Smart, rich family from over around Omaha. Perfect hair, pressed suits, squeaky clean, lots of smiles. A young, single, wealthy, well-connected attorney who was going places.

"Humph!" Erwin said aloud. Standing at the window with the rising morning light on his rumpled brown suit and the tingle of whiskers on his cheeks, Erwin suddenly felt impoverished and frightened. It is a feeling that has swept over him since he was a boy. He has learned that it doesn't last long. That it goes away if he refuses to think about it.

He was born in 1915 to the owners of the local mercantile, Erwin and Sally Benson. Through the years some people who knew his father called him Junior, but Erwin never liked it. His dislike must have shown, because from the beginning his enemies called him Junior to try to get his goat. He knew enough to ignore them, but they reveled in the contempt on his face. Except for the two years he spent at law school in 1932–33, he had lived in McDermot his whole life. Married a local girl, Lucy Adams, and loved her still, even though he buried her ten years before. They raised three good kids—gone off to Minneapolis and Chicago because there was nothing for them in McDermot. There were grown grand-kids now, about the age of Erwin and Lucy Benson when they came back from Lincoln after law school.

They were back in McDermot in time for Erwin to practice law for a couple of years before the rains stopped completely. After things dried out it took only a year for his practice to go bank-rupt. By then there was a little daughter to think about, and he was looking for work out of state when Governor Hanes appoint-ed him prosecutor in 1937 because there was no one who would run for the job. He had been the youngest prosecutor in the state then, and now was the oldest. Of course, in the beginning the job was to foreclose on farmers and ranchers for the banks. But Erwin Benson wouldn't do it, and that was the first time politi-cians in Lincoln got mad at him. There was an almost immedi-ate movement to remove Junior Benson from office, but he held on until his term was up, and by that time he had felt the first stirrings of an independent orneriness he would later become famous for. He informed the political machines that he had got-ten to like the job and ran for another term. In those days there were more farmers and ranchers than there were bankers and politicians, so he won by a landslide.

In the last few elections his margins of victory had narrowed, but if for no other reason than longevity and that famous orneriness, he was still a force in Lakota County. He had some power.

The coffee was perked and the usually stale office now smelled of rich French roast. Linda Anderson, his secretary, assistant, and political advisor of thirty years, would be there in an hour, and by then he wanted to have two briefs read. She'd start tidying up the instant she arrived and the stillness would evaporate. Mornings were his time to think, and as he poured his first cup he wondered if he had ever really craved power or if it had just collected on him from the years. He couldn't recall a time when, at the back of his mind, he didn't have the desire to stick it to the sons of bitches. He knew that was a species of power-craving, but the question Erwin wrestled with as he sat down at his cluttered desk was, how do you know the sons of bitches from everyone else? It was a tricky question, and he was aware that a lot rode on the answer. Some would say that *he* was the son of a bitch, and that bothered him. But he didn't let anyone know it bothered him—that was very important. He tried to use his power judiciously. Tried to prosecute the guilty parties and tried to make sure they paid for their crimes. Usually his job was straightforward: the bad guys broke the law and he made them pay. But sometimes the good guys broke the law and then he had to decide if they should be prosecuted or not. That approach worked much better when Lakota County had only two thousand inhabitants. Everyone knew the good guys from the bad guys back then. But the coast people had discovered McDermot. The rest of the county, the ranches and the little towns, were dying on the vine, but outside money had found McDermot. The population was growing by ten percent a year. The decision to prosecute was hard, and sometimes Erwin Benson wrestled with it for weeks.

He was fully aware that the determination of guilt is supposed to be left to the judiciary. The way it is laid out in ninth-grade civics class is neat and simple. Even law school makes it seem clean. But the real world was sometimes very different. He considered the real world as he sipped his coffee and looked out his window at the brightening sky. He smiled at the solid evidence that the sun was going to rise once again. Then he looked to the clutter on his desk and began rummaging for the briefs he had been wanting to study.

❧ 2 ❧

The night was shotgunned with stars, and even though it was August, the speeding Ford Expedition pushed a cool cushion of air over the road ditch as it passed. The gust laid the brome grass flat and buffeted the ears of the jackrabbits that ducked down and winced as the kids whizzed past. The car made very little noise, just a whoosh and the lingering whine of tires against the blacktop. Inside, the radio was blasting a song the kids knew from MTV. The radio signal was fading as they put miles behind them, and the girl tried to tune in another station, but there was no tuning knob. Ford Expeditions are all digital. She was not used to such a radio. The boy was driving too fast to help. He tapped his hand to the staticky beat, shrugged his shoulders, and laughed like he was perfectly content. The girl pecked at the radio's buttons and finally found another station. Then she turned up the volume even higher and moved in as close to the boy as she could. He took his hand off the steering wheel and pulled her tight. Her hand settled high on his thigh.

Stealing the car had not been their plan. They hadn't intended to do anything except drive the boy's pickup to the deserted end of the bluffs and spend a few hours exploring each other's bodies as an anesthetic for the pain that would come when the girl went off to college. But a tire went flat and the boy pulled out all the tools before he found that the spare was flat too. He threw the tire iron into the gravel. "Shit," he said, "that's the way it always is."

The night was warm enough, and the girl was happy to walk the remaining quarter mile to the park. But the boy was antsy and disappointed. He had pulled two cans of warm beer from behind the pickup seat and they sipped as they walked. The boy talked about the high school basketball team he would play on come winter. It was the only reason he had gone back to school for his senior year. But their looming separation was heavy on his mind and he grew more serious, talking about whether or not he would stay in school after the basketball season. "You're off to college on a big-time scholarship and here I am, still killing time in McDermot."

It was true enough that there wasn't much for either of them in their hometown, but she knew he had to have a degree to do anything. She told him that after he graduated they'd get their chance, that they could get out of western Nebraska and never come back. The girl told him she had no idea what she would do when she graduated from college, but she wanted to do something and she intended to do it with him. She toyed with her beer as they walked but didn't like the taste. Still, it was nice being there on that warm summer night. She felt grown up, like everything was going to work out.

They lost interest in the beers before they got to the park, and when they came to their special place, where they liked to lay and watch the stars, they found another car in their spot. They stood in the road and watched the car windows for movement that never came. The kids came together and had begun to kiss each other on the face and neck when they heard voices far off, through the trees, and near the river.

"They're down on the river." The boy left the girl and moved to the driver's side of the Expedition. He peered into the open window. "They left the keys," he whispered.

"Tad, we can't."

The boy held his finger to his lips. "Just a little ride," he said and slipped in quickly so the overhead light was on for only an instant. "Hop in."

They knew it was crazy, but they stole the Expedition without hesitation. The first thing Tad said after they squealed away from the park was that he was going to get into a lot of trouble. "I'll take you home," he said. "They might get me because of my pickup, but if they come for you, tell 'em I forced you into it." He was frightened but smiling with the excitement. "Take you home in style."

"I don't want to go home," Annie said. She slid over and under his arm. They were going fast by then and they were both scared. The radio was tuned to the station that the Expedition's owner had been listening to. Annie turned it up and was surprised that she recognized the song. "I don't leave for a week," she teased. "Let's just go to Salt Lake."

"Salt Lake?"

"Why not?"

He shrugged and smiled. "I got school tomorrow."

"Then we'll just pretend we're going to Salt Lake."

They were headed south and Tad knew that Salt Lake was more west. He was pretty sure you went over into Wyoming, to the interstate highway, then crossed the continental divide, where you hit the Utah line. He'd never really thought of Salt Lake except as the place full of Mormons. "Salt Lake it is," he said and gave the Expedition more gas.

It was just after the radio station faded out and Annie finally found another station that they passed a Nebraska state patrolman coming from the other direction. They were not paying attention and trying not to give a damn, so they didn't notice it was a patrol car when it passed or see it swing around in the rearview mirror. They were going fast enough to be several miles ahead of the patrolman by the time the flashing red lights came on. When Tad finally saw the lights he thought the policeman was chasing someone else. Then it dawned on him that they were busted. "Oh, shit."

Annie looked at his face, then over her shoulder at the distant flashing lights. Then they looked at each other and, even before she spoke, Tad mashed the accelerator to the floor. "You can beat him," Annie said and turned toward the front to watch the telephone poles and black haystacks flip past.

They were on Highway 27, following the Pawnee River. The lights of McDermot had just disappeared in the rearview mirror when suddenly there were three deer standing in the headlights. The Expedition was instantly among them. Everything was going lightning fast. But for Annie, as soon as the first deer skittered off the road, motion slowed and she could see exactly what was happening. Tad had missed one deer by swinging left. She felt the car braking, sliding a little, then straightening. She saw the second deer hit the front left fender and fly off the road, tumbling in long flailing loops up and backward. They were still on the road, but Tad could not miss the last deer. They hit it dead center and the whole world shifted to the ditch. The Expedition was still on its wheels when they went through the barbed wire fence along the pasture. Then they were airborne and everything went silent.

The next thing Annie knew she was sitting in the prairie grass with the patrolman's flashlight in her eyes. "Do you know your name?" he said quickly.

"Annie Simmons."

"Anyone with you?"

"Tad Bordeaux."

The deputy swung the flashlight toward the wrecked Expedition. It was upside down and looked as if it had dropped from the sky. The flashlight beam focused inside the Expedition to where Tad hung limp over the steering wheel. The deputy didn't want Annie to see so he pointed the light away and onto the left front tire. She would always remember it rotating slowly in the feeble light.

𝒲 3 𝒲

Once in a while Steve Thurston would call out in the night. When they were together, Gretchen Harris could feel him rolling and she knew he was dreaming again. As soon as he cried out he'd jerk up to a sitting position with his green, hooded eyes wide open, and stare straight ahead into the streetlight outside her window. There was always the need to comfort him, but she found out early that he wouldn't talk. She wanted to help him, wanted to ease his pain, but his silence made her suspect he was dreaming of another woman. If he was, he wanted to get away from her. He would never lie in a cold sweat wondering where he was or what was happening. The dreams were too familiar to frighten or disgust him. Like the ache in his knees or the stubble on his chin, the dreams were part of him. Gretchen remembered one particular morning when she lay in the dark and watched him swing his long legs over the edge of the bed. She wanted to touch him but something in his posture told her that her hand would not help. She knew from the beginning that, no matter how this man moved her, there was something in Steve Thurston that no one would touch. He allowed himself only the luxury of rubbing the back of his neck with his own hands. He squeezed the muscles hard and let his eyes go shut again for just an instant.

Gretchen watched him stand up, naked, with just the yellow glow from a distant streetlight illuminating the white parts of his body. He'd often told her that he felt like an old man, but when he bent to search for his clothes, he looked solid enough. Better in Gretchen's eyes than the shirtless young men who worked for him. She watched him without a word, taking in the square shoulders and the long muscles of arm and leg. The muscles had enough definition left to create a mosaic of soft shadows on his skin. Gretchen watched the back of his head and recalled, from the night just passed, the shaggy, salt-and-beach-sand hair against her shoulder, his warm breath tumbling across her chest and over her nipples. He found his jeans and slipped them on like slipping into water. In the nearly three years of their intermittent intimacy he had never worn underwear. The rough jeans pulled over the soft parts of his body and then there was the gentle slap of leather on denim as the heavy belt found the last loop. It took a moment for him to straighten out his work shirt—one sleeve was pulled inside out—and she heard the tiny sound of his callused hands against the denim.

When the shirt was straightened he pulled it on like a winter jacket, collected his boots and socks, and began to leave. "Hey," Gretchen said. He turned as if caught in the act of something vaguely shameful and smiled the little-boy smile she loved.

"Need to get out of here." He glanced at his watch. "Running behind. Jake will be getting up soon."

"I know. I just wanted to say good-bye."

The smile came again and Steve moved back to the bed with boots still in hand. He lay down on top of Gretchen and pressed his stubbly cheek firm against hers. He let himself relax completely for a few seconds and his weight felt warm and Gretchen wanted him to stay just where he was. His breath was in her ear. "Good-bye, baby." Then he was up and moving out to the kitchen where, if Jake caught him, it wouldn't look so bad.

Gretchen lay staring at the ceiling, trying to sort out what she felt. Part of it was inadequacy. She was a hometown girl, and even though Steve was also from McDermot she felt he was somehow suited for a different world. She tried to express that to him once and he only looked at her, bemused. From then on she kept those thoughts to herself. Now, from the kitchen she heard his feet slip into the boots with soft pops. Then a little, gentle heel tapping on the tile floor to settle the jean cuffs over the boots, the suck of the back door opening, and the concussion of its closing. She rolled over and looked at the illuminated digital clock. It was five thirty: a good half-hour before the first hint of sunrise. Gretchen snuggled back into the covers and closed her eyes to see if sleep would come again.

Across town another woman was waking in a different way. Eleanor Stiener's coffeepot had just begun to perk. It was fully automatic, and the perking had been preceded by a melodic alarm that eased her into the day. The sheets were sheer and the pillow was satin. She awoke with a clear head and a mind that leaped into activity. As on many other mornings, she had been dreaming in the past, and it took her thoughts a moment to catch up with the present. At first she suspected it was just one of those old local legends. But somewhere in the hills above the Pawnee River there was supposed to be a deteriorated but elegant stone house. A week or so after she moved from Chicago she thought she might have found a photo of the house. But there were two photographs, filed in separate folders, at the McDermot library. One was of the beautiful old Victorian house, its lower level made of huge stone blocks and its upper level covered with what looked like cedar shingles. A second photo was of a different house, smaller and unfinished but made of the same stone as the Victorian. A lone, nondescript man stood by the still-unhung front door. Eleanor had always been a local history nut; she never could get enough of where people came from, who owned what house, who remodeled it, when, why? She liked the hard facts of history and tried to stay away from the personal stuff. But here in McDermot she'd found that the personal stuff was mixed so tightly with the hard facts that sometimes they couldn't be separated. She could not determine which of the pictured houses was the one of the local legend that fascinated her so.

The stones in the fuzzy black-and-white photographs were certainly hard facts, and the look on the face of the man who stood beside the half-finished house was nearly as hard. There was nothing written on the back of either photo, just a note on the outside of the folder that said, "Early Homesteaders—Lakota County." The dimensions and style of the Victorian suggested that the picture had been misfiled, except for one detail. The stones were not only similar to those of the unfinished house but also very similar to the stones in some of the oldest buildings on McDermot's quaint main street.

When Eleanor asked the librarian about the photo of the unfinished house, she held her glasses up high on her nose with an index finger and looked hard at the image. Finally she admitted that she couldn't vouch for the truth of the story of an old bachelor who had built a stone house to win the favor of a woman who finally jilted him. She couldn't even guess if either of the pictured houses could be the house of the legend. But another nose-long look at the photo made her think that, judging from the background, the unfinished house in the picture might be above the Pawnee River breaks. Somewhere south of town perhaps. Eleanor knew the Victorian house in the photo was very old for Lakota County, but the librarian felt sure it too was indeed in the county. She believed it also might have stood on the breaks above the Pawnee River, and that it might still be out there.

It didn't take long for Eleanor to find her way to the Pawnee River breaks. The first day she drove the road south along the river, she got the feeling that these rolling hills held magic. The topography was different from any landscape she had ever seen. From a distance it looked fairly flat, but as she grew closer she saw that the land pitched at surprising angles. Most of her life she had lived in Chicago, married to a mortgage banker who still practiced in a prestigious partnership downtown. They had lived in Oak Park in a huge old house built forty years before Nebraska was even a state. She had always thought of Oak Park as home. But when she saw the Pawnee River breaks she felt oddly at ease, captivated by the gentle curve of land, fascinated by the ever-changing shadows.

The divorce was five years in her past. Eleanor had had the misfortune of coming home sick from her volunteer job as an arts administrator to find her husband of twenty-two years in bed with one of her best friends. The details are not important except to say that after a cruel and vicious time in court, she needed a fresh start. She began searching the Internet for a job and found that the newly formed McDermot Area Arts Council was looking for a director.

The idea of simply picking up and moving frightened her. She hadn't traveled that much alone and was probably even more shattered by the divorce than was apparent. She was nervous about going to Nebraska for the interview, but something seemed to be pulling her westward. She was apprehensive, but once she arrived she was pleasantly surprised at how lovely and historic the little city of McDermot really was. For a variety of reasons, such as safety, a sense of community, and lower taxes, people from all over the country had been moving to town recently. There was a new and vibrant awareness of the arts and the culture. The old railroad depot had been tastefully restored and served as the Arts Council headquarters. The potential excited her. It could all be delightful. What was perhaps an even more pleasant surprise was that the Arts Council board seemed to like Eleanor, too.

By Thanksgiving break of his sophomore year at Grinnell College, Eleanor's only child, Allen, was pressed into service moving his mother to the middle of nowhere. After the months of attorneys and fighting, she'd ended up with an amazing settlement, a fraction of which would have bought the nicest house in McDermot. But Eleanor wasn't ready yet to commit to a house, so she moved into one of the new condominiums that had been constructed on the south side of town. It was a beautiful condo with a marvelous view of the bluffs and the river. Though it was brand new and had never been lived in, she had the place completely remodeled and appointed with leather and stainless steel furniture shipped in from Denver. The kitchen too was stainless steel with granite countertops. Skylights were installed so the yellow winter light would bathe a couple of watercolor landscapes she'd brought from Chicago. When Eleanor was finished, despite the fact that it was new and without history, she was sure that she owned one of the loveliest homes in McDermot. She wasn't sure if that said more about her taste in decorating or about the town of McDermot.

But nice as it was, the condo couldn't take the place of the big, old rambling house she had overseen in Oak Park. She would sit at the window after work with an iced tea, or perhaps a cocktail, and look out over the Pawnee River. The fact that she did not miss her old life surprised her, but she was not surprised to realize that something was missing. It was impossible not to feel that the missing piece was out there, somewhere among the shadows of the rolling river breaks.

When she took on the volunteer position of president of the McDermot historical society, she began to learn that although the town had only been around a little over a hundred years, it still had an impressive history. The other thing she learned was that unlike Oak Park, most of McDermot's history had taken place outside the town, in the country, among the pastures and coulees, dependent on such things as water, weather, and grass. The town had seen small booms and busts in mining, agriculture, and even timber. From time to time money had come to the area, and as a result there were some nice older homes. In her spare time she haunted the community collection at the public library, pored over family histories transcribed from tapes, and published her research via copy machine for modest dissemination. She began to track down the Victorian house in the historic photograph. The first good clue was a newspaper article, dated June 1889, announcing that construction had begun on a stone "mansion" southwest of town. Those first months, after she'd settled into the Arts Council job, she drove the roads of Lakota County and spent a disproportionate amount of time driving southwest along the Pawnee River.

It was on one of those country drives that Eleanor caught sight of a large old house of pale red sandstone and weathered shingles down a long driveway above the river. In the beginning, having come from the suburbs of Chicago, she was shy about snooping, but with each trip past the house she drove slower and slower. After many such trips she finally ventured up the quarter-mile-long driveway. When it was clear that the house was vacant, she drove boldly into the yard and took a good look at the deteriorating gingerbread porch, the wooden shingled turret, and the tall, beveled glass windows. Though in sad repair, it was, by almost any standard, grand. She walked the neglected yard and reached out to touch the stone walls. There was warmth stored in the soft red stone, and Eleanor Stiener was sure that the house was redeemable. Once she knew the place was real, she began asking the right questions. The locals called it the Butler place, but according to county records, someone named Carlton Lindquist from Fredericton, New Brunswick, was paying the taxes on the house and over two thousand acres that surrounded it. After a little more research Eleanor found that the house was eligible for a historic restoration grant and she wrote Lindquist to inform him of what she'd found. She hinted that she might be interested in buying the place if it could be severed from the bulk of the land. She never received a reply. As time passed she came to think of the house with a pity usually reserved for living things. Still, on many mornings, when awakened by soft prairie light coming through the skylights of her condo and by the smell of the waiting coffee, she slowly realized that she had been dreaming about a lady of a manor house, walking the hardwood floors of the stone Victorian, overlooking the valley of the Pawnee.

4

His uncle, Arvid Thurston, was the first person Carl Lindquist saw when he got home for good after a thirty-year hiatus. Besides the obvious effects of age, the only discernable change in Arvid's appearance was a tic he had developed that caused him to study his hands a great deal more than Carl remembered. That first day home, in the fuzzy morning light, he watched Arvid roll his hands slowly as if he were trying to remember where all the scars came from. Arvid leaned back against the yard fence after greeting Carl, and as if he were searching for residue from the handshake, he looked down and pondered the deep lines and the ropy veins.

His hands weren't really dirty. Like a lot of the old-timers, he had always been clean and, most days, freshly shaved. When Carl was just a child Arvid told him that no matter how tough things get, if you shave, you feel like you're still human. It made no sense to Carl at the time, but now, after thirty years in a real world not half as severe as Arvid's, he understood. "It helps to slick back your hair too," Arvid had said. "Even if it's thin and gray and not much left." He was addressing his own two boys, Steve and Bob, and their older but less rugged cousin, Carl. Arvid's wife had been the sister of Carl's father. The Thurstons were Carl's extended family. The old folks were all products, in one way or the other, of the Dirty Thirties. Carl and his cousins had missed the thirties by a decade, but on that morning of Carl's return the memories of the fifties were thick around the Thurston place, and he remembered with some pain how hard those years had been. It was the reason he had gotten out.

There was a little oil and grease ground permanently into the skin around Arvid's fingernails like some aborted homemade tattoo. That had always been a standard feature with the old-timers, too. To get an idea of their lives you had to ignore the stains and look down the length of each finger. Consider the knots. What made the knuckles swell? How had the skin gone waxy and thin?

The first Saturday Carl was home he drove the three miles over to the Thurston place rather than walk the mile and half through the pastures the way he used to do. He'd already run into cousin Bob so he knew a little about what had happened to the place and to Arvid, and to Bob and Steve. Carl and Bob had been excited to see each other and jabbered about several things at once. But when it came to the fact that the Thurstons had fallen on hard times and that a stranger had offered them enough for the ranch that they had to agree to sell, both men went silent. Half the original Butler place had slipped out of family hands, and that fact forced the cousins to suffer an instant of silent realization. The world had shifted, as it always did. But this time it was not redeemable. Ranches broke up all the time, but they were never put back together.

Carl was interested in borrowing an air compressor to power the spray gun he had rented in town to paint the porch of the old house. The sun had been up for less than an hour, and though the air was calm, it was still cool. Carl found Arvid leaning against the gatepost of his front yard. Well, it really wasn't his front yard anymore. By then, it belonged to an attorney named John Tully, but Arvid still lived in the house. According to Bob, Arvid insisted on keeping the right to live there. It was actually a simple life-estate clause in the sales contract, very common in such situations, but Arvid acted like the idea was his, and that it had been a masterstroke of negotiation. Actually it had been Tully's suggestion, and he figured that he was the one who had made the good deal. The house wasn't much, and Tully needed a hired man anyway.

"I still do the work around the place," Arvid said, "but now I work for wages paid by Tully." He laughed and spit a speck of tobacco off the end of his tongue.

To John Tully, the wages were insignificant, but Arvid was not as dull as Tully might have thought. "The good counselor thinks he gave me a screwing," Arvid said. "But he's not so smart. I'm making more now than I ever did owning the place."

He leaned against the gatepost wearing his ancient cowboy boots, jeans, and a worn jean jacket. Carl had forgotten how cold High Plains summer mornings can be and he was shivering. But Arvid, for all his years, was still as macho as they come. "Didn't want the good counselor to catch me inside twiddling my thumbs," he said when Carl chided him about standing out in the cold. "I'll be plenty warm once he shows up." He hunched up and rubbed his hands together. The dry skin caught and crackled. But the gesture couldn't have generated much heat.

"No gloves?" Carl asked.

"Hell, it's summer." Arvid spread his fingers out and looked at them as if he had just gotten a manicure. The index finger on his left hand had only part of a nail and Arvid stared at it closely. He held up the finger and volunteered a story that Carl already knew.

"Been that way for 'bout fifty years. You were probably a little young to remember, but I'll bet you heard me holler all the way over to your house. Pinched the son of a bitch between two fuel barrels on a hangover morning. First and last time I ever let myself get talked into switching to beer from Black Velvet—phewy. Whiskey on beer, never fear, but beer on whiskey is goddamned risky."

Arvid's hands were still stretched out in front of him, and much to Arvid's embarrassment, Carl reached out and touched the hollow place in the meaty pad of his uncle's right one. There was a question in the touch, and Arvid answered as if he'd heard it clearly. "Cold February day," he said. "When I was maybe fourteen. A horse nibbled too deep into a handful of corn. Good old horse though, wasn't his fault. Too cold to feel it." Carl knew that story too, but he was glad to hear it again.

Then Arvid flexed his fingers. "Still works," he said. "Better than any tool you can buy at Hardware Hank's." He laughed, "Guess that's where the word handy comes from."

"Amazing," Carl said, looking then at his own soft hands, "what we ask a pair of hands to do in a lifetime." He was matching Arvid's brand of metaphysics with a little of his own, and that must have frightened Arvid. The old man pulled his hands back to his body. "Why are some hands asked to do one thing and other hands asked to do something completely different?"

Arvid shoved his hands into the pockets of his jacket. "I don't know," he said. "Just the way it is." He shook his head as if to clear away all residue of the Pandora's box he had opened. Then, in the nick of time, they heard the first clattering of John Tully's diesel pickup.

Back on solid, physical ground Arvid laughed. "Just like an attorney to buy a fifty-thousand-dollar pickup truck to run back and forth to his new ranch. Just the outfit I woulda got if I woulda won the lottery." He pushed away from the gatepost but continued to mumble, "Four-wheel drive, Cummings engine, dual wheels on the back, extended cab."

Carl Lindquist smiled through his woolly beard. The grin made Arvid react. "But I couldn't afford nothing like that." He looked away but added, "And I got real shit to haul. The good counselor never carried anything heavier than his goddamned briefcase, but he got the heavy-duty springs anyway." He moved out to meet Tully, pushing off hard with his good leg and dragging the crippled one like a sack of grain. "Don't want to get mistaken for a lawn ornament," he mumbled.

The pickup came around the corner and pulled to a stop just four feet in front of them. Carl had been back in town only a few days, but he'd noticed a huge number of pickups like Tully's and a lot of eyes shielded by fancy sunglasses like the ones that stared out of the pickup cab at him. "How goes it, Arvid?" Tully was buoyant—a type A barrister and no doubt glad to be outside and away from his work for a day. There was classical music on the radio—Mozart—and the devilish side of Lindquist hoped Arvid would say something like, "Can't complain about anything but that fucking music." But of course the old man said nothing at all.

Carl stepped up to the pickup and thrust out his big hand. "Carl Lindquist," he said. "I'm moving in to the place just upstream. Be your neighbor."

"You bought it?"

"I should have said I'm moving *back* into the place upstream."

"Hell," Arvid put in, "little shit was born in that house." He was already climbing into the passenger's side of the pickup. "He come over to borrow the air compressor. That okay?"

"Sure," Tully said. "Want to be neighborly."

"Well, good," Arvid said. He tapped his fingers on the dash. "Let's get this show on the road."

"Going to start getting cold at night," Tully said only to fill the silent space. He was wearing a trim stockman's hat and a denim shirt and dropped the pickup into gear with his hand draped over the shifter. With another big smile Lindquist stepped away from the pickup, but Tully didn't move.

"Ponds will be freezing up in a couple months," Arvid said, to acknowledge what Tully had just said.

"That's one of the things I wanted to talk to you about," Tully said. "I've got it on my list. We'll have to bring the cattle out of the south pasture soon."

"Yep."

"We'll let them drink from the heated tank in the corral. That's a good idea, don't you think?"

"You bet."

"Good," Tully said. He nodded his head and glanced at Lindquist. He should have been moving by then, and Carl got the impression that part of this conversation was for his benefit. "Now I also have, on my list," he raised his eyes and read from a notepad held under the visor above his head, "reset corner post and gatepost."

"I got the tools laid out." Arvid pointed ahead and to the left. "Over there by the machine shed."

Carl took a couple more steps back and raised his hand.

"All right!" Tully said with more enthusiasm than was necessary. "Hey," he said, "great to meet you." Sounds of a piano and oboes were seeping from the speakers hidden in the pickup's dashboard and Carl wondered what Arvid was thinking. To him it must have sounded like icicles being knocked from an eaves trough with an iron pipe.

"You too, sir." Carl pointed at him and smiled. "I'll bring the compressor back as soon as I'm done."

5

They mostly seemed like memories, and they came to Steve Thurston deep in the night or in the daytime when he least expected them. They came when he was driving a nail into a two by four, or just waiting at a stoplight. It was a sort of déjà vu: sometimes things he had seen with his own eyes, sometimes things he knew had happened but he could not have seen. Sometimes he had no idea where the feelings came from. When they came at night as dreams, they could wake him from a sound sleep. In the daylight, his eyes narrowed into the distance and he sat paralyzed, even with traffic lined up behind, the cars blowing their horns.

One of the memories came over and over. It usually was triggered by a scraping sound—a slightly bent blade of a summer fan touching a particular place on the housing, a shop owner shoveling snow on the sidewalk outside his store. Unless he fought it, the scraping became the sound of a power take-off shaft on a 1946 John Deere tractor. The greasy shaft rubs against the shroud that shields it from careless fingers, shirtsleeves, and loose-fitting coveralls. The shaft is not supposed to touch the shroud but the metal is bent down, pushed against the high spot on the universal joint where a generation of Thurstons have stepped to mount the tractor from the rear: something everyone knows you shouldn't do, but everyone does. The power that turns the shaft starts in the iron heart of the tractor and moves to the rear with a force as constant as the wind. Steve could hear the pulse of the tractor beating out in scrapes of steel against steel.

If he let the memory go that far he was suddenly thirty years back in time and studying that shroud through the eyes of the kid he once had been. The steel is worn nearly through. He looks close at the coupler that connects the tractor to the implements it pulls. When the knuckle comes around he hears it scrape, scrape, scrape against the protective shroud. He was always a careful boy, and he had told his father about the weakness of the metal many times. Arvid agreed that it needed fixing, but he was not a careful man and never found the time. So, on a Saturday morning in the fall of 1966, when the temperature was in the midfifties and the long prairie wind was gentle and out of the west, Steve woke early. He was determined to unbolt the shroud, pound it straight, build it back up with welding rod, and replace it before his father woke up and came out to do the chores.

He was a halfback for the McDermot Pioneers, who had lost a close game the night before to their conference rival, the Grandby Broncos. Steve hadn't played well. When he made a touchdown in the first quarter, the crowd had begun to cheer, "Thurston, Thurston, Thurston." It was a cheer they used to do for his brother, Bob, when he played two years before. Now Bob was in Marine boot camp, but for a few minutes it felt as if a Thurston would again carry the Pioneers to victory. But Steve fumbled twice in the second half and there was no more cheering.

Even though Steve was exhausted after the game, he didn't sleep well. The football kept slipping in slow motion out of his hands. All night long the ball bounced crazily away, over and over: an endless, disastrous replay. Even when he came from the house that morning, limping from an injury he hadn't realized he had, he could feel the Bronco's hands that held him and see that damned football squirting out and tumbling out of reach forever. He could see the ball that morning in the light of the Nebraska sun, still low behind the river bluff. The ball tumbling away, bouncing crazily. Away and out of reach.

The shroud is held on with three five-eighths-inch bolts. In the dream he feels the sweet release as the lock washers give way and the nuts begin to back off in the socket cradle. The nuts and bolts drop to the dusty ground beside the machine shop. He picks them up in his right hand and wiggles the shroud off with his left. The weight of the shroud surprises him. It had been worn to half its original thickness by years of friction and it is as light as cardboard. Steve carries it into the far recesses of the shop where the anvil rests like a chunk of granite on a cottonwood block and welding tools hang on rusting ring-shank nails. An old two-pound hammer lies on the anvil, a relic stolen two decades before when his father worked a winter in the big gold mine in Deadwood, South Dakota.

The heft of the hammer is pleasant, the way it makes a young man's forearm muscles expand and pulse. The shroud slides over the coned end of the anvil where horseshoes were once rounded and shaped to fit the feet of workhorses long gone from the ranch. When the hammer comes down on the bent steel of the shroud it rings like the ricochet of rifle fire: pang, pang. And Steve thinks of his brother, Bob, due to ship out any day for Vietnam. Pang. He wonders if Bob will ever have to kill a man. Pang, pang, the shroud begins to straighten. Will some little yellow man kill him? Pang. That doesn't seem possible. He drives the hammer down harder, lets it bounce, plays with the elasticity of the steel. Pang, pang, pang. They'd never get Bob. He lets the hammer rest and thinks about his older brother, taller and broader than he is, but with the same rusty hair. His mind is on Bob, getting ready to go off to 'Nam, but the air is still filled with noise. Pop, pop, pop. No, they could never touch Bob. Steve figured Bob would have that war all wrapped up by the time he graduated from high school, even before he was eligible for the draft.

Only when he lifts the hammer again does he realize that the sound in the air is not coming from the hammer and anvil.

Pop, pop. Suddenly he knows that the noise is the sound of the old John Deere warming up in the cool prairie air. He drops the hammer and runs toward the sliding metal door at the front of the machine shop. It is like in the football game, he runs with every ounce of strength, but it is not fast enough. He is slogging through water, and as he runs, the tractor's popping gets louder, then slows. He's running as hard as he can, but it is not good enough. He is too late to stop his father from trying to step up to the tractor seat. The foot finds no familiar shroud and slips against the power take-off shaft. The engine lugs down as the power take-off shaft begins to wind up his father's pant leg. The coveralls twist cruelly, tight enough to stop the engine and the leg is wrenched unnaturally down and back. Steve's father looks up at him with eyes a son should never have to see.

6

Jake was always a thoughtful kid. Of all the blessings of Gretchen's life, this was the one for which she was most thankful. Some of her friends' children used their absent fathers to get at their single mothers. They could make a mom feel way less than adequate. But until the age of twelve at least, Jake had played none of those nasty tricks. In the six years after the divorce, Gretchen had made Jake's needs her first priority. She supplied the clothing, toys, love, and braces. More even than those earthly needs she had tried to set a good example. Originally she had three rules from which she hoped everything else would flow: She made her bed every day, she went to her job at the newspaper even when she didn't feel like it, and though she never thought she was religious enough, she attended mass most Sundays. Those rules gave them some structure. The little house was half paid for. It was neat and clean. Jake was happy, active in everything, especially basketball, but still she wondered if her rules were enough.

There was the problem of her relationship with Steve Thurston to consider. Manhood had begun to stir in her son and Gretchen knew that a good example was important. Jake's father, Eddie Harris, reminded her of that fact every time he called, which was not often. He had moved to Denver and saw Jake only occasionally. Though he was chronically many months late with child support and had needed the urging of a judge on three occasions, Eddie would shower Jake with gifts when the spirit moved him. He'd drop Jake off after rare father-son weekends and leave Gretchen to deal with the aftermath of his extravagance. Eddie was a Disneyland dad, only spending time with his son under circumstances that were sure to make him popular. His interest in Jake picked up a few years before, however, when he heard that Gretchen was seeing Steve Thurston. He had known Steve mostly by reputation, and when he heard that a man with so little to show for his life was seeing his ex-wife, he suddenly became a fountain of moral advice. Gretchen agreed that it wasn't right for Steve to sleep in her bed while Jake was in the house, but she didn't admit anything to Eddie. She told him it was none of his business and refused to talk about Steve in any context. But secretly she wondered if it might not be a mistake to be sleeping with Steve at all.

When they first met he had seemed stronger, more reliable, but now Gretchen was not sure he was a good bet for anyone's future. Few could resist being attracted to him, but Gretchen had never thought of herself as one who was particularly attracted to looks or sex appeal. The truth was, in the few years that she had known Steve, he never did much but get by. He had always worked part-time jobs in town, but at least when he was still living and working on the ranch, she knew where to find him. Now he was prone to surprise absences of body and mind. They said Steve was once a good cowboy, but even he admitted, "Cowboys are mostly museum pieces, and getting worse." He was kind enough. He could be thoughtful and was honest, but for some reason that Gretchen did not understand, he had never committed to anything like a long-term job or a woman. In the early days of their relationship she thought she had felt that changing with their familiarity, but in the last year he seemed to be drifting away. Eddie, one of the great losers in Gretchen's experience, had called Steve Thurston damaged goods. She felt like arguing but she didn't bother.

On the morning that Gretchen's life took its fateful turn, she heard Jake moving around the kitchen as usual. He was making morning coffee for his mother, and the smell of toast floated into the bathroom where Gretchen fixed her hair and applied as much makeup as she could bear. The other reporters at the *McDermot Gazette* teased her about her stingy ways with makeup. They called her "nature girl," but that wasn't it. She never felt like a nature girl. It was just that too much makeup made her feel like she was somehow lying, like she was pretending to be someone she was not.

Jake knocked on the bathroom door. "Mom?"

"Come on in, honey." Gretchen opened the door and pounced playfully at her son. She wrapped him up in an exaggerated embrace and made a long series of kissing noises on his neck. Jake struggled, but not hard. "God, Mom." He was still young enough to giggle nearly uncontrollably when his mother acted silly. "Oh, God."

"No, no," Gretchen said, "just call me, Mom. Do you love your mommy?" She tickled him—a tradition since Jake was very young. "Do you love your mommy?"

"Ahhhh."

"Say you love your mommy."

"Ahhhh. I love my mommy. I love my mommy."

"Oh, you're so sweet." Gretchen kissed him loudly and let him slide, exhausted, down the wall to a sitting position. Then she stepped over him on her way to the kitchen.

When Jake recovered, he came into the kitchen too. They stood at the counter, Gretchen drinking coffee and eating toast while Jake devoured a bowl of cereal and an orange. School had just begun for the year and the logistics of getting to and from had not yet been established. "Are we driving this morning?" Gretchen asked.

"Nope. It's Robert's dad's turn."

"Basketball tonight?"

"Practice."

"What time?"

"I don't know, maybe seven to nine."

"Well, is it seven to nine?"

"I think. I'll call you at the paper if it isn't. You're driving."

"Taking or picking up?"

"Pick up, I think."

"Okay. Supper at six and I want your homework done before you go to practice. Understand, rubber band?"

"Got it."

A car's horn sounded just as the telephone began to ring. Jake leaped for his backpack laden with thirty pounds of books and basketball equipment. "Bye, Mom." He was out the door before the phone rang the third time and the house seemed instantly empty. It settled hard on Gretchen that Jake would soon outgrow days like this.

The phone rang again, and even though Gretchen knew she had to hurry to answer it before the answering machine, she hesitated. It was still only seven thirty, too early for telephone solicitors or social calls, and as soon as she said hello, she sensed in the following silence that the call was important.

"Miss Harris? This is Ida Miller." The voice was breathy. "From the hospital. I'm one of the ER doctors."

"Have we met?"

"Not really. I heard you were asking some questions." The tension in the woman's voice was clear, but Gretchen had no idea what she was talking about. The week before, she had interviewed a few people with an eye toward doing a feature on the regional hospital, but she didn't remember an Ida Miller.

"I was up at the hospital a week ago," she said.

"Look," Ida said. "I can't talk right now, but we need to get together while I've got my nerve up."

"Nerve up?" Gretchen hadn't planned to write anything controversial. She'd asked a few questions about the hospital's relationship to minorities, patients, and staff, but that wasn't the focus of the feature.

"Yeah, I need to sort of unload, and if I don't do it now, I may never do it."

"Well, sure," Gretchen said. "Let's talk. What time would be good for you?"

"I'm just finishing my shift. I get off in twenty minutes."

"You want to meet for a cup of coffee?"

"No. Nothing public." Ida exhaled into the phone. "How about the county park. Out by the Bluffs."

Gretchen hesitated. Ida Miller seemed too dramatic, too serious. On the other hand, what could it hurt? She glanced at her watch. There was time before she had to be at work. Besides, if there was a story in this, it was work. "Sure. What time?"

"Say, eight fifteen. Right there by the pond with all the ducks."

"I know it. I'll be there."

Ida hung up without saying good-bye, and Gretchen was left uneasy. McDermot was a small city but growing wildly. Wealthy people were moving in from all over, trying to escape violence and corruption. And of course, violence and corruption followed their wealth. Oddballs collected, and reporters at the *Gazette* had attracted unwanted attention. Gretchen was no celebrity, but as a feature writer she had a public persona. There could be someone out there with an ax to grind, who knew what?

She thought of all this as she drove her Jeep toward the rendezvous with Ida Miller. At the last gas station before the road to the Bluffs Recreation Area she stopped to call into the newspaper.

It was still early but Ryan Hooper, the editor-in-chief, always got to work early. She didn't want to raise concern unnecessarily but she wanted someone to know where she was. The *Gazette* had been promising cell phones for its reporters for a couple of years, but nothing had come of it. She pulled up to the single island of pumps. The Jeep needed gas anyway.

As the gas pumped into the tank she walked to the pay phone along the side of the building. She hated outside pay phones in the winter and on windy days, but that morning the sun was warm and the air was still. Standing in the sunlight for a few minutes seemed like a good idea. But when she got to the phone the old twenty-five-cent machine had been replaced by a new fifty-cent model—another sign that her old hometown was becoming a different place. She didn't have the right change so she returned to the Jeep and finished pumping the gas.

She paid at the counter and by then was running behind. Even though the required fifty cents was in her hand, she almost decided to forgo the call in the interest of promptness, but she forced herself to return to the phone. The phone was picked up on the first ring. "Hooper."

"Ryan, it's Gretchen."

"Yeah, what's up."

"Just wanted you to know that I'm on my way to meet with a woman."

"Congratulations. You finally gave up men."

"Someone who says she has some information on that hospital story we were talking about."

"Congratulations again. Why are you calling?"

"I wanted you to know where I was."

"Where are you?"

"On my way out to the Bluffs."

"Okay, what's this about?"

"It's a woman named Ida Miller. Says she's an ER doc at the hospital. She's being secretive and weird and I wanted someone to know where I was."

"You think she's a crackpot?"

"I don't know. She just sounded tense on the phone."

"Okay, let me get this down. Ida who?"

"Miller."

"Ida Miller at the Bluffs. You call me as soon as you're done with the interview. You don't call by nine thirty and I'm on my way out there."

"Thanks, Ryan."

"Get to work."

By the time she got to the parking lot for the Bluffs, Gretchen was five minutes late, but there was a lone Dodge minivan pulled up near where the trail to the duck pond began. It looked right except that the minivan had a license plate from Pennsylvania. For safety's sake, Gretchen jotted down the number on a notepad and slid it behind the Jeep's visor. She took another notepad from her briefcase and left everything else on the seat. Only a couple of years before, she would have left the car unlocked, but times had changed. So she clicked the door locks down as she stepped out into the warm sunshine.

Having grown up in McDermot, she knew the Bluffs like her own backyard. It was a hangout spot since before Gretchen was born. Eddie and she knew it well—perhaps too well. Notwithstanding the miserable four years of marriage that were the fallout from some of those hot summer nights with Eddie, she loved the park. Two-hundred-foot-high bluffs loomed up over a half dozen channels of the Pawnee River. Those hovering cliffs, combined with the thick woods along the river, created a sense of safety, a kind of hidey-hole that made a person think the rest of the world could never find them. There were paths running in and out of the willows that grew near the water, and since she was a child, Gretchen had played along that river. She had always felt at home there, but that day she hesitated for just an instant before setting off on the path that wound away from the parking lot.

The path made a turn around a group of enormous cottonwood

trees and came to the edge of the Pawnee River. She recalled how, in spring, those cottonwoods shed their silky seeds and the air was oddly filled with enough whiteness to make Gretchen think of winter. She hadn't thought of those warm spring "snowfalls" for years, and the memory enchanted her. Just ahead was a wide spot in the river, called the duck pond, where Eddie and she, madly in love, had skated during the real winters of their youth. But those cold, snowy winters had disappeared like their youthful love. Autumn days held no hint of winter anymore. They tended to be like this one, the air was warm and the pond still sported its summer fringe of green and growing cattails. On the observation deck built over the river, with a dozen ducks swimming below, stood a tall, middle-aged woman. The sight of her stopped Gretchen in her tracks and as fast as she had stopped she was embarrassed. Not only was Ida Miller still dressed in her light green hospital scrubs and white shoes, but more surprising, she was black. It wasn't that Gretchen was uncomfortable around black people, it was just surprising to see a black doctor in McDermot.

By the time Ida Miller turned fully and saw her, Gretchen was walking again. They met at the steps that led up to the observation deck and Ida held out her hand. "Gretchen?"

"Yes. Sorry I'm late."

Ida waved the apology away. She had light brown eyes, a laser-like stare, and she wore horn-rimmed glasses fastened behind her neck with a golden chain. "I'm glad we could get together," she said. "I'm not permanent at the hospital and I wasn't going to say anything."

"Not permanent?"

"I'm a traveler—a locum tenens." Ida could see that Gretchen was not understanding. "Could we walk?"

"Sure. I'd rather." Gretchen stepped backward down the two steps and onto the path.

Ida came down too—her soft-soled hospital shoes made almost no sound. "Sometimes public hospitals have trouble with staffing," she said with a smile. "For the last six years, I've traveled around. The kids are off on their own and I can get a job about anywhere." Ida said nothing about a husband, and though Gretchen noted that lapse, she didn't ask. Ida smiled in what might have been a gesture of thanks. "There's work for me just about anywhere. I wanted to see what this country is about so I decided I'd just move around. Stay a year here, six months there. There's a lot of places that are growing too fast and need docs like me."

Gretchen was not sure she wanted to hear Ida's story. She was afraid it would make her ashamed of the citizens of McDermot. "How long have you been here in McDermot?"

" 'Bout six months."

"When will you leave?"

"Not sure." She held a finger to her cheek as she walked. "I sort of thought about staying."

"But now you're not sure because of what you want to tell me?"

"Not really. It's happening everywhere. I just wanted you to know that it's happening here too." She grinned to herself. "But I always keep my bags packed."

"I'm sorry," Gretchen said.

They'd been walking along a wide, flat section of the river, coming up to a place where, in the middle of the nineteenth century, a group of prospectors supposedly crossed over. The water slowed and the back-eddies were dotted with errant grasshoppers struggling for the banks. Ida looked at Gretchen out of the corner of her eye. "How can you be sorry? You don't even know what I'm talking about."

"Well, no." A fish rose from the depths of the pond and snapped one of the grasshoppers from the surface. But it was too fast to see, and both women turned toward the sucking sound in time to see only the whirl.

"This isn't about me," Ida said. "If that's what you're thinking."

Gretchen fumbled for a word but finally just nodded. "Okay, what do you want to tell me?"

"Well, something happened this morning that might interest you. Should interest everyone. There was an accident out on the highway. Boy got hurt pretty bad. Good chance he's going to die."

Gretchen's notebook was in the pocket of her jeans but she didn't bother reaching for it. "What's his name?"

"Bordeaux. Came in the same ambulance as his girlfriend. Her name was Simmons. She wasn't hurt bad, but the boy had bad cranial trauma. Big-time neurological stuff."

Gretchen hoped she was wrong about where this was going. Bordeaux was a Lakota name. "What happened?"

"The boy came in all busted up and we did what we could to get him stable, ran the right tests, decided he probably needed a craniotomy. Leastways he needed a specialist like we don't have at the hospital and he needed one fast."

Gretchen knew a little about what Ida seemed to be getting at. The hospital had recruited its first neurosurgeon about three years ago. It had taken several hundred thousand dollars in equipment and perks from the nonprofit hospital to lure him away from where he was. It was a big story for a middle-sized Great Plains town, but the new story was that the hospital was having a hard time holding onto its specialist. The neurosurgeon whom the community had gone out on a limb to recruit was now part of a group housed in a new clinic set up to compete with the area hospital that had recruited most of them. "High Plains Medical Clinic?"

Ida rolled her eyes. "That'd be the place. Right across the street, and those guys are 'sposed to be on call for this kind of stuff. It's my job to get the Bordeaux kid the best care I can, so I call over to HPMC and after a few false starts and being put on hold for a few minutes, I get the neurosurgeon. It's Dr. Cring, who happens

to be the director of HPMC. They've connected me to his home."
Ida stopped walking and turned to Gretchen. "Now I want you
to know that what I'm about to tell you doesn't have my name
attached. It happens all the time. I don't get paid what the specialists over at HPMC get. I still need a job, understand?"
Gretchen nodded. "Off the record."

"Off the record." Ida nodded back, smiled, and continued walking along the trail that began to bend away from the river and
under the canopy of cottonwoods. "So by the time we do the ER
evaluation and get the kid stabilized it's a little after five o'clock
in the morning. Five sixteen to be exact. We keep records of all
that sort of stuff. Records about everything." She shook her head
as if the very thought of all those records exhausted her.

"Dr. Cring sounds like he's awake already. Those surgeons get
up early. Cring does a lot of administration now, but he's still a
hotshot surgeon and used to the hours. So he's up and I tell him
what the situation is, and the first thing he asks is what's the
patient's name. As soon as I tell him, he tells me to call Flight
for Life and get him flown to Denver immediately."

"That's unusual?"

"Yes!" Ida said. She raised her eyebrows far above the horn-
rimmed glasses and rolled her eyes. "Even a hotshot surgeon
can't tell what's wrong with a person without looking at them."
A crack in her professional bearing had developed, and Ida took
a moment to regain her composure. She cleared her throat. "Usually a doctor needs to at least evaluate a patient before he sends
him off."

Gretchen was confused. "I'm not sure I understand what you're
you saying."

Ida tilted her head down and looked over her bifocals. "Cring
didn't want to treat him."

Gretchen nodded but still wasn't sure what Ida was getting at.

Ida shrugged. "He's done the same thing with Black Elk, Janis,

Two Bears." Ida shook her head again. "And he's not the only one."

"So HPMC is refusing to treat Indians?"

Ida held up both hands. "No, no, no, no." They had made a loop on the trail and she stopped at nearly the same place she stopped before. "This is way simpler than a race deal."

Gretchen stared blankly. "If not race, what?"

Ida shook her head in disbelief. "It's money, girl. Sure, HPMC doesn't want to work on Indians. But it's incidental that they're Indian. Who they don't work on is poor people. Uninsured people. Underinsured people." They stood two feet apart. Ida had worked herself up again and Gretchen wasn't sure how to take what she was hearing. "Cring knows an Indian name when he hears one and he knows the best he's going to get is Medicare rates. Wise up," Ida said. Her eyes were dark with anger. "These guys are carpetbaggers. What do you think that new clinic is all about?"

Gretchen began to wonder again if she had a nut case on her hands. "I have no idea," she said.

"The whiz-kid specialists get all the private payers—the well-insured folks—and, hello, the regional hospital gets stuck trying to provide the same care for half the money. It's called cherry picking."

They were moving again. Their cars were just ahead. "We end up with a two-tiered health care system," Gretchen said.

"On the mark."

"And you think I should write a story about Cring."

"It'd be nice, but I know how these things go." They'd reached Ida's car. She put one hand on the hood as if she was feeling the heat that the sun had imparted to the metal. She had calmed herself down. "I just had to say something to somebody, had to get it off my chest." She took her hand off the car hood and held it out to Gretchen. When they shook hands, Ida's was very warm.

"I wanted someone with some power to know about what happened this morning."

Someone with some power? Gretchen had never thought of herself that way and the shock of the responsibility made her want to respond to Ida with strength. She thought about reassuring Ida that something would be done, but she was realistic enough not to promise.

"Thanks for calling," was all she could say. They smiled at each other and Ida started to get into her car, but Gretchen stopped her with a touch. "What happened to the boy?"

Ida looked directly into Gretchen's eyes and it was then that Gretchen realized that Ida was older than she had thought. She was likely a grandmother. "Last I heard," she said, "he was in the airplane on the way to Denver. All alone and fightin' for his life."

7

The construction business around McDermot had been good for several years, and in some ways the boom had saved Steve Thurston. Since the ranch had been sold and the money used to pay the debt that had accumulated since before he could remember, Steve had been working full time as a carpenter. He liked the work all right. It was good to see his labor amounting to something. Day after day he watched the new suburban houses going up. The sites changed from simply country, to empty lots, to houses with conveniences that he could hardly imagine. The project he was working on was a big, post-and-beam house for the man who started the Internet access business in the area. He happened to be a realtor of long standing in the community, and there was no way to know if the money for the house came from the Internet or from the real estate office. It didn't matter. The house was huge and expensive and the contractor Steve worked for figured they'd be busy for most of the winter.

Even though it was a warm day and real winter was probably several months off, there was a feeling in the crew that they needed to hurry and get the house closed up. They were all born in the panhandle of Nebraska, most came off ranches, and all knew it was important to be able to move inside when the nice days started to evaporate. The plumbers were working now, and Steve was on the roof, ramrodding a couple of guys who had just graduated from high school. They were ready for the plywood sheeting that went over the rafters. The next step would be tar-paper. Soon they'd be ready for the colored steel roofing that was all the rage in new construction. Steve had seen steel used for high-end houses years before on a rodeo weekend over at Jackson Hole, but he never thought he'd see it in McDermot. This house would have a light-blue steel roof. It would be the first light-blue steel roof within two hundred miles.

But first they had to get the rafters sheeted. The day was per-fect for handling the four-by-eight-foot sheets of plywood: there was no wind, and even though it was warm, it wasn't unpleasant. A pallet of fifty sheets of plywood had been lifted with a forklift onto the flat roof of the garage, but old-fashioned muscle power was the only way to get each sheet up on the roof for nailing onto the rafters. It was tricky because some of the pitches were steep. Steve was forever telling the crew to be careful. They didn't need any accidents. He knew the boys' parents, had known the boys all their lives. For some reason that Steve could not even guess at, they looked up to him and usually did what he said. That meant that, in some odd way, any accidents would be his fault.

When they got the sheets into position, Steve tacked them with a hammer and nails from his belt. When a row was tacked up they brought the pneumatic nail guns from the garage roof and fastened everything tight. They would leave the corner piec-es—the ones that needed to be cut to fit—for last. At that point Steve would go down to the ground where the circular saw was set up and the boys would start calling down the dimensions for him to cut. They calculated that the sheeting would be done by the end of the day.

Once Steve got the boys busy with the nail guns he took a moment to rub his face and stretch. He took off his ball cap and, with his fingers, combed back his damp hair. With his shirt-sleeve he mopped his forehead above his sunglasses. He nev-er really liked working on roofs: at the age of forty-nine, all the

45

climbing up and down was beginning to take its toll. He never imagined he'd be doing this kind of work at his age. It was always assumed that he and Bob would be running the ranch. No one in the fifties and sixties had actually promised it would turn out that way, but they all talked about how Steve and Bob's generation was the luckiest ever. To Steve and Bob that meant ranching and a chance for a life as good as their parents'. Steve thought about that and in two seconds had come to money. No, it wasn't the money that made a life better. He had more money than Arvid had ever had. Silver dollars, he thought, but silver dollars thrown into a hollow barrel. Even if you could fill it, it was still a hollow barrel. He'd grown up expecting something more than a hollow barrel. But whining didn't do shit. Circumstances changed. This new world rewarded different people for different things and men like him were no longer on the list; they had to get what they needed in other ways. It was a shame, he laughed, that he was too old to rodeo.

Standing at the very peak of the house Steve again ran his fingers through his moist hair. There wasn't much gray and it was still pretty thick, but that didn't matter to him the way it used to. Just thinking about getting old got him wondering again about what he should do about Gretchen. In some moods a good woman with a ready-made family seemed a real possibility, almost like a good idea. But sometimes he felt choked down and it didn't seem like enough. His opinion flipped from one day to the next, always had. Today he wasn't sure and simply replaced his cap and pulled it down tight.

A longing for a quiet life had forever been in his dreams, but when he tried it for even a few days he would wake up antsy, staring into the distance. He had thought it would come with time, but somehow it seemed worse than ever. The thought of Gretchen and Jake caused everything inside to tighten and he had to admit that he didn't even know what he wanted to do with his own life, let alone Gretchen's or Jake's. They deserved more than he was giving but he wasn't sure there was any more to give. A breeze came up and reminded him that if an early winter caught them with the roof still not done they'd be up there laying blue steel with icy hands, balancing on icy beams. Worrying about weather the way he did was a flashback to ranching. He looked out over the river valley below and thought how wonderful it would be to have a house like this out on the old ranch, instead of a rusty green mobile home parked in the midst of fifteen others on the edge of town.

A pickup truck came down the still-unfinished driveway kicking up dust. Steve paid little attention, but the boys stopped working and peered down at the outfit. Ever since a couple of years before, when a crazy woman Steve had met at a topless bar up in Rapid City appeared with his lunch and a couple bottles of beer, people had taken a particular interest in his visitors. The boys working with him today were in high school when that happened, but it was still a small town. People loved good stories and being around the people they thought could supply them.

The whole thing was embarrassing. It was part of that mixed-up feeling Steve got when he thought of Gretchen and Jake. Hell, most of his life he hadn't known if he was coming or going. "Somebody for you, Steve?" The boys chuckled.

"Never mind. You two just keep nailing."

In fact, it *was* someone looking for him. When he looked closely he recognized the pickup of his brother, Bob. Steve was a little amazed that Bob had come all the way to the job site, a little amazed that he even knew where it was. They lived together in the rented mobile home at the edge of town but Bob was seldom there when Steve was there. Hard to say where Bob spent his time. He didn't talk much. The pickup turned around in a wide spot thirty yards up the driveway and parked pointing back out toward the road and as far to the right side as he could safely go. Bob didn't get out but he waved out the window for Steve to come down.

"You guys keep going, I'll be back in a minute." Both boys had stopped nailing and were trying to see who was in the pickup. "It's my brother, okay? Back to work."

Bob stayed in the pickup and let Steve walk all the way to the driver's side window. Steve peered into the pickup cab and found his brother wearing a dark blue watch cap like a sailor would wear in the winter and a fatigue coat even though it was seventy degrees. His long graying hair hung out behind in a ponytail. There were old telephone numbers written in dust on the dashboard and an opened jar of kosher pickles on the seat beside Bob's leg. "Yo, bro," his brother said. He was smiling, showing his poor teeth. "Guess what?"

"I give up."

"No, guess."

"I can't guess. I got nothing to go on."

"Guess who moved back to the old place."

"What old place?"

"The Butler place."

"Not Carl."

"You bet. Old Carlton retired from his teaching job. I seen him when I went out to say hi to Dad. He's moving in, fixin' the place up. Says he's going to hunt birds and read books for the rest of his life." Bob laughed and banged his steering wheel with both hands. "Ain't that something?" He reached into the pickle jar and pulled one out. "Ain't that something?" he said again and bit off a third of the pickle.

Cousin Carl was a few years older than Bob, but since the two ranches were right next to each other, and in fact had been one ranch until their grandparents had divided it between their children, all three of them were pals until Carl went off to college. Steve had always figured that Carl escaped the draft with a college deferment. That was fine with Steve; he'd dodged it when the lottery came into being. Only Bob got caught in the mucky middle. It gave Steve the creeps to think how those years played out, but he had to smile remembering Carl Lindquist. He'd seen him only a handful of times in the last fifteen years. "So how is the old professor?"

"Fine as frog hair," Bob said. "A little fat. Big beard. Still hanging out with those bird dogs. Spouting a little poetry."

"Is he getting ready to hunt those prairie chickens?"

"Oh yeah, he's champing at the bit. Says he's looking forward to seeing you. Wants us to go out hunting with him"

"I'm going out home to help sort cattle on Saturday." Steve pulled up short at what he'd said. It wasn't really home anymore, but he wasn't ready to call it the Tully place. "I'll stop in and see old Carlton."

"That's cool," Bob said. He laughed again and tapped the steering wheel with the heel of his hand. "Ain't that cool?"

"Yeah," Steve said. "That's cool." Then, "Hey, why don't you come out Saturday too?"

Bob shrugged. "I might."

Steve nodded. It was best not to push Bob. "Like old times."

Bob straightened up in the driver's seat. "So, I just stopped by to tell you about Carl 'cause I thought you'd get a kick out of it." He looked out the window at the construction site. "So, how's the job coming?"

"Good. We're going to have her closed up by winter."

"You got lots of time. Going to be an Indian summer." Bob was still looking at the building. "Big job, huh?" He took another pickle from the jar. "Want one?" He held the pickle up for Steve.

Steve shook his head. "You need some work, Bob?"

"Naw. I don't think so." He hadn't worked since the ranch was sold and the cows had gone to the sale barn. "Shit, working for some rich fuck don't get you nothing but dead."

49

"So does eating nothing but pickles."

Bob smiled at his brother. "Well, there it is." He looked back to the house and the boys nailing on the roof. "Don't worry, little brother. They can't starve me. I got my benefits."

"You earned 'em."

"Yeah, guess I did." He moved his eyes from the building back to his brother. "How 'bout you? You okay?"

"I'm okay." They looked at each other for just an instant.

"Weird fucking world, ain't it?"

Steve smiled. "Yeah," he said. "Weird fucking world."

Bob started the pickup. "Don't fall off that roof," he said. "Don't get drunk with the professor."

"You worry about yourself."

"I ain't worried." Bob pulled the gearshift into first and moved slowly away. He drove like an old lady. When he stopped at the end of the driveway only one brake light came on and Steve made a mental note to tell him about it.

8

Ryan Hooper was in an editorial meeting all morning so Gretchen had to leave a message on his voice mail. First she told him that she hadn't been murdered, then she said she needed to talk with him concerning the hospital story. She suggested lunch, but he didn't get back to her until after two o'clock, via e-mail.

"Lunch won't work. Coffee? 2:30 bagel shop?"

She e-mailed back, "Sure."

It was a quarter to three when Ryan finally came into Bluffs Bagels. He was a thin man with a light beard and thick glasses, but surprisingly hearty. Like most of the men raised around McDermot, he was a hunter and a fisherman. He even played some high school sports. He was two years younger than Steve, ten years older than Gretchen, so she hadn't known him growing up. Ryan was a good high jumper in high school and really smart. He'd gone off to college and come back and married a local girl. If he would have kept going he would have ended up at some big-city newspaper. The word was that he was a shoo-in for publisher when the present publisher retired. That would be good for Gretchen. Since she had chosen to marry Eddie Harris and had given up on college in her senior year, she was lucky to be working at the *Gazette* at all. She was the only reporter without a degree and she would never be anything else.

Hooper waved and went to the counter to order. He called over his shoulder to see if Gretchen wanted anything. She was almost finished with the cup of coffee she really hadn't wanted.

She shook her head and watched Ryan banter with the girl behind the counter. What is it with men? How can even a happily married man like Ryan flirt so carelessly? How can they be so good at it and then honestly be surprised when it turns out to be less than benign? It was a phenomenon that left Gretchen smiling and shaking her head when Ryan came to the table.

"What?" he said.

"Nothing."

His tray held three bagels with cream cheese, peanut butter, and honey on the side, plus a triple latté drink of some kind. Another phenomenon: Ryan could eat like this all day long and never put a pound on his lanky frame.

"So, what's the deal," Ryan asked as he smeared the cream cheese on an everything bagel. "I see you didn't get abducted by Ida Miller."

It was like Ryan to remember the doctor's name. "No, I wasn't abducted, but I got some interesting information."

"Yeah?"

"Yeah. What do you know about Dr. Cring?"

Ryan shrugged. "Neurosurgeon of some kind. Recruited heavily by the . . . ," he indicated quotation marks with his fingers, "'nonprofit' hospital. Stiffed the good people of Nebraska by taking what amounted to a signing bonus and is now the managing stockholder in a . . . ," he put more quotation marks in the air, "'for-profit' hospital—excuse me—'clinic'."

"You know all about this?"

"Some. This is the last frontier for the medical industry—only real center for two hundred miles in any direction, free of little encumbrances like managed care. Land of the libertarian. Milk and honey." He took a big gulp of his latté. "That much is not a story, if that's what you're thinking. Old news. Health care out here at this point in time is like the mining industry was a hundred years ago, only the people involved don't get as dirty in a real sense. Metaphorical dirt is another question."

"So, Cring and his buddies get their clinic built and set up and take the better cases?"

"Clinic is a euphemism. Makes it sound like it's not competing with the hospital. You bet they'll take the better cases. The ones that pay better, that is."

"And that's legal?"

"Come on, Gretchen. That's free enterprise. You wouldn't expect a mechanic not to choose the cars of the people who pay him the most."

"But doctors?"

Ryan shrugged again. "They're business people too. Half the doctors in this town are trying to get in with Cring. They're just a little behind the curve and they're nervous—sweating like Mike Tyson at a spelling bee. Got to remember: libertarianism is the grandchild of anarchism. The politics over there at H P M C would scare a grizzly bear."

"But can they refuse treatment just because someone's insurance pays less."

Ryan had been licking the honey off his fingers, acting like he wasn't paying a lot of attention to what was being said. It was a way he had of remaining noncommittal when discussing a story. But now he stopped and looked at Gretchen hard. "Refusing treatment?"

"I don't know. That's what Ida Miller said."

"Refusing treatment is a different matter." Ryan was still staring at Gretchen. "But let me tell you something. Accusations like that are tough to prove, they won't get a positive audience from the editorial board, and there are doctors over at that clinic making well over a million dollars a year. They buy the best legal help available." He smiled. "Not to mention the money they spend for advertising in the *Gazette*."

Gretchen sat back in her chair. The coffee was cold but she took another sip anyway. "A doctor in this little town is making a million dollars a year?"

"More than a million and there are several."

"And they still can't be bothered to save a young man's life?"

Ryan shrugged. "Latter-day Mr. Peabodys."

"So is refusing care a story?"

"Very dicey."

"Are you going to tell me not to look into it?" Gretchen was getting up, thinking now that she was running late.

Ryan shook his head. "I'm not going to tell you that, Gretchen. But don't get to thinking you're some *McDermot Gazette* version of Bob Woodward. It's a tough story. Chances of it seeing the light of day are slim."

She stood over him. "Well, I'd like to ask a couple simple questions of a couple people, nothing too heavy." Hooper shrugged, reserving judgment. "I'll report back to you before I write a word."

"Okay," Hooper said, "fine." He waved the last of his bagel in the air. It was his way of saying good-bye.

9

Don and Eleanor had been working all morning on an upcoming area arts show. It was the second year of hosting the juried show that Eleanor had initiated when she came to McDermot. A tremendous amount of work went into the show: a hundred applicants, twenty-five winners, fifty pieces, and out-of-state judges. They had just finalized the winners, and it was only a matter of time until the pieces themselves began coming into the gallery. Eleanor had a poetry reading scheduled for that weekend, and she had a dozen people to contact in connection with that. But since the showpieces had finally been chosen, Eleanor looked at Don and nodded toward the window. It was a beautiful late-summer day. They both stood looking at the blue sky, fingers of pale green cottonwood branches reaching down across the frame to the windowsill. Warm sunlight angled across the stark floor of the gallery.

"We've been working a lot of overtime on this show, Don. You must have a few errands you've let slide. I know I do. What say we take the afternoon off?"

Don looked hard at her. He didn't trust what he was hearing. Eleanor was known for being a workaholic. She took very little time for herself. When he saw that she was serious, Don jumped at her suggestion. "Please, Eleanor. Don't make me take the afternoon off. Don't make me go outside into that horrible prairie sunshine. I'd rather stay inside all afternoon. Please, oh please, don't throw me into the grass patch."

Twenty minutes later Eleanor was approaching the Butler place on the gravel road that wound east along the river. She still wore her linen slacks and satin print blouse, but she had shed the tailored coat and let her dark hair free to blow in the wind through the car window. She drove barefooted, and when she caught a glimpses of herself in the rearview mirror, she was surprised by the glow of youth that still flickered in her eyes and emanated from her skin. She had always enjoyed the reputation of being a beautiful woman. Some had called her handsome, classy—even classical. A lot of that had to do with her long, willowy frame and high cheekbones. It had been an advantage in life—something Eleanor had always considered an unearned gift.

The road she traveled followed one side of the wide valley that was cut eons before by the Pawnee River. The Butler place stood on the south rim of the valley, several hundred yards off the road, so that she was always surprised to come around a curve and see it looming on the horizon. The bay windows and dormers commanded the valley below, and she assumed that all the land between the ridge where the house was built and the river was part of the ranch. Modernists might have seen the tall gables as too imposing for the landscape, but the mindset of early twentieth-century architects was much different than that of contemporary builders. To Eleanor, the vertical lines, the shingled walls, the huge porch, the slate roof, and the gingerbread trim were magnificent. But oh, the house was in poor repair, and as always, the closer she came, the sadder she became.

A huge cedar post at the edge of the road, which once must have supported a mailbox, marked the beginning of the long, tree-lined lane that led to the house. She pulled onto the lane as she'd often done before and started up the incline toward the house. In her car was a picnic basket with bread, wine, and cheese. Eating afternoon lunches in the overgrown yard of the Butler place had become a rare but favorite treat. She would stretch out in the grass, dreaming of what the place had been and what it could be again. Now she guided her car under the neglected trees that lined the driveway, and she thought of all the prairie winds, freezing temperatures, and wilting sun blasts that had reduced them to little more than gnarled sticks. Someone had planted and cared for them, but trees were not a natural part of the prairie uplands and they needed constant attention. The trees had been trying to grow on their own for decades, each summer's growth drying and dying back to less than it started with in the spring. The grass was wearing them down, and would no doubt eventually reclaim the grove.

She was looking out the car window at the trees, wondering whether they could be brought back by careful cultivation and watering, when a big orange and white dog jumped from the underbrush. The dog paid no attention to the car but ran in long graceful bounds, zigzagging out into the prairie grass. Eleanor's car was nearly to the front yard when the big dog slowed, then came to a complete stop and stood stock still on a small grassy rise a hundred yards into the pasture. Its head and tail came up as if it had just won the Westminster dog show and a gallery of photographers was about to begin snapping pictures. Eleanor craned her neck to watch, wondering where the dog had come from and when it would start running again. She let the car keep rolling, and when she looked back up the driveway that curved around to the back of the house, she was shocked to find two pickup trucks parked near the back door. A large bearded man, with an enormous cardboard box in his arms, stood behind one of the pickups. Another man, this one with a gray ponytail, stood out near one of the dilapidated sheds.

No one had ever been around the house before, and at first she felt like they were intruders. But the man with the cardboard box looked directly at her and the broad smile on his face made it impossible to be frightened. By then she was within only a few dozen feet of him. He set the box down on the hood of the pickup and stepped out in the open. A Red Sox t-shirt stretched across his wide chest. Stout, hairy legs emerged from paisley shorts and ended abruptly in a pair of large, bare feet. Eleanor tried not to look at his legs as he held up a big hand in a self-assured wave.

On the strength of his friendly gesture Eleanor drove ahead and parked beside the pickup. She was nearly rigid with embarrassment but determined that it was best to just tell this man exactly what she was doing, so she stepped out of her car and thrust a hand out before her. "Hello. I'm Eleanor Stiener. I just came out to look at my favorite house. I just love it."

The man was perhaps sixty years old, with gray eyes and graying beard and hair. He smiled again. "I'm Carlton Lindquist. I own this place."

Eleanor's embarrassment immediately deepened. She hoped he didn't recall the pretentious letter she had written him. "Oh. Well, I'm the president of the historical society. I mean . . . well, really, I administer the local arts council but my interest in your house is from the perspective of the historical society."

"Yes," Lindquist said, "I believe I got a letter from you a year or so ago."

"Well, yes. I think maybe I did write to you."

"Sorry I didn't respond. The last year's been a little hectic for me. Tying up loose ends."

"Are you moving in?"

"Yes, finally. I'm moving back in. I was raised here."

"You were? You're not a Butler."

"My grandmother Christine Butler married Lars Lindquist."

"Ahh. But you grew up here."

"Took off right after high school. Came back whenever I could, mostly this time of year. I like the prairie, especially in the fall."

"It's lovely."

"But I've had a career that's kept me away."

"Oh?"

"Just retired." The smile burst out of his beard again. "I'd invite you in but I'm not quite ready for guests."

"Oh, no. No. I just like to come out here to get away from town. Now that I know the place is occupied I'll leave you in peace. I mean . . . well, you're fortunate."

Lindquist let her finish, then looked right into her eyes to make sure she understood that he was serious. "I wasn't just making polite conversation. I'd love to have you visit." The gray eyes were steady and they made Eleanor uneasy. "Eleanor Stiener, at the Arts Council office, right?"

"That's right." She leaned back into her car to fish a card from her purse mostly to get away from the pressure she was feeling. When she handed him the card he read it with great seriousness.

"Uh huh," he said. "May I call you when I get this place livable?"

Eleanor was thrown completely off balance. "Well, I . . . " She had to think for an instant. She wanted to say something fresh and witty but had to settle for "Well, sure. Call me." She moved backward toward her car and was almost inside when she remembered the big orange and white dog. "Do you have a dog?"

"I sure do. I like dogs."

"Me too. I don't mean I have one. I mean I like them. Is yours a big orange spotted one?"

"That's Tolstoy. Did you see him?"

"He was out in front of the house. Standing out in the grass like a statue."

Lindquist moved quickly for such a large man. "Wonderful," he said as he stepped past. "He's pointing birds." But he was not addressing Eleanor. He was already nearly around the corner of house, walking boldly, even without shoes. Eleanor exhaled and took a last look around the yard and up at the house. The other man, who she had forgotten about, stood shyly near the shed and turned away when she looked his way. She got back into her car and started out the driveway.

The dog was still where he had been, and now Lindquist was standing fifteen feet behind him. He didn't look Eleanor's way, and she kept driving because she didn't want him to think she was nosey. But she saw Lindquist step up beside the dog and stroke it several times before walking out in front. The dog didn't move, but from the grass at Lindquist's feet a large bird and half a dozen slightly smaller ones sprang into flight. They filled the yellow air around Lindquist and his dog, their silver wings flashing. The birds swirled up and around, decided on a direction, and closed their ranks. The man and the dog remained still but stood taller as they watched the birds disappear downcountry.

❧ 10 ❧

The construction crew worked a half-day on Saturdays, but on the first Saturday in September Steve took the whole day off. The first Saturday in September was the day the Thurstons had always weaned calves on the ranch, and though this year was different, he intended to help his father just the same. He called Gretchen on Thursday to remind her that he wouldn't be around Friday night. She knew the day was planned and that Steve had to be out at the old ranch house by five thirty, so when he said he planned to be in his own bed early Friday night, she shouldn't have been surprised. But when he mentioned it on the phone the line went cold. He knew suspicion was something she couldn't help. It had something to do with her ex-husband, who had not been completely faithful to her. It had to do with his own track record too. But more than that, it had to do with a feeling within her that made her think she was inferior. It made no sense, but low self-esteem never did. Steve didn't know how these things worked, but he understood that much. He also knew that his demands for independence did not help.

There was a woman Gretchen knew named Carolina Riggins. Steve had dated her years before he and Gretchen got together, and once in a while he still saw her around. She meant nothing to him, but right away when Steve reminded Gretchen about weaning calves, she brought up Carolina's name. She wanted to know why he couldn't come over Friday and he told her he needed sleep, he'd be working until six and up again at four thirty. "Right," she said, "Say hello to Carolina for me." Steve didn't say anything. He'd been in that position before. There was no sense trying to defend himself, because if he did, things just escalated and pretty soon her accusation would become a fact in her mind. If he let it go it would pass and be forgotten. Gretchen didn't mean what she said. She couldn't help it.

It had gotten worse lately. He didn't even try to talk her out of that craziness anymore. When he had tried, it seemed the more they talked the madder they got. The conversations degenerated into potshots that neither of them meant. Pretty soon they'd forget where the argument started and they were right in the middle of the crazy life they were both dead set against. Backtracking through one of those arguments was impossible. So, after a year of occasional nights that threatened to tear them apart, they had learned to dance away from the dangerous stuff. That Thursday night they disengaged quickly and hung up the phone, even though neither of them was satisfied with the conversation.

By four thirty Saturday morning when Steve woke up in his little mobile home he still felt unsettled. He thought of calling Gretchen and, though he didn't know what he'd done, try to make it right. But her irrationality might not have subsided yet. She might take the opportunity to accuse him of just getting in from a night with Carolina or who knows who? The thought of her sharp tongue made him think he deserved a night like she imagined, and in his early morning fog he wondered what Carolina was doing just then. He was making coffee in a half-conscious state. The curled and stained linoleum was cool against his bare feet, and he wore only a pair of jeans. The radio was tuned to the cattle market report out of habit and the sun was just pushing up a glow from below the horizon. His father was no doubt doing the same thing in the old family house. He wondered why he couldn't move back in with Arvid. They were just two old bachelors, neither one of them fit to live with anyone else.

One good thing about leaving the ranch was that for the first time in his life Steve had a little money because he didn't plow all his extra cash into the ranch. He was a decent carpenter and a good worker. He didn't get paid like the people whose houses he built—he wouldn't know how to spend such money—but he got paid okay for what he did. It was an honest job for honest pay and in a lot of ways it beat the hell out of ranching. When Bob and Steve were trying to make a living with cows, he never could afford a decent pickup. But as a full-time carpenter, he was driving a practically new one, and he enjoyed the way it accelerated and how tight the steering was. He drove the river road out to the ranch a little faster than he should have. The sun was barely up and there was no one on the road. With his coffee tight between his legs he pushed the speedometer up to seventy and let his almost-new pickup float.

Two mule deer stood at the side of the road, and Steve slowed in case they decided to make a jump for the opposite side. That was unlikely because they were on the prairie side of the road where mule deer feel safe. The other side was cottonwoods and plum thickets, the domain of whitetails. If it was whitetails on that side of the road, he would have expected a mad dash across the road in the direction of the river, but the mule deer simply stood and stared. He thought of the two kids that hit the deer with the stolen car. He wondered if they were mule deer or whitetails. Gretchen was worried about the one kid dying, maybe that played into her mood. It crossed Steve's mind that if the kid had known how differently the two types of deer acted, he might have driven right past them and nothing would have happened. But nobody cares about that kind of stuff. Probably those kids never even saw the deer until it was way too late.

The road made two more bends before the Butler place came into view. If Steve had time, he would have stopped in to see if Carl Lindquist really was home. Maybe he'd come back that afternoon, once the calves were cut off and the cows were driven to the back pasture. Maybe Carl would hear the calves bawling for their mothers and come over to the house. It would be good to see "the professor." He always had a little different take on life and Steve loved to hear him talk. It was good to listen to the professor, and it was good to talk too. Carl Lindquist was known for being a good listener.

Two miles beyond Carl's driveway was the turn to the Thurston place. The Tully place now. Steve slowed drastically because there was always a chance of a family group of grouse dust-bathing in the gravel of the driveway. That morning there were no grouse, only a group of noisy magpies in the buffaloberry bushes. They flitted wildly as the pickup passed, and the older ones headed out across the prairie in their trademark roller-coaster flight. Steve had to laugh. Magpies had split personalities: crazy suspicious in the country but tame as robins in town where they fed in dumpsters.

There were two old pickups in the yard, and for an instant he didn't recognize the second one. It was parked behind Arvid's, so not until he'd traveled far enough to see the bashed-in taillight did he realize it was Bob's. Steve wasn't expecting him to be there. He'd hoped he'd make it, but even when the three of them were running cattle together, Bob could not be counted on to show up when there was a job to do. It wasn't that Bob was lazy. He was once a good worker, but it seemed like being counted on to go to Vietnam used up all the dependability in him. But nothing about Bob bothered Steve, really. He didn't mind taking up a little slack for Bob if he had to. He was just glad they'd all be there together at weaning time, even though they'd be weaning someone else's calves.

Arvid stepped from the house with his coffee cup in his hand. No need to smell it to know it was half Black Velvet. Steve was as sure his father's coffee cup contained whiskey as he was sure that Bob's contained cocoa. Bob stood holding his cup just like the old man, and Steve couldn't help thinking that in some ways they were alike. But as they moved forward to meet him their likeness evaporated. Bob moved like a shadow and his father walked with the limp that changed everything. "Well, let's get this show on the road," Arvid said. "We're burning daylight."

The horses were in the pasture beside the barn and came ambling toward the fence when the three men approached. Steve went to the old granary while Bob and Arvid gathered up bridles and saddles from the shed. To get to the granary he had to pass the workshop, and as he did, the memory of that day long ago when he was still in high school came to him and along with it came the remembered sound of scraping. Metal against metal. Scrape. Scrape. He picked up his pace to get away from the shed—to kill the memory before it took hold.

There was a gallon pail in the granary, the same one that had been in the granary for thirty years, but for some reason there was no grain in the granary. There never had been. The horse grain was kept in the steel barrel that stood against the corral rails. Steve dipped the pail half full of oats as he passed the grain barrel on his way to where the horses stood stomping and pushing against each other, jostling for the first shot at the oats. Bob was carrying saddles from the shed and tipping them up on the swells on the ground beside the hitching rail. Arvid came with the bridles. This was one of the things Steve liked to remember most. It was still long before most other people were out of bed and the three of them were beginning a day of working together. "You want to ride Blacky?" Arvid asked.

"Sure," Steve said and nearly laughed. Of course he'd ride Blacky. Bob would ride Elsa. Arvid would ride Jack. It had been that way since all the horses were three-year-olds. Now that they were all past twenty, there was no reason to change.

They let each horse have its share of oats, then led them to the hitching rail. On the ground, the saddles balanced upright with saddle blankets lying over the cantles. They looked like some sort of monuments or like someone had abandoned them there a long time ago. Each man slid in beside his own horse and began the ritual of preparing it for gathering cattle. Bob talked in murmurs to Elsa. Arvid swore gently at Jack. Steve stroked Blacky, stood very close, and didn't say a word.

When the horses were saddled, they led them to the summer pasture gate. Arvid reached into his saddlebag for the pint bottle that was always there. He held it out to Bob, who shook his head, then to Steve, who took a little swig. Arvid downed two fingers, licked his lips, and put the bottle back in its place. He wiped his face with a shirtsleeve. "Let 'em out," he said.

Bob was holding the gate for the horses when the sound of a pickup engine drifted over them. It was a diesel but only Arvid recognized it. "He was supposed to be studying up for a trial," the old man said mostly to himself.

Tully's shiny new pickup pulled into the yard, and he waved in a stiff little salute through the windshield. He leaned out the window. "Hold on," he yelled. "Wait for me."

He was a nimble man with nervous strength. In a flash he had an aluminum ramp set up at the tailgate of the pickup and was backing his ATV toward the ground. Once it was flat on the driveway, he revved the engine and let it slow to an idle, sliding off to retrieve the black and orange helmet from the rear of the pickup. He looked silly with the bulky visored helmet atop his shoulders, but Steve shrugged. Didn't hurt to be safe. Like the pickup, the ATV was new and shiny. All the old-time ranchers hated the damned things, but even though the sound of an ATV was an insult to animals and countryside, more and more of them were replacing horses. "Easier to catch" was the joke, but the joke was never delivered with levity. Tully's ATV didn't roar, like the lightning bolts on the gas tank suggested it might.

It purred, and the horses didn't shy when Tully pulled up beside them. "Couldn't stand working inside," Tully said. Then he waved his hand to indicate the rising sun and the yellow light on the distant, eroding buttes.

Steve could see by the way Bob turned away that he didn't like Tully. But Tully didn't seem to mind or notice. His face was beaming like a kid's and Arvid smiled and nodded. "Morning, cowboy." They all nodded but Steve was disappointed that this man had interrupted his day with Bob and Arvid. Of course it was Tully's place, and when Steve saw how happy the guy was, he couldn't stay mad.

11

There had been considerable changes in McDermot's downtown since Carl Lindquist was a boy, and he tried to comfort himself with the thoughts of Heraclitus: There is nothing permanent except change. Still, like everyone, he supposed, it seemed to him that his town had lost something. It was a different kind of loss than the loss experienced in the fifties, or thirties, or the 1890s. The loss since the fifties was not, as they say, in terms of brick and mortar. He was a kid in the fifties and by the time he left for college in 1965 only Main Street was still active. Back then the side streets were lined with failed businesses from the times when McDermot was a mining town and, more recently, a thriving farm and ranch community. At age eighteen it was hard for Carl to believe that McDermot could lose much more. That was thirty years before people from big cities began nosing out places like this, a quarter century before the nation's prosperity began to pounce on places with relatively unsullied natural resources and population densities that could sustain civility. McDermot was fortunate to have the Pawnee River and the miles of accompanying bluffs. It was a scenic environment, and Carl concluded that what he was noticing in his hometown was another boom. The scenery boom, he thought. The solitude boom. Could panoramas and sunsets be mined like precious metal, trees, or topsoil? He tried not to worry about it. He would be dead before McMansions lined the bluffs.

By the time Carl came back from his exile, the downtown was relatively lively again with businesses finding enough profit—or outside money—to restore a few buildings that had been neglected since the postwar boom. Driving through his hometown, Carl saw the obvious changes that nearly anyone would say were for the better. Carl knew at a glance that his hometown had become the kind of place where summer softball leagues are popular and children are encouraged to play soccer instead of football. Snowplows were parked discreetly behind businesses, chain restaurants were being built at the edges of town, and people traveled almost everywhere by car. Things were shinier. On Main Street, people moved on the sidewalks that he remembered as nearly empty. But there was something missing: the pedestrians moved faster, they didn't stand on the street corners and chat like he remembered. They bustled between the newly restored buildings and nodded fleetingly to each other beneath the billboards advertising this and that useless item. "God! I do hate being such a cynic," he thought. "Curmudgeonhood is a curse."

One of the restored buildings was the address on the card that Eleanor Stiener had given him. Certainly he had known the building as a boy, but he drove by it twice, looking for a parking place, before he recognized it as the railroad depot behind which he had smoked his first cigarette. The little district of remodeled warehouses seemed to be a popular area. There was no place to park and he had to pull the pickup around the corner and down a half block. The day was warming, so he rolled down the passenger-side window to be sure Tolstoy got plenty of air. "Guard the wagon, boy." He rubbed the dog's big silky head. No need to lock the pickup. No one would bother it with "Leo" riding shotgun. Though Leo was facing forward, he looked at Carl out of the corner of his eye. Carl knew the look was demure coyness, but strangers often mistook it for the detached gaze of a crazed canine.

Carl strolled toward the railroad depot where he hoped to

surprise Eleanor Stiener at her work. Oddly, he had had to gather courage before heading to find Eleanor. He knew he was being forward, and at least twice he had nearly convinced himself to give it some time. But there had been something in Eleanor's face that haunted him. It was not the obvious beauty or the undeniable innocence that conspired with the beauty that would not leave him alone. Perhaps it was imagined, but Carl Lindquist believed he had seen something familiar in Eleanor's dark eyes. Perhaps it was his own penchant for mystery, but behind the erudite confidence of Eleanor's smile, Carl believed he had seen loneliness. It caused him to forget his usual caution. It attracted him like a magnet.

As if by providence, the first new store he passed was the High Lonesome Flower Shop. Without breaking stride he changed direction, entered the building, and walked directly to the cut-flower case. A woman about the age of his former students came from around the counter with a smile on her face that made him slightly nostalgic for those first few weeks of class when the freshmen were innocent enough to be openly interested in all they came across.

"Can I help you?"

"*May* I help you."

The girl smiled. "Excuse me?"

Carl smiled back, not at her, but at himself. "Never mind," he said. "It's just an old habit. Something I need to get over." The girl looked plainly confused and Carl took pity on her. "Yes," he said with a cheerfulness that approached the genuine, "you can help me. You certainly can. First, I need your advice. You look like a young lady who is used to receiving flowers."

She smiled again, her confusion behind her. "Once in a while." Now she was cagey. "Not really that often." She blushed and Carl was charmed.

"Well, as you can see," he said, "I'm an old man." The girl

generously shook her head and he couldn't help reflecting that a mere gesture from a woman can flatter a man of any age, but the more years on the man the more likely he is to notice and appreciate. It took him a moment to get back on track. "Old," he said. "But not too old to try my hand at attracting a particular lovely woman with a bouquet of flowers."

Now the girl smiled in a different way. A smile as old as the Rift Valley, Carl thought. She was amused but clearly took this situation seriously. She even winked. "We've got long-stemmed roses."

Carl fished his glasses from his shirt pocket. "Are they nice?"

"Very nice." She moved to the case and slid the door back. He still held his glasses in his hand as the girl leaned forward, but he slipped them on just as she bent over to collect a bunch of roses. He couldn't resist a quick glance at her perfectly formed posterior. Old man stuff, nothing serious.

Then the roses were under his nose and the odor was strong enough to clear his brain. "I'll take a dozen," he said. "No. Make it two dozen."

"Two dozen?" the girl was incredulous. "They're three dollars apiece."

"A bargain at any price." He pointed back into the case. "And throw in one of those yellow beauties for the sake of caprice."

"For what?"

Carl opened his mouth to begin an explanation but realized that it was no longer part of his contract. He let his face relax into a smile. "For the hell of it," he said.

The girl glowed. She was primping the flowers and heading for the counter. "I'm betting this works," she said, almost to herself. "Your lady friend is going to say yes."

Carl tagged along behind her. "But you don't know what I'm going to ask."

Now the girl was behind the counter tucking the yellow rose into the bouquet. "Don't matter," she said.

"Doesn't matter."

"Yeah." She tilted her head and smiled. "That's what I said."

❧ 12 ❧

Since Jake had basketball practice and Steve was helping his father with John Tully's cattle, Gretchen was adrift. Something was making her uneasy. She puttered around the house, cleaning things that were already clean, until she realized she was thinking of Annie Simmons and her boyfriend, Tad Bordeaux. She'd done some checking and found out that Annie was a good student with good prospects. The teacher she'd talked with shook her head when she spoke of Tad Bordeaux, but she smiled too. "He was always one to take a risk," she said. "Not a bad kid, just devilish." She looked at Gretchen and raised her eyebrows. "One of those boys who are hard to resist. Annie was as attracted as the rest of us." Then she shook her head. "She'll come out of it once she gets to the university."

"The University of Nebraska?"

"Full ride. Academics. Very rare." Another shake of the head. "She's a good kid. Needs to get over this accident and get out of this town."

Talking with Annie's teacher transported Gretchen back to her own high school days. Back then, when Jake's father was mentioned, eyes had rolled in the same way. That had always made Gretchen want to find out more. So with the men in her life out doing what they loved, she found herself thumbing through the McDermot phone book.

There was only one Simmons listed and the address was on

the north edge of town, an area Gretchen knew from growing up locally and from working at the *Gazette*. It was the part of town she was always told to avoid as a child: the part of town that yielded far too many tragic news stories. It was where the disenfranchised people of McDermot lived, where the broken families, the drifters, and the Lakota people lived. The address was only five minutes from her house, and she knew her curiosity would lead her to at least drive past the house. But before she committed to the drive, she called Ida Miller.

The phone rang five times before it was picked up, and just before Gretchen heard Ida's voice, it occurred to her that Ida might be sleeping, that she had likely just gotten off her shift.

"I'm sorry," Gretchen began.

"Sorry?"

"For waking you."

"Oh, you get used to it. I can get back to sleep in a few seconds."

So, Gretchen thought, I did wake her. "I'm sorry."

"Sorry, schmarry. I'm glad to hear from you. I figured they'd have put the kibosh on you. Maybe worse."

"They?"

"Your boss. The A M A. Somebody."

"Not yet. I'm still interested in your story."

"You heard he died." Gretchen stiffened. She had not seriously considered that possibility and it struck her that Tad Bordeaux was just a boy, only a few years older than Jake, the same age as Eddie when she had loved him with such intensity.

"No," she said flatly. "Nothing like that came into the paper."

"No reason to notify you. He died in Denver."

"But he was killed here."

Gretchen didn't know why she said that. After an awkward pause, Ida exhaled. "Sure was." She sounded suddenly tired.

"When did he die, Ida?"

"Last night. I called down to Denver and talked to a nurse. He lasted almost a week but he was pretty much gone by the time he left our hospital." Another sigh. "Time is real important with those head injuries."

There was another lull in the conversation. "I'm going out to Annie Simmons's," Gretchen finally said. "Do you know her?"

"No. Just saw her that night. Pretty thing. Young."

"I'll want to talk with you again." Gretchen knew she was speaking but felt disengaged from the conversation.

"I don't know how much I'll be able to say."

"We'll just do what we can."

"It's all we can ever do."

It was warm enough to wear shorts but Gretchen chose a pair of blue jeans, running shoes, and a cream-colored t-shirt. It wasn't professional dress but it was Saturday and she was doing this on her own time. She tied her hair back in a ponytail, pulled it through the adjustment strap of her Yankees baseball cap, and checked herself in the hall mirror. Not bad, she thought, then playfully, how could Steve resist?

The canvas top on the old Jeep was a pain in the neck in the winter, but on beautiful days like today, it made the Jeep into a toy. She popped the doors off and leaned them against the wall in the garage. They needed to be kept handy. Winter could come in a flash. She laid the top back carefully because it was already showing signs of cracking at the fold. Again she thought of winter. Despite the great technical swing toward comfort and security, winters, even the modern, diminished winters, were still a powerful presence in Lakota County. Winter, spring, summer, fall: though people tried to pretend otherwise, or simply didn't realize it, weather still dominated most lives around McDermot. That day the weather was glorious enough to have a positive effect on Gretchen. It nearly brought her out of the uneasy mood she had been in since the night before. She strapped the top down, grabbed the roll bar with both hands, and swung into the seat. As soon as the engine came alive she turned on the radio and tuned it to an oldies rock station. As if conjured just for her, the drumroll introduction to "Born to Run" was in full swing. She laughed at herself. Gretchen knew she was not born to run, but she liked the thought of it, and when she put the Jeep into reverse she let it squeal a little rubber as it jumped out of the garage and into the warm September sunlight.

All the way across town she left the radio volume up high. She loved the music but the other reason she didn't turn it to a reasonable level was that, right now, she didn't want to think too much about the story she was working on. That instant was the first time she thought of it as a real story. The Pulitzer Prize was not in her future. Still, she took journalism seriously and had a tendency to get very involved with the work. Whether it was a story on a new restaurant or a story about orchids, she made herself believe it was important so she could do her best. It was easy for her to see this new story as important but it was difficult to see it in print. She was not an investigative reporter and the thought of trying to be frightened her. Still, she hated to give up a story once she'd invested time in it. But as she drove, she told herself that stories got killed for one reason or another all the time and it was often not the fault of the reporter. "Forget all that," she thought. "Just do the work."

The Simmonses lived on Cherry Street, one of the main drags in an enclave that was not quite ghetto and not quite integrated with the rest of McDermot. There were a few nice homes on Cherry Street but most of the houses showed the telltale signs of poverty in their crabgrassy lawns, peeling paint, and broken screen doors. The Simmons house was more prosperous than most, but still, there was a car up on blocks in the side yard, a porch with a broken step, and a two-tone side wall where a well-meaning handyman ran out of paint. A Christian fish symbol hung beside the front door.

A well-dressed woman in her early forties came to the door and waited silently for Gretchen to state her business. "I'm looking for Annie," she said. "I want to talk to her about Tad Bordeaux."

"Who're you?"

"Gretchen Harris from the *McDermot Gazette*."

The woman shook her head. "We just got back from Denver. I don't think she wants to talk to you."

"I wouldn't blame her," Gretchen said. "I'm sure she's very upset."

"Yeah," the woman said. "She thinks her life is over, too."

Gretchen nodded. She had no trouble understanding how an eighteen-year-old girl could feel that way. It would be hard enough even after you learned a little about life. "I won't stay long."

"You going to put her in the newspaper?"

"No, I just want to know what happened."

The woman stared through the screen door. Gretchen didn't try to influence her decision with her expression. They looked each other over and in the woman's eyes Gretchen saw two things: she too was afraid that her daughter's life was over and she had no idea of what may have been the real reason for Tad Bordeaux's death.

Gretchen felt like she should let her know one thing. "I've got a little boy just a few years younger than Annie."

Annie's mother nodded slightly. She looked down at her feet, then up again. "Wait here, I'll see."

She was gone several minutes. When she returned she looked more like a concerned parent than the sad and skeptical woman who first answered the door. "She's in the back. You can just go around the house." Gretchen nodded, understanding that the woman was embarrassed about her home, and she turned to go.

"But please," the woman said. "Don't hurt her anymore. She loved that Tad, you know. They were counting on each other."

The derelict automobile in the side yard was a badly dented, late sixties Ford Mustang. A couple of kittens scurried under it as Gretchen passed, and when she stepped into the backyard another kitten ran for cover under a picnic table where a young, black-haired girl sat in a white t-shirt and bib overalls. When she saw Gretchen she stood up and turned toward her. It was hard to tell what she was feeling because her eyes were narrowed by fatigue. Gretchen feared it was resentment, but as soon as she grasped Annie's hand she knew it was not resentment that made the girl's eyes squint, but confusion and fear. Her handshake was weak and her eyes went soft and looked away.

Gretchen introduced herself and Annie nodded as if she knew the name. Her eyes never met Gretchen's but Gretchen understood she meant no offense and tried to pay attention to her body language. The way she stood, a little awkwardly, before she sat down, reminded her of Jake when he wasn't quite sure what to do. Gretchen had been thinking about this meeting since talking to Ida an hour before, but when it came to actually speaking, she felt as awkward as Annie or Jake.

"I heard about Tad."

The girl nodded. "I have to believe this is the way it is meant to be," Annie said. She sat upright on the picnic table bench and Gretchen joined her. She was cried out. Her eyes were red and her posture was drawn down with exhaustion. "I don't really believe in God the way my mother does but maybe she's right. He must have needed Tad up there for something or he wouldn't have called him." Her reliance on her religion was understandable to Gretchen but it was hard to listen to. For several reasons she felt terrible for this young girl, and found herself tapping a frustrated foot under the table. "They put him in an airplane, you know. Flew him fast to Denver, but it didn't work." Annie had no idea what had actually happened, but Gretchen had found out that the transfer to the airport took a half hour and the flight took an hour and a half. It was almost three hours before Tad received the care he could have gotten right there in McDermot. Dr. Cring and the staff at his fancy new surgery center had gotten an extra three hours of sleep that morning.

"So I just have to go on living," Annie said. She shook her head and generated one more tear. "I just hope it wasn't something I did, you know."

Gretchen reached out and patted her arm. "No, Annie. It was nothing you did." She let her hand rest on Annie's arm and sat quietly. But inside she was shaking her head.

"What happened that night?" Gretchen asked.

"Deer. We hit the deer."

"But before?"

"We were talking about school before we took the car."

"School."

"He wanted to quit," Annie said. "I told him he couldn't. But now look. I'm the one who's quitting."

Gretchen was confused. "Quitting what?"

"College. I'm supposed to go tomorrow but I'm not going."

"Give yourself a week. You can catch up."

Annie tried to smile but shook her head. "I don't know."

Gretchen patted her arm again. "It will be all right. Time," she said. "You just need time."

When Annie looked up, Gretchen was struck by how beautiful she was. Her eyes were large, and even though she had been crying, they were deep and very dark. Her skin was clear and healthy, and when she smiled it was impossible not to stare back at her with a kind of awe. There are few things more powerful than a young woman, Gretchen thought. She continued to stare, gazing as if mesmerized, into a nuclear reactor. Power comes early to women and it is brief. But for a short time the world stops to focus on their promise and energy. It is a power greater than that of the wisest old men. But they are almost always too young, Gretchen thought, to realize that power. By the time they understand, it is gone. She reached out and touched Annie's face. "You will heal," she says.

☙ 13 ❧

When the door of the McDermot Area Arts Council opened, it triggered a recording of the beginning of Gershwin's "Rhapsody in Blue." Eleanor heard it from her office but didn't give it much thought. She heard Don say, "May I help you?"

"I'm looking for Eleanor Stiener."

It was a man's voice that Eleanor didn't quite recognize. Ordinarily she wouldn't have paid any attention but something made her get up, go to her office door, and peek out. Don was looking up from his work at a large, bearded man holding a huge bouquet of flowers. A cross between a Viking and a hippie. It was Carl Lindquist, and at first, even though he'd asked for her by name, she thought he had come into the Arts Council office by mistake. Don's devilish eyes told Eleanor that he was thinking about jumping to his feet and asking if the flowers were for him. But Carl looked vaguely dangerous, so Don was not ready to try humor. He rose and came around his desk. "Oh. Are those for Ms. Stiener?" He moved forward to take the flowers. "How nice."

Carl held the bouquet out of Don's reach. "I'd like to give them to her myself. Is she in?" Eleanor ducked back into her office but kept listening. She felt somehow dishonest, but she could neither go back to her desk and wait nor step out to greet Carl.

"Oh." Now Don was blasé. "I think she's in. I'll check." He started to move away. "May I tell her who it is?"

"Tell her it's the squire of the Butler place."

"Squire. Yes, I'll tell her."

Eleanor hustled to her desk, sat down, and looked up as if she were clueless. By then Don was leaning against the closed door with his hands on his hips and a knowing smile on his lips. "You old tramp," he whispered. He pointed a finger at her and looked over the top of his glasses.

"What?"

"What? Oh, nothing. It's only Genghis Khan carrying a hundred pounds of flowers."

"What are you talking about?" she whispered with exaggerated coyness.

"I'm talking about the fact that you've been keeping secrets."

"Maybe."

"Does 'squire of the Butler place' ring a bell?"

Eleanor couldn't help smiling as she got up from her desk with all the nonchalance she could muster. "Maybe."

Don bowed away from the door and opened it at the same time. "My lady," he said as she passed. "I'll just find something to do here in your office."

Eleanor stepped out into the reception area and saw that Carl was looking at a series of framed glossy posters for concerts sponsored by the Arts Council over the past three years. He turned and his bright teeth appeared in the center of his beard. "Eleanor."

"Hello, Mr. Lindquist."

"Carl."

"Carl."

He stepped forward and presented her with the flowers. Behind her she shut the reception-area door in Don's face. But she was sure his ear was against the door, so she gave the oak a solid knuckle rap before stepping out to accept the flowers. "And blushing roses for your brow."

She'd received a few bouquets of flowers since her divorce, but never accompanied by a poem. "Bobby Burns?"

"Actually, it's Blake."

"Wonderful."

"With a touch of editing from Lindquist."

She took the flowers and looked up at him. "Better still," she smiled.

"Well, yes." Carl said. He took a deep breath. He was surprised to find himself flustered. Never mind, he thought. "I didn't come just to deliver flowers. I'd like to ask you to dinner."

"Dinner?"

"At my house. The Butler place to you historical types. The restoration is a long way from being completed but the grouse season is about to begin and I'd like to cook some up for you."

"Grouse?"

"Grouse. Don't worry, I'm an experienced if not talented cook. You'll enjoy it."

Eleanor's face was still in the bouquet and the roses smelled divine. "When?"

"My social calendar is not exactly full." He shrugged. "About any night next week would be fine with me."

"I like to be in bed early on weeknights." Eleanor blushed at the unintended double entendre. There was an awkward little pause and she imagined a tiny moan from behind the office door.

Carl did not let her embarrassment slow him down. "Would next Monday work? The season starts on Saturday and it would give me a couple extra days to finish the floor."

"I hope you kept the original oak." Eleanor said without hesitation.

"Of course." Carl smiled and raised his eyebrows. "Monday?"

"Monday will be fine."

Relief exploded on Carl's face. "That's the deal then," he said.

"What can I bring?"

"Absolutely nothing."

"I'd like to bring the wine. I have a nice wine cellar."

"Well," Carl said, "in that case how about a bottle of Terra Valentine, cabernet. A 1999?" He smiled at his own joke, knowing the wine was rare and extraordinary.

"Ahh, don't have the '99." She faked consternation. "Would you settle for a '97?"

" '97 Terra Valentine? Surely you jest."

"Not about wine."

Carl mumbled but finally spoke. "Well, yes. A '97 would be wonderful. I just didn't know there was any left."

Another smile. "Would six o'clock be too early? I love the sunsets over the Pawnee River from your yard."

"Six o'clock would be grand." He looked as if he was going to say more, but he came up blank. Eleanor began peeling away the paper from the flowers.

"Thank you," she said. "They really are lovely."

"It is my pleasure," he said. "It truly is. '97, huh?"

" '97 Terra Valentine. I'll bring two bottles."

There was another little awkward silence. "Well, then," Carl finally said. "I'm going home to work on the floor and the menu." He smiled broadly, started to say something more, but instead only nodded his head.

As soon as the door closed, Don leaped out from behind Eleanor's office door and, like a teenager, danced around her, pointing. "Trampy, trampy, trampy."

Eleanor smiled from behind the flowers. "Oh, Don. You're just jealous."

☜ **14** ☞

The cattle were in the usual places for that time of year: the high flat against the west fence, the wheatgrass ridge, the draw leading down to the big dam. Arvid and Bob loped their horses in a wide loop to put the animals between them and the corral, now a mile and a half away. They'd pick up any stragglers in the buffaloberry bushes. Tully and Steve set out for the high flat with the intention of pushing the main herd south and joining up with Arvid and Bob's bunch at the big dam. Then they'd move the combined herd down country and into the corrals where the calves would be cut away from their mothers for weaning. It was a time of year that made Steve light-headed with an odd, calm energy.

Blacky's registered name was Montana's Black Dancer, a name that had always stimulated a lot of ribbing from his friends. "What's the breeding of that horse?" they would ask. It was a straight line for the next guy to say. "Looks to me like he's out of Montana by Trailer." They told the joke hundreds of times but Steve never let it get to him. He knew it was because they envied him for owning such a horse. Strong and smart, Blacky had once been sort of famous. Steve had roped from him when Blacky was young and Steve had been in his prime. The silver buckle that Steve always wore had been won while riding Blacky. Back then, the lanky black horse had been one of a half dozen that Steve had ridden regularly, but he'd never had a horse to compare to Blacky.

Now he was Steve's only horse and getting too old for hard

riding. But he was still surprisingly strong, and when they started up the hill, through the rough country that led to the high flat, he was able to keep up with Tully's Kawasaki. It wasn't until the land leveled off that the old boy started to fall behind. But Tully didn't race ahead. He realized that Blacky was flesh and blood, that his heart, lungs, and muscles were no match for steel pistons. He seemed to realize that Blacky's strength had limits and that Steve had to conserve it for when they might have to run to turn a crazy cow. But it was hard for Tully to idle the engine down enough to let the horse walk. While Steve kept his heels lightly in contact with Blacky's ribs to stretch his walk out as much as possible, Tully made circles out into the grass and back. Steve had ridden the same route a hundred times but this was the first time he'd felt anxious about speed. It wasn't that Tully was pushing, it was mostly in Steve's head, and he tried to forget it.

When they came over the last knoll, where the high flat opens out like the top of huge pool table, Steve signaled Tully to go on ahead, run around the cattle that grazed a quarter mile ahead, and start bringing them back. He'd move up to the left and see that no wise old cow took her calf over the top and into the brushy draw where they'd be hard to find. Tully understood Steve's wave and shot off in a curve that would bring him to the far end of the flat and push the perimeter cattle to the center in the process. It was just the right move. Tully seemed to have some cow sense.

When they first talked about selling the place, Arvid had put great store in the fact that Tully claimed to be a farm kid, that his father had run a dairy in the eastern part of the state. "He's a farm kid with capital," Arvid said. "He might be able to hold this place together. Ranching without capital is like shooting pool with a rope. Don't work." He shook his head. "Ask me, it's 'bout time we cashed out to a farm kid."

"Probably had Mexicans milking about five thousand cows," Bob said. "Running a dairy these days ain't necessarily like being a farm kid."

Arvid just waved away Bob's grumbling. "He can't help the fact that he's rich. It ain't no crime in the United States."

"But that's what it leads to."

"Ain't going to mouth fight with you," Arvid said. "You're just ornery."

"So are you."

Steve laughed to think of Bob and Arvid arguing. Then he nudged Blacky into a slow lope to get into better position to pressure the cattle in the right direction. Tully and the ATV were already buzzing back and forth like an eight-hundred-pound sheep dog. The cattle were beginning to drift away from them and toward the dam where they'd meet Arvid and Bob's bunch. Steve was in the spot he liked best: a gentle presence that keeps the cows moving honestly. There was no need for fast movement or whooping and hollering. The cattle felt him back there, and that was enough. The gathering would come off without a hitch unless the big, old Hereford bull that Tully bought to use on the cows started causing trouble again.

Arvid and Steve had tried to cut the bull away from the cows in late July when they were moving the other bulls to a separate pasture. That day was nothing like today. These cattle were moving nicely and the cowboys didn't have to think much. But back in July, they learned that Tully's prize bull had a mind of its own and didn't like to be pushed. The bull repeatedly broke back from the other bulls to lope long and heavy back to the cows. When they pushed the bulls hard, he quit the bunch and headed for a deep brush patch in the bottom of one of the draws. There he stood until Steve urged Blacky into the prickly brush and drove the bull out while Arvid tried to get behind him with Jack. But the headstrong Hereford dove back into the brush time and again, until both Blacky and Jack were white with sweaty lather. "Piss on him, Dad," Steve said. "Let him stay out here 'til fall."

The bull's tongue was hanging out but Arvid wasn't ready to

quit. "We can't let him get away with this," he said. "He'll just get meaner. Chase him out one more time. I'm goin' to catch his back legs and drag his ass to that bull pasture."

Arvid was right. If the bull thought he could get away with pushing people around, he'd just get worse, but Steve wasn't sure that either of them had enough horse to pull the huge old Hereford anywhere. Arvid acted like it would be a cinch and shook down a loop of lariat. He looked old and battered sitting there on his old horse. Steve wasn't sure they had enough roper for the job either. Arvid was thin and his hat sat up on his head like it was a size too small. His Adam's apple was prominent in his scrawny neck. Who was the guy his father reminded him of? The guy who fought windmills. Ten years before, either of them could have heeled the bull and either horse could have dragged him about anywhere. But that was ten years before. Now, after all the changes, Steve didn't think much of their chances of making the bull do anything. But his father's jaw was set and so he took Blacky around to the other side of the brush and forced him to wade in one more time. The bull spun to face them, smashing brush with his horns like it was so many toothpicks. He swung his heavy head in a slow, powerful threat but Steve swung the knotted end of his rope and snapped him across the nose. The bull turned with a snort and broke from the brush just as Arvid began to swing the lariat around his head. The bull hadn't taken three jumps before the rope snaked out and neatly circled his hind legs.

Arvid would have caught both heels if he had been a little quicker. But he was a half beat behind, and the rope tightened on only one leg. The old man dallied on the saddle horn anyway and turned Jack hard toward the open pasture. By the time the slack went out of the rope Jack was moving at a ninety degree angle from the bull's path with all he had left, and when the rope tightened, the Hereford was pulled violently sideways. He almost went down, but instead, Jack was pulled backward far enough to give the bull some slack. The heel came loose, and when the lariat snapped back, the loop rolled limp and useless into the grass. Steve thought that was the end of it. But something in the bull's brain switched to a different frequency. He swapped ends like a cat and came at Arvid and Jack with horns lowered and legs churning. He caught Jack's rump with a horn on each side and knocked the horse sideways and nearly off his feet. Steve was already riding to help but had time to imagine what the bull might do to a downed horse or an old man afoot.

By the time he got there, both Arvid and Jack were safe. They'd made it to a small knoll that the bull refused to climb. He stood his ground, head low, eyes aflame, pawing, and blowing snot on the dust in front of him. "Goddamn his snaky ass," Arvid said from the top of the knoll. The old man was shaken but trying to build a new lariat loop as Jack danced under him.

"Forget it, Dad. We'll just leave him be."

"The hell," he said.

"Just leave 'im. He ain't hurting a thing." Steve had ridden up alongside Arvid and had his hand on Jack's bridle. With his eyes, he made it clear that he wasn't letting go until Arvid coiled the rope and tied it back to the saddle.

Now, as Steve walked Blacky slowly across the high flat, he shook his head at the memory of Arvid's face. He had seldom seen him like that since he was a boy, since before Bob went off to Vietnam. Arvid had been full of fire, mad as hell at the bull, but after a minute the sparks seeped back out of him. By the time the rope was coiled, his old hands had begun to tremble. That's what he remembered most clearly, his father's trembling hands. "That son of a bitch is dangerous," Arvid sputtered. "If this was still our herd I'd shoot that rotten Christer dead as hell." But it wasn't their herd anymore. It belonged to the man on the ATV whizzing back and forth across the grassy flat that also now belonged to him.

89

The cattle were moving just the way they'd planned. Tully was pushing them along happily. He was doing most of the work. Blacky and Steve were walking slowly, just keeping pace with the last cows and moving in the same direction as the herd. It was like cutting a board on the construction site with a handsaw. The second person doesn't need to do much, just hold up one end of the board to keep the saw from pinching, and the first man's job becomes simple. The cattle had been moving along in pairs, the calves slightly alarmed and sticking close to their mothers' flanks. The cows were all Black Angus and the calves were called black baldies, jet black with the white heads of their Hereford fathers. Now, as the pairs came together, the cattle blended into a river of black, the clean white calf faces bobbing along like Clorox bottles. They were heading downcountry in the direction of the dam where they'd rendezvous with the rest of the herd.

Steve cued Blacky to a stop on a small hill overlooking both the flat where Tully continued to push cattle in front of him and the dam where a few pairs were beginning to collect from the other direction. He let his hands, with reins held lightly, fall to Blacky's neck. This was one of the highest spots on the ranch and was always one of Steve's favorites. Blacky knew the routine. They'd remain there on the hill for a while and Steve would move around in the saddle to see in every direction. The old horse lowered his head cautiously, remembering his early days as a cow pony when he was never allowed to eat while there was a man on his back. Those days were gone; Steve was twisted in the saddle looking back at the Pawnee River and didn't pay any attention when Blacky sneaked his nose deep into a tender bunch of wheatgrass. The old-timers claimed that the low ground and river bottom in front of it was the flat where old Henry McDermot found the original herd of Lakota horses. It was said that the Lakota had stolen them from the Pawnee, who likely got them from the Apaches, who got them from the Spaniards. But Steve was only clear on the part about McDermot, because when he was younger he had stopped with Blacky on this very hillside and looked down toward the river. He had actually seen the colored horses blotching the green flat above the cottonwoods. A few Lakota boys had been sitting on wise old horses at the periphery of the herd. The boys took their job seriously and scanned the surrounding hillsides for Crow raiders. But they did not expect white men because none of them had ever seen a white man. They did not see McDermot's men winding stealthily through the cottonwoods. They had no idea that such a small group would ever try to steal their horses in broad daylight. They had only heard of repeating rifles.

Steve believed he had seen the Texas cowboys coming up on the boys. Somehow he had known that the longhorns were several miles south. He had heard them chewing the hard and nutritious northern grass, felt them gaining weight like they had never done in Texas. He had smelled the trail on McDermot's men and knew they looked on this herd as a bonus for months of driving wild cattle. They shot the first two boys from the cover of the trees and ran the other two down as they tried to gallop back toward their camp. He had watched as Joe Butler, his great-great-grandfather and Henry McDermot's foreman, rode to within ten feet of the last boy and shot him twice with a pistol before he fell. Steve has always believed that he watched Butler shoot the boy once more in the head as he tried to crawl to cover.

From his favorite hill on the ranch Steve had squinted his young eyes and had seen the first warriors come over the hill from what would become Butler's homestead. Fire from the trees thumped into them and their horses squealed as dead men reined them roughly to the ground. Twice that afternoon the Lakota tried to recover their horse herd, but they could not get close. Within days the longhorns grazed the river bottom, and McDermot's men have never really left.

Now, Steve looked back to the latest, tamest incarnation of cattle, and saw a single red smear in the otherwise blue-black stream running to the stock dam below. It was the bad Hereford bull that refused to leave the herd in July. The bull was happy where he was, and moved along as docile as any of the cows. Steve didn't expect any trouble from him. At least not until they got to the corral and started to cut him off—probably not even then. Tully was pushing the cattle ahead, and Steve's position on the little hill had ceased to be helpful. He pulled Blacky's head out of the wheatgrass and started down to intercept Tully. He moved slowly, trying to sort out what he knew about the land from what he felt.

The ATV was making uniform short passes behind the last of the cows and Tully was smiling like a schoolboy alone on a skating rink. When he noticed Steve, he smiled even wider and pulled the machine to a stop. "They're going good," he said.

"Just right," Steve said, "but let's let 'em bunch up and mix with Dad and Bob's."

Tully nodded and pulled the helmet off his head. His face and hair were sweaty, and some dirt kicked up by the ATV wheels had collected on his neck. He pulled one leg over the seat and sat sidesaddle. "They're going good," he said again.

Steve nodded and Tully pushed his short, brown hair back under control. "God," he said, "what a day." He indicated the entire earth and sky with the sweep of his hand.

"Beauty. Sure is."

Just then Arvid appeared behind the last cow coming off the east ridge. Bob came up from the right and filled the open space behind the whole herd. "Time to go?" Tully asked.

"Time to go. Push 'em easy. They should line right out for the corral."

John Tully and Steve fell in with Arvid and Bob at the back of the combined herd. Now Bob and Steve rode together, pushing the herd from the center, and Arvid and Tully worked the flanks to keep the animals together. The cattle moved like Steve had expected they would, the older cows leading the way through the last open pasture gate and the rest of the herd following them into the corral. The cattle swirled into the largest pen of the corral and Tully whizzed up and shut the gate like he'd captured a grizzly bear.

But there was still a lot of work to be done and the Thurstons, who had weaned calves for scores of years, fell to the job silently. Because he was the oldest, Arvid took the position at the sorting gate. Bob and Steve stayed on their horses and pushed the cattle gently his way. Tully parked his ATV, took off his helmet, and crawled up on the fence, ready to help his calves be sorted from his cows. But he wasn't sure what to do and saw immediately that things were under control. He sat on the top rail to watch and learn.

"Look at that son of a bitch," Bob said as they stood still at the back of the herd. Arvid had swung the gate open to entice a cow away from her calf.

Steve didn't know what Bob was talking about. "The cow?"

"No, that damned Tully."

Steve looked at Bob to see if he was serious. "What are you talking about?"

"That damned Tully sitting up there like a chute rooster."

"It's his chute."

"No shit."

"Watch that bull," Steve said and pointed to the big, horned Hereford.

"I been watching him. What the hell's he doing in there?"

Steve eased Blacky to the left to hold the cattle toward where the calves were being neatly cut into one pen and the cows into the other. "We tried to take him out when we took the other bulls off, but that bastard's got a mind of his own."

"Candidate for a Spam can," Bob said. He too moved left. "That's what I'm talking about. What the hell's he keeping a bull like that for?"

At the front of the herd an old cow tried to get into the wrong pen and Arvid swore and slammed the gate in her face. That caused all the cattle to shift and the riders backed their horses to make room for the wave of excitement that swept through the herd. The cattle calmed quickly and the riders moved up again. "That's a high-test bull," Steve said. "Expensive, good bloodlines. Finest kind." He smiled, knowing his comments would irritate Bob.

"He's got a wild look in his eye and those horns are a thing of the past."

"Well," Steve laughed, "he's in good company."

"Shit."

"He's good-looking, though. Throws nice calves."

"Well, there it is," Bob said.

Sometimes it was hard to tell exactly what Bob was getting at, but Steve got the drift. Bob didn't like Tully, and he didn't like his taste in bulls. But really, Bob was simply hurt. Tully seemed all right to Steve and he thought about telling his brother that Tully couldn't help it that he'd done something with his life. But that would have been cruel to Bob and just another way to whine.

Arvid worked the cutting gate like the old professional he was: calves into the left pen, cows into the right. As the pens filled, Tully came off the corral fence to help keep the penned animals back from the gates until finally it was only three calves, two cows, and the Hereford bull left to sort. They let the cattle mill until the three calves wandered over toward the cutting gate looking for their mothers. When the distances were just right, Bob spurred Elsa in between the calves and the adult cattle just as Arvid opened the proper gate. The calves shot through in an instant and Arvid slammed the gate just in time to stop the cows and bull from following them into the wrong pen. He waved his arms. "Git, you ugly sows." The cows spun and retreated, but the bull shook his head and took two more steps toward the old man. "Git, you son of a bitch!" Like an old fool that Steve didn't know, his father limped out toward the bull and waved his arms again. Instantly the boys rode between the bull and Arvid. The bull spun and went back to the cows. Arvid, who was too far from the safety of the fence, brushed his hands off as if he just turned the bull with brute strength.

"He goes out that way." Arvid pointed to a gate that led to the pasture where the other bulls lounged in lush grass and watched the proceedings. "Let's try to cut the two cows off first. You boys move that bull to the other end while me and the counselor work on the cows."

It was a reasonable plan that Bob and Steve understood right away. They slid their horses between the cows and bull while Arvid opened the cow gate. Tully stood just inside the cow pen holding the others back. "Give 'em a little push," Arvid called.

Steve turned Blacky, and the cows scooted toward the open gate. But with amazing acceleration the bull charged after them. Bob rode to turn him but the bull wouldn't be dissuaded and when Steve looked to his father, the old man was standing with his jaw out and the gate opened wide, waiting for the cows to pass into the pen before slamming the gate in the bull's face. Behind him Tully could see what was happening and moved to get out of the way. Steve spurred Blacky toward the charging bull. "Shut the gate," he yelled. But Arvid held his ground until the cows passed. Steve forced Blacky into the running bull and the good old horse hit him chest first with all he had. The impact staggered the bull but the old man refused to leave the corral until he had closed the gate behind the cows.

But it took too much time and the bull regained his balance and began accelerating in his attempt to follow the cows. Suddenly

Steve felt sick and helpless. Bob and Elsa had moved between the bull and their father, but the bull rolled around them and there stood Arvid, defiant but crippled, in the bull's line of charge. Motion slowed and once again he heard the scraping of the power take-off shaft against the tractor's safety shroud.

But the bull ignored Arvid and left the ground fifteen feet from where Tully fumbled to latch the gate behind the cows. Two thousand pounds of beef went airborne. The bull sailed headlong toward Tully but fell short of clearing the gate. He landed with one front leg over the gate, and they heard a terrible crunching sound. The gate crumpled but somehow held the bull, stopping him only two feet from a wide-eyed attorney wearing new work gloves.

Blacky and Steve moved to help shield Arvid as the bull staggered backward. By that time Bob had opened the gate to the bull pasture, and together the two horses drove the Hereford from the corral. When that gate was shut behind him, and the bull was trotting out to join his comrades, Bob and Steve rode slowly back to where Arvid and Tully stood shaking their heads near the edge of the corral.

Arvid was acting as if nothing had happened but Tully was fired up. "Wow. The bull jumped over the moon."

"The bull that needs a bullet in his brain," Bob said under his breath.

Tully's head was bobbing. "Wow," he said again. "He's a beauty, isn't he?" No one responded. "That's a bull. This is what I call living."

Bob raised a finger, readying himself to speak. But Tully's cell phone rang just in time to keep him silent. Steve stared at Bob while Tully grunted into the phone. He spoke for only a few seconds, then, as if he had suddenly become a different man, he clicked the phone shut and started across the corral. "Got to go," he said. "Park that ATV over by the shop. Something's come up."

That was all he said. He left them in the corral watching the shiny new Dodge swing around in the yard. Arvid moved to the fence, reached through the rails, and tipped the old grain barrel over far enough to reach under it. Tully was just out of sight down the driveway when Arvid retrieved a bottle of Black Velvet from the darkness under the barrel. He brushed a little dirt from the bottle and cracked the lid. He didn't bother to offer Bob a drink but pointed the open bottle at Steve like it was a loaded pistol.

🦋 15 🦋

The sun had barely set and the bottle of Black Velvet was nearly gone. Carl had heard the freshly weaned calves bawling for their mothers and had gone to the Thurstons to help, just in time to miss the work. But in time to help with the Black Velvet. Now Bob, Steve, Arvid, and Carl sat in the kitchen, hunkered over the enameled table like they used to do when Carl was a kid. Mrs. Thurston was gone, of course. Fifteen years. Carl's folks too. The four of them were all that was left of the first family to settle the valley. They were all a lot older and without women but it somehow felt the same. Maybe it was the whiskey. After all, this kitchen was where they all learned to drink.

There was a chill in the air outside so the wood stove in the corner was ticking away with wood scraps Steve had brought from his construction site. Carl sat across from Arvid, his hands flat on the table in front of him, with a silly Black Velvet smile on his face. "So how the hell you been, Arvid?

"Only fair. Things been a little tough since you lit out."

Carl laughed. It had been a long time. "I saw it coming," he said.

"You always were a little smarter than the rest of us," Bob said.

From the recliner near the blazing stove Steve added his two bits' worth. "Bullshit, only difference between him and us is that he learned how to read."

"And it wasn't easy," Carl said. "Not with the temptation of goofing off with you guys to rise above."

Arvid got up and poured everyone but Bob another inch of whiskey. "I still can't believe you were a professor," the old man said. "Don't they have any standards?"

"Of course they have standards. To be a professor you have to be afraid of physical work and able to find adversity in any situation. You have to be politically correct and sensitive to all sorts of delusionary points of view."

Arvid sipped his drink. "What the hell's a professor do, anyway?

"Profess," Carl said. "Some profess one thing, some profess another."

Steve said, "What'd you profess?"

Carl unbuttoned his shirt. "I professed literature."

Arvid said, "There you go with that reading again."

Steve asked why Carl was unbuttoning his shirt. "It's hot as hell in here. I professed Romantic literature."

"Like them Harlequin romances?" Arvid pointed at Bob. "The boys' mother used to read them. God rest her soul."

"See?" Carl said. "There was someone in this family who could read. But no, no Harlequin romances. Keats, Byron, Shelley. People you wouldn't know. Authors no one knows. That's why I professed them."

The whiskey was deep into their brains. Carl caught Steve trying to focus on him. He was trying to understand what Carl had just said. It was hot beside the stove and Carl took off his shirt. Steve put another handful of wood scraps on the fire for some unknown reason. He knew he should have gone home. Gretchen would be thinking up some story to complicate his whereabouts. She would be silent for two days, then come out with a story he would not be able to fathom. But now it was too late to go home. It was still possible to drive—the roads were deserted—but it would be dangerous and now he did not want to go. It seemed too hard. He only wanted to sit in the house where he was born. Just sit.

Arvid held the whiskey glass in both hands. It was the way he always drank whiskey. He must like it warm, Carl thought. He took small sips, never big swallows. Steady, sip, sip, sip. All day, all night, Carl supposed, since the tractor crippled him. Maybe before. That's what's going through Steve's mind, Carl thinks. Trying to remember if his father ever drank whiskey before the accident. But Carl figures that he did. He always drank too much, but it was losing the boy's mother that accelerated things. Mary Thurston had been sick with cancer and by the time she died Arvid was drinking a bottle a day.

"Well," Arvid said. "I profess that one of us has to check them calves pretty soon." Carl knew what he was talking about. He remembered about weaning calves. It was unusual to have problems but sometimes the calves got restless the first night without their mothers. They have to be calmed sometimes. In the old days the cowboys sang to them. Now it was usually enough to move gently among them with a flashlight.

Arvid turned around in his chair and fished a deck of cards from the drawer behind him. They all knew what was up and didn't have to talk about it. Carl recited "Ode on a Grecian Urn" while Arvid shuffled. Only Steve listened. "Thou still unravished bride of quietness / Thou foster-child of Silence and slow Time."

Steve took a sip of whiskey and looked at Bob. "You'da been a good professor too," he said. "If you'da had a chance." Nobody paid any attention to him except Carl. Steve took another drink. Carl had stopped his recitation and sat leaning hard to hear what Steve was saying. "Why wasn't I a professor? I had a chance. Why wasn't I shit?" Steve was sitting in the recliner over by the stove, hot as a three-dollar pistol, and spoke only to himself. "Had to work. Dad crippled, mother sick, brother in the war." His voice became even harder to hear. "Lazy, scared of books, thought I knew it all. Horses, cows, junk tractors, pickups, women." He stared at the stove and his head swam.

Arvid dealt four cards from the deck. They were all facedown, but everyone in the room knew the jack of hearts was one of them. The other three didn't matter. It was a game that Carl had seen played only in that house. Not a game really. A way to teach responsibility, maybe. A way to keep the bitching down. A way to get a job done. Steve leaned back and took a card from the table. They each took one. One of them had the jack of hearts. "It's no great shakes," Carl said.

"Professoring?" Bob asked.

"Decent work. But no great shakes." They all looked at their cards and put them back on the table. Whoever got the jack had to check the calves. Nobody said what they got. It was part of the game. Arvid just collected the cards and folded them back into the deck. Whoever got the jack could have denied it, could have forced another hand. But that never happened.

"I should have been the professor," Arvid said. "Hell, I'm the only one that knows anything around here."

"True," Steve mumbled. At the edge of his vision he saw barechested Carl watching him. The image blurred and Steve realized that he was very drunk. It was hot enough to boil water where he was sitting. After he spoke, it was silent for a few seconds, then suddenly Steve pushed up from his chair. The room spun slowly and Steve felt that the whole ranch was twisting away. It was the feeling that the Lakota must have had as they felt the burn of the bullets in their flesh and slipped from their horses. It made Steve sick and he stumbled from the kitchen and out onto the porch. Carl sensed that he needed help and was close enough behind him that the night air hit them nearly simultaneously like a bucket of ice water. It was bracing but didn't seem to have the same effect on Steve as it had on Carl. Steve babbled about a bull and a place up on a hill where you could see the horses. "History and all," he said. "The end of it." He looked sick and found the porch rail with both hands. Bob came out on the porch too, but he didn't stop. He stepped off into the night carrying a flashlight and Carl knew that he was the one who got the jack of hearts. Steve watched his brother through blurry eyes. "We're always going to be remembered," Steve said in a slur.

"We sure are," Carl said.

"Not you. Us Thurstons. They'll always call us the generation that lost the ranch." Bob had disappeared into the dark and Steve bent forward to vomit. Carl pushed back against the wall to avoid the splatter.

The poor boy, thought Carl. Whiskey poured out of him, and when he raised his head Carl was not surprised to see the tears pouring too. "Everything is mushy," Steve said. It was an exorcism of sorts. "I can't get any traction." He leaned and vomited again. When he stood up Carl moved to his side. His chest was cool and clammy, but what the hell? He put a big hairy arm around Steve's shoulders and held him tight. "You're fine," Carl said.

Steve was embarrassed and sick but Carl didn't care. There was still vomit on Steve's chin and he couldn't stop the tears. He tried to pull away from Carl's hug, but Carl refused to allow it and that made the sobs start again. Finally, Steve raised his hands to his face. "I'm sorry," he said. "It was me let the place go." Then Steve clutched Carl with a free hand and twisted in the grip so that Carl had to look into his swollen face. "You still got the other half. You'll protect it, won't you?"

Their eyes were only inches apart, and they held like that until Carl's head began to nod. "I will," he said. He made himself sound convincing, but the question had sobered him. He had never protected anything and he knew it.

"I'm sorry," Steve said again.

Carl pulled him even tighter. "It's not your fault," he said. Carl wanted to say something meaningful, something about fate, destiny, and the dispassion of an ever-changing world. But the idea would not jell, and Professor Lindquist had to settle for just the hug.

2

❧ 16 ❧

Carl Lindquist opened his shotgun and removed the two shells. It was a beautiful gun—an original Parker twelve-gauge side-by-side—and though he had owned it for fifteen years he still marveled at the tight hinge, the way the shells slid so perfectly from the chambers, the grace of the walnut grip. No question. The nicest object he ever owned. He closed the gun, pushed it through the barbed wire fence, and leaned it against one of the wooden posts. "Whoa, boy," he said. Tolstoy was a long-legged Ryman setter who, atypically, liked to run. He was perfect for an older man living on the prairie. He was the son of the daughter of Carl's first good dog and was as beautiful as the Parker. The big dog was already on the other side of the fence and starting off for the next draw, but when he heard Carl he stopped and waited. His kennel name was Leo—dogs like short names best, and besides, in the field he and Carl were informal. Carl considered himself to be on the rotund side, stout, jolly, substantial, call it what you may. Any euphemism will do. Whatever it's called, he thought, it makes crawling through barbed wire fences a pain in the big ass. Sometimes literally.

"Awk," he said to Leo, "these fences are getting lower and the wire tighter every year." Leo turned his head quizzically and Carl could see he was being humored. The dog was gentle and well trained, but he was still a bird dog and he wanted badly to get going. Once Carl was through and had picked up the Parker and replaced the shells, Leo started to creep toward the open prairie. He was beginning to gain speed but stopped when he saw Carl raise his hand. "Hang on, buddy." It was a hot afternoon, the first day of sharp-tailed grouse season, and Leo was panting heavily. Carl reached into the game pocket of his hunting vest, gently moved the grouse he'd shot a half hour before, and located the squeeze bottle of water. "Have a drink, boy."

Leo was exasperated to have to delay the hunt, but once he got a taste he remembered he was thirsty and lapped the stream of water out of the air and drank a pint without spilling more than a few drops. When Carl took the bottle away Leo licked his jowls and wiggled all over with appreciation. The dog-man relationship is symbiotic, Carl thought. Dogs have trouble with consecutive thinking and men have trouble with everything else. When Leo's panting was reduced to little more than a few puffs a minute, Carl leaned and rubbed the big silky head. He was about to send the dog on when the sound of a gasoline engine spoiled everything. Leo heard it too and looked to the south where an ATV was moving along a ridge toward them at breakneck speed. "Hmmm, looks like the new squire has detected poachers on his fief." Carl went back to rubbing Leo's long ears. "That would be us, boy."

They waited at the edge of Tully's property until the Kawasaki roared to within a few feet. "Some fine day," Carl thought, "gasoline will be too expensive to waste on something so vulgar." Tully killed the machine and pulled off the shiny black helmet that reminded Carl of a medieval knight. The notion of a noble protecting his domain was enforced. "You know where you are?" Tully asked without preamble.

"To the extent that any of us knows where we are," Carl said.

"Then you know you're on my land." He hadn't recognized Carl.

"I do, counselor." Carl held out his hand. "I believe we met a week or so ago at Arvid Thurston's home. I'm Carl Lindquist. Your neighbor."

"Oh, of course." Tully spoke as if it just came to him. But he was flustered and Carl knew he had gained the upper hand. He wanted Carl off his ground but he wanted to be neighborly. "I saw you out here. Didn't know who you were. Wondered what you were up to."

"First day of grouse season. It's a passion of ours." He put his hand back on Leo's head. "This is my bird dog, Tolstoy." Then, to prime the pump for permission to hunt and perhaps to vent his displeasure, he added, "We've been hunting this land all our lives."

Tully thrust his hand out too fast toward the dog—the sign of a novice or a man with no feel for animals. Leo, who was the kindest of dogs, endured the faux pas but turned his head with disinterest. "Leo!" Carl said. "This is our neighbor." He shrugged. "Sorry, he takes grouse hunting pretty seriously. Guess he wants to get on with it."

Apparently Tully hadn't noticed the poor manners or the slight. "He finds the birds?" His voice was genuinely curious.

"You bet, it's his job in life."

"I'm a hunter too," Tully said. "Shot a bunch of ducks in the South." Carl tried to look interested but his efforts were wasted. Tully was forging on. "Never tried upland bird hunting but I've read about it." He smiled slyly and Carl saw a glitter of something he could like. "Always wanted to try it."

It was impossible to miss what Tully was getting at. Now he had Carl. There they were, standing on Tully's ranch—never mind that it had once belonged to Carl's grandfather and Carl had hunted it since before John Tully was born. The counselor was a wannabe bird hunter. He'd heard this was the true gentleman's sport, had received the Orvis catalog in the mail, but he had no real access. Tolstoy was Carl's access and he could be Tully's too. Of course Carl preferred to hunt either alone or with very good friends, but there was a business deal in the wind and he was cornered. "You'll have to come out with us sometime." He had to force himself to speak it audibly. "Season runs for six weeks. We'll be out most days, at least for a walk."

"That would be nice," Tully said. Then he pressed the negotiation. "I've got a friend who likes to shoot too." He started to lean forward to pet Leo but again he moved too fast and Leo ignored him.

"It's okay," Tully said. "Go on and hunt. I'll give you a call sometime, when I'm not busy." He pulled on his helmet, started the ATV, and lifted his gloved hand in a wave as the engine roared.

When the sound of the machine had faded Carl looked down at Leo. "Now there is a man who knows how to drive a bargain. A little too much for an old schoolteacher." He checked to be sure the shotgun was loaded, then reached down and tapped Leo on the back of the head.

"Find the birds, boy." He whispered the command, but the dog, disgusted with the delay, heard him perfectly. By the time Carl straightened up to follow, Leo was running at full speed.

He ran long and smooth, and Carl had to marvel at the dog's desire and drive to hunt. As if the pasture were laid out with grid lines, Leo worked back and forth into the wind. Carl was an unapologetic anthropomorphizer. This animal was happy, he thought. Leo's nose was always high, searching the breeze for an essence that Carl could only imagine. How does it work? A human is lucky to smell a sizzling cheeseburger at twenty feet. Leo was detecting, at a hundred yards, the negligible scent of a bird feather, sorting it out from a thousand other smells, then triangulating its location perfectly. A good dog worked and concentrated harder than most men did in their careers.

This was what Carl had spent his life dreaming about—the leisure to hunt and to walk the hills of his youth. Books, bird hunting, and the occasional company of a woman were all he wanted. As he walked he tried to think of what else was important and for another fifty yards he pretended that those three things were all that mattered. But Carl Lindquist was honest enough to admit that these were his passions and that other people have their own imperatives. Some of them are worthwhile, he thought, though not many. As he watched Leo casting out along the edge of a plum thicket, family, home, and the duty of defending them were the only things that came immediately to mind.

The sun was beginning to settle toward the west and the light was bright but defused in the shade of the plum bushes. Leo moved parallel to the centerline of the draw eighty yards ahead, through the snowberry that feathered up through each side-draw. His head bobbed laterally as he ran, searching the breeze that filtered through the plums. He ran gaily until something invisible jerked him sideways as surely as if he had hit a glass barrier. The predator is in us all, Carl thought, as his attention sharpened with the dog's. His eternal march in Leo's wake slowed, and he watched as if wood nymphs might appear from the brush. Leo took a few cautious steps into the wind, and then, as if the atmosphere had turned to Jell-O, he ground to a stop and his tail rose and froze. He stood stock still where the last plum runners began to show in the prairie grass.

Carl's mind began to whir. The grouse are pinned. They are using their first line of defense, concealment. If Leo has handled them perfectly and is not too close, they will remain where they are. If he is too close or the birds have been caught in thin cover where they are not comfortable, they might revert to plan B. He'd seen it many times and knew the birds might decide to fly at any time. He knew he had to hurry into shotgun range, but it still took him a moment of awe before he started toward the point. He tried not to rush, tried to enjoy this moment. It was the coalescence of elements that dominated his dreams and his waking aspirations. He tried to appreciate the colors of the land: the neutral tones that Thomas Hardy would have found in the powder sky and the buffeted grasses. He watched the dog, traced the curve of his upturned tail, and tried to take his time. He thought of savoring the breeze and the sense of anticipation that such moments crystallize. But all that is mostly for sitting in front of a fireplace with a single malt in hand. Fuck it. Carl hustled headlong toward the point, fumbling to check the shotgun and praying to pagan gods that the birds wouldn't get up too soon.

His breath was coming hard by the time he got to within range, and he knew he had to regain control. When he was close enough to be assured a shot, he stopped and spoke to Leo. "Atta boy. Easy." It was as much to calm himself as it was to calm Leo. The wind was quartering from the plum bushes, and like any flying machine, the birds would jump into it if they could. Carl moved to Leo's left side. I'm panting like a truck driver in a Pensacola whorehouse, he thought. But he had the presence of mind to reach down to touch the dog. Leo's body was frozen beautifully in place and the muscles of his back were hard as a horse's neck. The invisible birds had triggered all this, and Carl took an instant to ponder the power of a bird's aura. Sharp-tailed grouse have the power to turn dogs to stone and men to jelly. He forced himself to take a series of deep, slow breaths as he stared at the grass around the brush that harbored the grouse. As usual, he saw nothing, and as usual, his faith flagged. He wondered if there had been a mistake. But as usual, Leo said no. He stood rigid at the man's side. Holding the shotgun at the ready, Carl stroked the dog's back again. His hand moved gently down the spine and up the tail. "Good boy." Then Carl stood up straight and told himself again to be calm. Methodically he turned his ball cap around backward for better vision and stepped forward into the birds.

The grouse materialized and launched into the air a dozen strong. Instinct took over and Carl's eyes chose one bird. He was already swinging the gun, and when the stock touched his cheek, the hammer fell and the shell inside the chamber exploded with a sound that Carl did not hear. The barrels swung on through, past the puff of feathers, and Leo and Carl marked the fall together. But they didn't move until Carl breathed again. He took an instant to absorb it all, then reached down and tapped the back of Leo's head. "Fetch 'em up, boy."

As Leo searched for the bird, Carl thought he heard the calling of angels. No—an alien sound. It was far off but raucous as a jay. He scanned the distant ridgeline as irritated as a lover listening to the telephone ring. Leo was halfway back with the bird in his mouth by the time he located the sound. It was Tully, still sitting on his A T V, cheering as if he were at a sporting event. He had been watching the point and shot from a distance of a quarter mile and was now showing Carl that he had witnessed the whole thing and was impressed. Carl tried to ignore the cheers. He knelt to accept the bird from Leo, pet his head, praise him, and admire the incredible silver and smoky brown of the sharptail. He rotated the bird and looked thoughtfully at the marvelously adapted snowshoe feet. He lifted the bird to his nose and took in the scent of all that is wild about the prairie. The cheers continued from the distant ridge and finally Carl acknowledged them with a wave. As he waved and smiled, he spoke to Leo. "Crude son of a bitch," he said. "Couldn't tell a water lily from a floating turd."

✍ **17** ✍

Of course Erwin Benson heard about the death of the Bordeaux boy. A death associated with a stolen car is something that always gets the attention of the prosecuting attorney. But in this situation, unless he could prove that the girl was involved in the theft—which he couldn't—there was no one to prosecute. It was too bad the boy died, but Erwin would likely have brought charges against him if he had lived. Can't steal a car and wreck it in Lakota County without consequences.

Erwin tried to keep the fact that Tad Bordeaux was Lakota out of the equation. A defense attorney likely would have wanted to plead him to a lesser charge, but the state would have stuck to grand theft auto because that's what happened out there on that road. If Bordeaux got a showboat attorney the thing might have gone to a full-blown trial, but from what Erwin understood about the case it would have been more about the attorney's ego than about Bordeaux's well-being. The showboats would likely have stayed away from that one. No future in getting your ass kicked in public court. Bordeaux probably would have ended up with some young, idealistic court-appointed attorney just out of law school. There were three or four of them around town now, and secretly, Erwin admired their spunk. The trouble was, the young ones really don't figure out how it works until they're old ones. There were times in Native cases over the last few years that Erwin felt sorry for them and had challenged a juror that the defense attorney had okayed. Even though Erwin knew that the juror would be an asset to the prosecution, he had asked that he be removed because Erwin knew the family, and he knew that the juror was a racist from a long line of racists. Nowhere does the law function the way people think it functions. Erwin Benson didn't guess Lakota County was an exception.

But he never got to prosecute Tad Bordeaux for grand theft auto. Bordeaux died in a pea-green windowless neurology ward in the Mile High City, and at the time, few people thought much about it. A shame he died but it wasn't big news in McDermot. Few people even knew about it except the folks on the north side of town and an old fart attorney who made it his business to know everything that went on in the county.

The night he got word of Tad Bordeaux's death the old fart attorney was seated at a rolltop desk in the workshop in his house on Calvert Street. He'd been trying to figure out just how to get online but had taken a few minutes to think of Tad Bordeaux. In fact, nearly an hour had slipped away and the computer screen had long ago shut down. He looked up with some fear that he had done something wrong, then pushed the on button, which turned the damned thing off. He knew it was off because it said, "Good-bye." Even he knew what that meant, so he pushed the button again, the screen said "Hello," and he was back where he was an hour before.

The computer had been a gift from his daughter over in Minneapolis, and though he had grumbled, he had secretly been excited to set it up on the desk that he used only to fiddle with his fishing equipment. A cheap fly-tying vise was clamped to the edge of the desk and there were traces of feathers and wool on that side of the desk. But he didn't tie many flies. He didn't care for fly-fishing so much anymore. His eyes weren't up to the task of any of it, and besides, he had always liked the idea of warm water and really big fish. Who really liked standing in cold water to their waist, dressed in an eight-hundred-dollar Gore-Tex clown outfit from a company based in a part of the country where all the fish have already been caught? Modern fly-fishing was a consumer game for hopeless romantics. But heavy-tackle fishing aroused in Benson the atavistic desire to put meat in the freezer. It was the lure of warm water and big fish that had brought him to the Internet.

There was a constant chatter about Web sites in the office. His assistant, Linda, was no kid, but thankfully she seemed to understand the new technology. If she didn't, the prosecutor's office would have ground to a halt years before. Like a lot of people, she was a little obsessed with technology. She kept all sorts of mailing lists for the Democratic party on the office computer. It was probably an infraction of some sort but Erwin figured he didn't know enough about computers to say anything. Not only that, but the list of Democrats in Lakota County couldn't take up much space. Like in many places, progressives were hanging onto the cliff with just their fingertips, and frightened, feverish Christian fundamentalists were kicking at those fingers with hobnailed boots. Linda was the office expert on computers and talked about them constantly. Almost every attorney and police officer that came into the office mentioned them. According to what he had heard you could find anything on the World Wide Web.

He ran his finger down the checklist his daughter had sent along with the computer. The handwriting reminded him of her mother, Lucy, and he had to force himself to stay focused. Cursor here, double click there. He'd never gotten to the part where it said type in subject line before, but that night it happened. Bingo. He typed in "fishing" and hit return. One million three hundred and fifty-two thousand possibilities. He looked back down to the notes. Narrow the subject. Be specific. Hit "Search."

He typed in "warm water fishing." Still, a lot of choices came up, but the first one was a fishing lodge in Belize. He clicked on it, and bingo again. A smiling black man appeared. He stood on white sand with palm trees in the background and held a great blue fish as high as he could reach, but its tail still touched the sand.

❦ **18** ❦

Friday night was a basketball night. The McDermot seventh-grade Storms played the Eaglewood Bobcats at the McDermot YMCA. The game was at seven thirty, and Steve and Gretchen planned to meet there, as usual. Steve worked until dark. His crew was busy with the eave troughs on the enormous house out near the bluffs, and he wanted to finish because the weather forecast was for rain the next two days. Jake was going to a friend's house after the game, and Gretchen was looking forward to a sandwich and a beer, then going home to spend the night with Steve. She was hoping the rain would blow in early. If it did, she was going to suggest going to Steve's mobile home. It would be nice to listen to rain against the metal roof.

Gretchen had been thinking about the HPMC story all day and had gotten herself worked up. She hadn't had a chance to put ideas on paper, but as she sat in the stands at the YMCA watching the Storms warm up and waiting for Steve, she felt the need to begin writing and the first stirrings of pride. It could be a good story, provocative with regard to the role of the medical community within the greater community. She'd found statistics on the Internet that supported her subtle claim that individual health care is a public issue, that allocating services to the well insured harms the populace and ultimately drives up costs. She had a tendency to get a little carried away with expectations for a story and was fighting it. But she couldn't help suspecting that the biggest piece of the local services pie was going to the wealthiest and the cost was being borne by everyone. To write a story like that she would have to walk the line between a dry, fact-filled story and one that made the problem personal and immediate. As she sat waiting for Steve and for the game to begin, she struggled with a way to do it without mentioning Tad Bordeaux or Dr. Arnold Cring and his HPMC. She wanted readers to put two and two together but she didn't want to worry about incurring the wrath of the medical community. There was no doubt that that would jeopardize her job.

Halfway through the first quarter she looked up to find Steve standing at the gym entrance searching the crowd. He'd come straight from the job site and stood erect and dusty in his work clothes. She knew the particular jeans he wore, the faded green plaid shirt, and the scuffed boots. His cap advertised Caterpillar tractors and showed dark where sweat had repeatedly soaked through. She took a moment to reflect on the fact that men, especially men like Steve, could look great in a beat-up, battered state. It wasn't fair, but there was also something very wonderful about the attractive self-confidence men gained simply from working. Jake had already scored four points and she was in a buoyant mood. She watched Steve for another few seconds, then stood up and waved wildly. Being inside a gym with the sound of a crowd, the excitement of the players, a certain physical smell in the air, and the basketball banging the hollow floor, she was taken back to high school days as a cheerleader. Usually she did her best to keep that part of her life in the past, but that night it was a nice respite from the grown-up world of unprincipled doctors, cautious editors, shaky relationships, and tragedies like the one that befell Tad Bordeaux and Annie Simmons.

Steve made his way along the edge of the court and folded himself onto the seat beside her. He smelled of sawdust, sweat, and the canvas of his coat. She snuggled around his arm and brought him up to date on what had happened in the game so far. "Jake's guarding that big number 22. He's not very nice."

Steve laughed. "Nice?"

"Well, they're just little boys."

"Hmmmm."

They didn't play like little boys. They played rough and hard, and Steve was, as always, sucked in by the game. By the fourth quarter the Bobcats were down by five points and had started to press. Jake's coach seemed like a good guy. He was, after all, volunteering hundreds of hours of his time, but Steve mumbled something about wishing the kids were better prepared. Jake was the best dribbler on the team and brought the ball up court after the Bobcats scored the basket that put them just three points behind. But the Bobcats came out in a zone press—according to Steve that was a defense that should be passed against, not dribbled against. The Storms didn't recognize the difference, and the coach didn't yell out to tell Jake. When he tried to dribble, the Bobcats collapsed on him and number 22 took the ball away for another score.

That put the Storms up by only one with a minute to go in the game, and Steve was standing on the bleacher seat screaming, "Zone. Zone. It's a Zone. Pass and move. Pass and move." Gretchen laid a hand on his hip, but he didn't feel it. "Look up the court, Jake. Don't dribble. Calm down. Good passes." She pretended to try to quiet him, but in a way, she loved that he took Jake's games so seriously. And she knew that Jake was glad he was there.

Again the Bobcats collapsed on Jake, but this time he passed to the open boy and they got the ball across the ten-second line. "Yes!" Steve said.

There were only twenty seconds to go. "Keep passing," Steve screamed. "Run out the time. Make 'em foul you." People were looking at Steve, and Gretchen was gently trying to pull him down to his seat, but he didn't notice. "Make 'em foul you!"

And that was what they did. Jake went to the line, shooting one and one, with nine seconds to go. The crowd went completely silent as the ball arched toward the basket. Sinking both shots would have iced the game, but the ball bounced high off the rim and came down in the arms of the Bobcats' number 22.

"Get on him!" Gretchen screamed.

"No," Steve yelled, "don't foul."

Now they were both standing on the seats. The seconds were ticking away and 22 was moving the ball up court against Jake. Gretchen wasn't completely sure what was going on. She wanted to yell advice but didn't know what to yell. Finally, in frustration, she screamed, "WIN!"

Steve looked at her and smiled. "Win?"

They clutched each other's shoulders when Jake coolly pinched 22 off at the base line, and the clock ran down. There was a desperate fading jump shot, but it fell far short and missed everything. A mass of boys leaped for the rebound, but time had expired. The McDermot Storms came away winners by one point.

After a frenzied victory hug Steve and Gretchen collapsed onto their seats. "Jesus," Steve said, "I can't take it."

Gretchen closed her eyes in exaggerated exhaustion and pressed her forehead against his shoulder. "I need a drink."

"Me too," Steve said. But they did not leave their seats until they saw Jake come across the floor toward them. He had been jumping and high-fiving his teammates but had also been moving toward his mother and Steve. It was a tradition that he would come over and exchange a few words before running off with his friends. When he was younger he had hung around his mother a lot longer but now he had to remain cool. For that reason, and perhaps others, he stood closer to Steve. Watching Jake listen to Steve's critique of the game created a rush of mixed feeling in Gretchen. She kept the smile on her face but felt a sadness too. She stood silent as Jake reached out and hit Steve on the arm.

This was something new. He grinned and bobbed his head as if daring Steve to hit back. "Pretty cocky," Steve said.

Then Jake put his arm around Steve and whistled with studied nonchalance. "You know," he said, "after a tough basketball game a guy needs a little food."

This was between Steve and Jake, but Gretchen couldn't help herself. "Would you like to come eat with us?"

Jake rolled his eyes. "Well," he said, "Trevor and Jud and I were thinking about a pizza."

"You're hitting me up for cash?" Steve laughed.

"A basketball star has to eat." Steve was already reaching for his wallet and it crossed Gretchen's mind that she should stop him. But she loved watching the two of them so much that by the time she stepped forward, the transfer of funds had already been made.

Another pop on Steve's shoulder. "Thanks, big guy." Then Jake turned to his mother. I'll be at Trevor's. He stepped right up and pecked her on the cheek. "See you tomorrow."

He left them standing in the emptying gymnasium looking after him. It was a moment before Steve's hand touched her shoulder. "Still interested in a drink?" She'd been smiling but not until she faced Steve did her white teeth appear.

"Yeah. Somewhere close there's a glass of whiskey with my name on it."

They got their drink at Clyde's Steakhouse on Main Street. It wouldn't have been Gretchen's choice but Steve wanted to talk with Bob, and Clyde's was Steve's best guess at where to find him. Clyde's was just a bar with a kitchen in the back. The room was narrow, with a row of tables along the long wall and a bar on the opposite wall. The barstools towered over the diners and the waitresses pushed chairs out of their way as they delivered medium-rare rib-eyes and draft beers.

The place was packed, so Steve and Gretchen stood at the door, peering down the smoky bar toward the pair of pool tables at the end. "There are a couple of stools toward the end," Steve said. He looked to see if Gretchen was up for sitting at the bar.

Gretchen shrugged. "Sure. Is Bob here?"

"Can't tell." They moved through the maze of after-the-game softball players and golfers still there from happy hour. Steve claimed the two stools and flagged down a waitress.

"Couple Crown and waters," he said.

"And a Diet Coke." Bob had appeared from nowhere and was leaning against the bar between them. "Howdy," he said.

"Just the man we're looking for," Steve said.

"I'm in a pool game." He raised the cue in his hand to prove it.

"We can wait," Gretchen said. "We have to calm down from a seventh-grade basketball game."

"And eat," Steve said. "You hungry?"

"I ate chips."

"You got to eat more than that," Gretchen said.

Bob smiled. "I am." He pointed to a thin young man in super-baggy pants. His face was adorned with rings hanging from his nose, ears, and eyebrows. His hair was streaked with lavender. "I'm eating this guy's lunch." He took his Diet Coke from the waitress as she arrived. "Get this, would you, bro?"

"Hey," Gretchen said. "Let us order you a steak."

Bob looked fondly at her. "God, it's nice to have someone interested in your health. I'll have the steak fingers and fries." He wiggled his eyebrows and turned back into the crowd.

They watched him walk slowly back to the pool table as the young man paced, impatient for Bob to take his next shot.

The waitress had escaped and Steve was trying to wave her down again. "How about you?" he asked. "You hungry?"

"I could eat, but I have to look at a menu."

Steve plucked a dirty piece of paper from between the salt and pepper shakers. "You should have this memorized by now."

They ordered another Crown and water with the steaks they always ordered, then spied a table in the back. As they gathered up their drinks for the move, Gretchen looked down the bar and saw a severe pony tail she recognized. Carolina Riggins had somehow slipped into the bar unnoticed, a rare event in itself. It was not like her to stay unnoticed for long, and Gretchen watched to see if Steve would look her way.

He either didn't notice her or he saw her come in and was pretending she was a million miles away. In fact, he was watching his brother shoot pool and settled into the chair without taking his eyes off the table full of colored balls. Now they were only a few feet from the pool game and they held their breath as Bob pulled the stick back and stroked smoothly through the cue ball. It shot across the table, slapped the ten ball into the corner pocket, and backed up for a straight-in shot on the six ball. Steve hid a smile by raising the Crown Royal to his lips.

The next three balls went in with the efficiency of a metronome, but Bob stopped to chalk his cue before he shot the eight ball. It was a straight-in shot, and everyone watching knew that Bob needed no chalk. It was just a pause before administering the deathblow. A cat playing with a mouse. The pierced boy with lavender hair dug into one of his enormous pockets before Bob even stoked the ball. By the time the eight ball dropped he had tossed a ten-dollar bill onto the table. Bob walked to the back wall and put the cue on the rack without looking at the money.

The waitress pushed her way through with the food as Bob passed the pool table. He picked up the bill as if he had found it lying there. He was coming to join them when Carolina Riggins appeared from the crowd. "I want to play the winner," she said and tossed her head from side to side. Her blond ponytail flapped around nearly to her face and she stood looking at Bob with both hands on her hips.

"That'd be me," Bob said.

Both Steve and Gretchen saw her showing off but turned away. Gretchen felt like she might blow apart, thinking how good it would feel to snatch a handful of that blond hair and bang Carolina's head on the pool table.

"Well, chalk that cue, Bobby boy." Carolina walked toward Bob but he backed away, stuffing the ten-spot into his pocket.

"Play the kid," he said and nodded toward the boy in baggy pants.

"I want to play with you." She smiled at her own joke.

"Got to eat." Bob pointed to the table of food and Carolina's eyes followed his gesture.

"Well, hi!" she said as if she hadn't seen Steve and Gretchen sitting at the table. Gretchen let her eyes roll, though no one saw her. Carolina stepped over to the table. "Good to see you, Steve. Gretchen, good to see you, too." Carolina laid a hand lightly on Gretchen's shoulder, and Gretchen slouched lower, like a dog that has been mistreated. "You guys here to play pool?"

"No," Steve said. "Came to eat."

"Oh, oh, I'm sorry." She smiled broadly and winked. "I'm just going to kick this boy's ass." She nodded toward the lavender-headed boy who was racking up the balls.

"Great," Gretchen said. "You go kick his ass."

When Bob sat down, he and Steve dove into their meals like a pair of wolverines. They appeared to concentrate on the food and pretended to pay no attention to Carolina. It took a few minutes for Gretchen to calm down. For the first part of the meal all she could see was Carolina wiggling around the pool table, giggling at mumbled remarks, and offering up her tightly jeaned rear end as she leaned over for every shot.

When they left the bar the rain was just beginning, but Gretchen no longer wanted to lie in Steve's bed and listen to it hit on the metal roof. She'd had a third drink and had gone quiet. Steve acted like he didn't know what she was mad about. She insisted that she wasn't mad. She also told him she hated being made a fool of. He shrugged and took both hands off the steering wheel. "What?"

"You never looked at me once after your old girlfriend came in."

"Carolina?"

"Jesus."

The rain was coming down hard against the windshield. Steve shook his head. "I've had a long day. I'm not really up for this."

"And I haven't?"

"Haven't what?"

"Had a long day. I just sit around all day. That's what you think."

"Come on."

"You come on."

They drove in silence until they came to the intersection of James Avenue and LaCrosse, where they would turn to go to his trailer. "Well?" Steve said. The rain was coming misty on the windshield.

"Well, what?"

"Well, do you want to come home with me or not?"

The rain was pulsing in gentle waves that could have been sensual. Gretchen wanted to back the evening up, but she couldn't. "I don't care," she said.

"Well, fine," he said and turned the pickup hard toward her empty house.

Steve had fully intended to simply drop her off, and Gretchen had fully intended to walk to her door by herself. But as they drove, they knew that that was not the way they wanted the evening to end. Without a word Steve pulled the pickup into the driveway and turned the engine off. They sat dumbfounded in the darkness. What had happened to the mood they had been in during Jake's game? How could they get back to it?

The light rain gathered into droplets on the windshield and ran zigzag paths to the motionless wipers. "Do you want to come in?"

"Yeah."

"Well, let's not talk then. Just come in and make love to me." They sat in silence for another minute. "Yeah," Steve said, "guess that's best." As they stepped from the pickup, the rain increased. Now it was strong enough to make a drumming on the roof of the mobile home the way Gretchen had imagined. But the chance for that was gone. They walked in silence to the house and were thankful for a dry place to share the night.

❧ 19 ❧

Gretchen knew a few things about herself, and one of those things was that she needed to focus on the positive to do good work. The next week she would write the High Plains Medical Clinic story, and in preparation she would need to clear her mind. Steve and Gretchen woke up early Saturday morning. The rain had stopped and after a quick assessment through the bedroom window, Steve was sure they would work their usual half day. Gretchen experienced a twinge of guilt for being pleased by the fact that Steve would be leaving her alone. As he finished dressing, Gretchen began thinking about Annie Simmons and the circumstances that they had shared. Suddenly she felt a panic to warn Annie, to guide her away from a life in McDermot and out into the world. Gretchen sat in bed with the sheet wrapped tight around her and stared straight ahead.

"Gretchen! Hey, Gretchen, are you there?" It was Steve, dressed and ready for work. He was inches away from her face. "You're thinking about that story, aren't you?"

Her distant stare telescoped back until his face came into focus. She smiled. "Yeah," she said.

"I thought you weren't going to start on that until Monday. You told me this weekend was Jake's."

She nodded. "I did and it is going to be that way."

"Promise?"

"Promise."

He touched her cheek with his right hand and leaned to kiss her good-bye. The warm, damp night just passed crashed back in on her and she remembered how safe she had felt curled under his arm. But by then the kiss was over and he was moving. "I'll call you," he said.

"I'll be right here, me and Jake."

She lay in bed and listened to the sound of Steve's pickup until it had faded completely. The comparison of Annie Simmons and the much younger Gretchen Harris tried to find a toehold in her consciousness, but she shook her head and jerked the bedcovers back.

As she straightened the house, she refused to think of anything but Jake. An hour passed quickly. By the time Jake came home at noon it had begun to rain again and she insisted that he stay home, which he didn't seem to mind. Focus. She needed to spend time with her son.

She only allowed four hours of television a week—a proclivity that from time to time had earned her the title of the meanest mom in McDermot. But that afternoon Jake let her snuggle in with him on the couch, and with the rain misting the window in waves they watched an old movie until dark. It was one of those days when they both needed to be quiet and close—a rare sort of day since Jake had neared his teen years. He would have jumped from the couch if one of his friends knocked on the door, but no one knocked, and so Gretchen savored the closeness. It occurred to her that this might be one of the last days of Jake's childhood.

In the evening they baked molasses cookies and played like they hadn't in months. It was as if Jake, too, sensed the special nature of the day, and Gretchen found herself hoping that Steve would show up. She wondered if he had been able to work that morning. She hated herself for it, but she wondered why he hadn't called. They watched another movie and in some way she felt confident that Steve would walk in and snuggle down on the couch between them. He hadn't said he'd come over, but Gretchen came to believe he would, and she found herself getting more and more disappointed as the night wore on. Jake asked about him but such things are impossible to explain to a child. Gretchen didn't understand it herself.

Jake talked about going out to the Thurston ranch. He didn't quite grasp that the ranch no longer belonged to the Thurstons. He loved spending time with Arvid and over the last years they had formed a bond like all children should have with a grandparent. His own grandparents on Gretchen's side were in Arizona and Eddie's parents had retired to Florida. Arvid had filled the void. And like all little boys, Jake loved the horses and the country. Of course his link to all that was Steve, but he didn't come Saturday night and he didn't call. It must have been confusing for Jake. It was confusing for Gretchen, and she went to bed angry and suspicious of what Steve was doing.

After Mass on Sunday Gretchen felt good, but like some dopey schoolgirl, she went home and waited for Steve to call. That gave an opening for thoughts of Annie Simmons to try to get back into her consciousness. It all had to do with the knowledge that, very soon, she would have to knuckle down and write her story. She was able to keep her focus on Jake but it was less than perfect, and the uplift she'd gotten from church was destroyed. Jake must have sensed she was thinking of Steve because he asked if he could go out to the ranch and see Arvid and ride the horses. The day had cleared and by one o'clock Gretchen thought about calling Arvid, but she couldn't be so presumptuous. Jake had to settle for shooting baskets with his friends.

After he left, the house was particularly quiet. Gretchen was again feeling the pressure of the story looming in front of her like a dentist appointment. She would have to face Ryan Hooper for his blessing and that made her feel lonely and sad and angry with herself for feeling that way. Cleaning the house and doing the laundry didn't help. Finally she took a walk around the neighborhood, snooping in the backyards of families playing in wading pools and getting ready for barbecues. When she returned she went directly to the answering machine to see if Steve had left a message. The green light wasn't blinking, and despite herself, she grew angry. Finally, just after the sun had set behind the bluffs on the other side of the Pawnee, and fifteen minutes before Jake was supposed to be home, Steve's pickup pulled into the driveway.

Her first impulse was to run out to meet him. She wanted to throw her arms around him. She even got that swishy feeling in her abdomen and considered the feasibility of taking him into the bedroom before Jake came home. She wanted to lie back and have him unfasten her jeans and peel them down to leave her naked before him on her bed. But as quickly as those feelings came, they vanished and were replaced with a wave of red-hot fury. Where had he been? Why hadn't he called?

She didn't run to meet him. She couldn't. Instead she watched him come up the sidewalk and fought the feeling of resentment that threatened to wash over her. By the time he reached the front door she'd managed to calm herself, at least on the outside, but the fact that he pushed the door open without knocking jolted her again with irritation.

"Hey," he said.

"Hey, yourself."

Steve winced to hear the tone of her voice. "Go gently," he said. "I overtrained a little last night."

"That so?"

Steve walked past her and sat down on the couch. "Taken four showers today. Drank a barrel of tomato juice." He was trying to be funny, but trying too hard.

Gretchen couldn't help it. She stood in front of him with arms crossed like a poor soapbox actress. "Who were you with?"

"Come on."

"Just tell me. All I ask is honesty. You've made it perfectly clear that I shouldn't ask for anything else."

"Jesus, Gretchen, you wonder why I don't want to make a commitment?"

"Just tell me who you were with."

"This is going to be a shock for you. It's going to ruin your day."

"Have a party, Steve."

"I went to Grandby to look at that job I told you about. Remember?"

It rushed in on her that he did say something about going to Grandby. She should have simply apologized but she couldn't. "But you were drinking, right?"

"Right."

"All day?"

"Well, yeah."

"No phones in the bars?"

Steve raised his hands. "You're right. Sorry. I had a few beers. Jesus." A car door slammed and they heard Jake calling good-bye to his friends.

"And I suppose you were drinking by yourself. In the phone-less bars."

Steve closed his eyes and she knew he was trying not to speak, but his temper had been ignited. "I don't have to tell you who I was with." In fact, there *had* been a girl. They'd danced and he'd let his leg slide between hers. She had pushed back and they had kissed in the parking lot. He didn't remember her name and didn't care to.

Gretchen sneered. "Feeling a little cornered? Is that why you blow up?"

"Go to."

"You're so easy to read."

Could she really read him or was she simply always suspicious? What did it matter? Steve was standing up. "You got it all out of proportion. You're guessing. Making things up in your head." But the front door opened and Jake bounded in with his ever-present gym bag over one shoulder and a shopping bag in his left hand.

Before he realized that Steve was there, he began to talk. "Hey Mom, look what I got." His glance came up and caught the rage in the eyes of them both.

"Oh," Gretchen said unconvincingly as she moved to meet her son. "Let's see. Is this school stuff?"

Steve wanted to come too but he was too angry. "So what are you doing? Spending all the money you mooched off me?" He was trying, but he sounded like he was reading from a script.

"No, that was for pizza." Jake spoke slowly, feeling his way through the tension. "This was lawn-mowing money."

Now the hangover was heavy on Steve. Jake—too much like his mother—reached out and punched him very lightly on the shoulder. "You know that pick–and–go thing you were teaching me? I think I got it. It works." He was trying hard, too.

"Yeah?" Steve said. His eyes had come up and met Gretchen's. There was still frustration in them, but the venom was gone. "Dribble as close to the pick as you can. The pick person has to turn with the ball. It's the only way it works."

"Got it." Jake said. He had maneuvered the shopping bag to the edge of the couch and Gretchen knew he didn't want Steve to see what was inside. Discreetly, Gretchen took the bag and moved to the kitchen. Jake and Steve went on talking about basketball. When she looked into the bag, she found an inexpensive handkerchief with a daisy embroidered in one corner. Now they were talking about riding horses on the ranch and tears had welled up to teeter on Gretchen's lower lids.

❦ 20 ❦

The day after Carl asked Eleanor to dinner at his ranch she was at the library ten minutes after work. She had her notepads and pencils, ready to do the compulsive research that she loved so much. Carl had been on her mind for over twenty-four hours, and she was not only surprised but also a little embarrassed. The thoughts were nothing really risqué or lascivious, but titillating. It was hard to say why he affected her that way. The fact that he was a professor of literature perhaps, his massiveness, the hair, the shy-boy eyes, the unassuming smile. These were things that Eleanor hadn't thought of for years, and as with most attraction, there was a synergy at work. She had always believed it was not any separate characteristic that attracted one person to the other. It was the whole package—more than the sum of the parts—loaded with the potential for surprise. She wondered who he really was, what his life was like in Fredericton, New Brunswick. Why Canada? Had he been married before? Did he have children? What about the house she loved so much? In fact, her little research project may well have been mostly a displacement activity. There were still four days to pass before the grouse dinner, and in the interest of self-esteem, she needed something to think about other than Carl Lindquist. She was, after all, hardly a schoolgirl.

To be honest, what she was doing there at the McDermot Public Library was not true displacement, because it had a strong connection to this Carl Lindquist. She awoke that morning with a question as heavy as a bowling ball on her chest. Why call Carl Lindquist's ranch the Butler place? She was at the library to find out who Butler was. She'd run into this before in the McDermot area. Houses, farms, and ranches were often referred to by the name of their first inhabitant. European inhabitant, of course. Some of the houses in town had been lived in by a single family for generations but were still called by the name of the builder. She suspected the same thing with Carl's ranch, but wanted to know the story. The second question she woke up with that morning had to do with grouse. What *was* a grouse, anyway?

The ornithological question was easily answered. Peterson's *Field Guide to Western Birds* had a whole page of drawings of grouse. It took a little reading to figure out that Carl was likely referring to sharp-tailed grouse—a pale, speckled, brown grouse of prairie brush. The picture looked a lot like the picture of a hen pheasant. That was positive. She'd eaten pheasant and found it bearable to good. The other question, that of the origin of the Butler place, was a little more difficult. Mary Jane Nelson was the chief librarian, and because Eleanor had spent quite a bit of time in the library since she came to town, they had become friends. She bent the rules for Eleanor. Strictly speaking, she was not allowed to be in the Special Collections room by herself, because some of the documents were fragile or one of a kind. The policy was to request that the librarian bring them out to the reader. Nothing in the Special Collections room was to be checked out. The collection was comprised almost exclusively of local and state history and contained a great deal of information that existed no place else on earth. Eleanor loved that idea and loved the fact that Mary Jane had slipped her a key and asked no questions.

Suddenly Eleanor was alone with handwritten and mimeographed accounts of early settlers. She could smell sod cabins and woodsmoke in the pages and it took her only an hour to learn that Carl's father, Ralf Lindquist, had died in 1972 and that his father was Lars Lindquist from Spencer, Iowa. Then she hit pay dirt—an obituary from the *Pawnee Democrat*, dated January 11, 1932. It was a long, detailed account of the life of one of the first citizens of McDermot, Edward Butler, who had arrived before statehood.

According to the writer, who claimed to have known Edward Butler, there was no county at the time—so no records—but Edward had apparently ridden into the country from Texas as the foreman for Henry McDermot. Later he carved out a ranch of over ten thousand deeded acres and additional sections of open range that would later become government lease land. That seemed too big to be Carl's ranch, Eleanor thought, but then she discovered that Edward had a daughter. Where he found a wife it didn't say. The daughter was Christine, and in 1904 Christine married Lars Lindquist.

Eleanor was so proud of herself that she squirmed in her seat. There was a nearly uncontrollable urge to call Carl and tell him what she'd found out. But of course he knew this family history. What was she thinking? She was thinking that she wanted to talk to Carl Lindquist, for God's sake.

She came out of the Special Collections room and handed the key back to Mary Jane who was busy with a little old man who wanted to know how to use the computer to find a book. "So what's a grouse?" Eleanor asked, to flaunt her new knowledge.

"Verb or noun?" Mary Jane said as she guided the man's hand on the mouse.

Eleanor laughed. "Noun."

"Bird."

"Actually," Eleanor said, "its a pheasantlike bird of the prairie brush."

"Boyfriend?" Mary Jane asked over her shoulder.

"Why do you say that?" Eleanor was surprised and embarrassed.

"Grouse, pheasants, partridge—they love that kind of stuff."
Mary Jane was watching the screen and still guiding the old
man's hand. But the old man was looking up at Eleanor and nodding his head.

❧ **21** ❧

The High Plains Medical Clinic was the newest large building in McDermot. It wasn't as big as the regional hospital, but it was fancier. The corporation that owned the clinic also owned another six acres on the hillside behind the gleaming steel and brick building. As Gretchen pulled her Jeep into the slick new asphalt parking lot, she saw orange survey stakes peppering the hillside to the east. More construction was obviously planned. Maybe Steve would end up working there on that sunny hillside.

It was clear that the High Plains Medical Clinic was doing a land-office business, especially when its physical plant was compared to the nonprofit regional hospital housed in an aging building just across the street. Gretchen took a moment to compare the two buildings. The location of the High Plains Medical Clinic seemed calculated to diminish trust in the public hospital. Both she and Jake had been born in the regional hospital, so it held a special spot in her heart. But she had to admit that the new building gave the impression of being dedicated to high-tech, cutting-edge medicine, while the old hospital seemed dated and starved for funds. If what Ida Miller told her was right, those impressions were well founded.

She had called ahead and put her name in for a public tour of the new facility. Though Ryan Hooper, who advised her to go slow, was the one who suggested the tour, she was not there as a newspaper reporter. If they recognized her, of course she wouldn't try to hide it, but she hoped she wouldn't be recognized. Her own inclination was to be direct, but Ryan suggested a low-key approach. In some ways she would have liked to begin by simply speaking with Dr. Cring but she couldn't do that for two reasons. First, Ryan Hooper would fire her if there was even a hint of accusation before she had more evidence to back it up. Second—and she was trying not to think this way—she suspected that any man who could get the HPMC built and control it was the kind of man who could slither or bully his way out of almost anything. That kind of confrontation always left her weak.

The reception area of the HPMC was massive, with a high ceiling supported by beams as big as the cottonwoods along the Pawnee River. The entire fifteen-foot-high back wall of glass looked out on the river and the prairie beyond. The floor was a dark, rich oak laid out in boards pinned with wooden pegs. In the main foyer was a larger-than-life bronze sculpture of a man in flowing robes ministering to a woman on a sickbed. The sculpture stood on a wooden pedestal two feet high in the center of the room. Gretchen moved closer to look up at the two figures depicted in metal. The sculpture was powerful in its evocation of both the suffering of the patient and the concern of the physician. The patient's anguished eyes turned up to the doctor's thoughtful gaze. A bronze plaque attached to the wooden pedestal read: HIPPOCRATES. Below the title plaque was a second plaque inscribed with the Hippocratic oath. The first rule was *Do no harm.*

Gretchen looked back up at the face of the robed physician, then back to the first plaque. "Hippocrates," she said aloud, but in her mind she spelled it Hypocrites. Instantly she was ashamed of herself, both personally and professionally. Everyone deserved the benefit of the doubt, and she couldn't let the thought of Annie Simmons or Tad Bordeaux change that.

It took a few minutes to find the HPMC office where the public tours of the new facility began. She wandered past rows of offices and finally found a handful of interested citizens enjoying coffee and cookies while waiting in a plush lounge. A tall, red-haired woman in a tasteful black skirt and white blouse was flitting among them like a flight attendant in the first-class cabin. When the woman saw Gretchen, she excused herself from the older couple she was talking to.

"Ms. Harris?"

Gretchen was not surprised to be recognized, but her paranoia whispered that this woman had been tipped off. "Yes."

"With the *Gazette*, right?"

"Well, yes."

"I noticed your name on the list," the woman said. "We're so glad you came out to see us. I'm Betty Bechtold, community relations." She took the woman's proffered hand and shook it. "Would you like some coffee?"

"No, thank you."

"Well, let me get some information for you." She walked quickly to a small table filled with pamphlets, collected one of each, and was back before Gretchen had a chance to do more than glance at the others in the room. They were mostly older people, people who might well find themselves patients at the HPMC in the near future. They were likely there to see what they would be getting into.

"Here you go." Betty Bechtold handed the pamphlets over. "They tell a little bit about the facility, the equipment, the staff, all that." She smiled, turned to the others in the room, and raised her voice. "We're going to start now. It will be a quick tour of some of the patient rooms, the galleys, an operating suite, and a peek at the administrative offices. If anyone needs assistance or has questions, just ask. The entire building is, of course, very handicapped-friendly." Gretchen fell into line behind the couple whom Betty had been talking with when she arrived. They were both well-dressed and gray and Gretchen decided to stick within earshot of them to gauge their reaction as a sort of curb to her own prejudices.

The tour was well organized, efficient, and clearly designed to give prospective patients the impression that the entire facility was run that way. The couple in front of Gretchen was taken by the grandeur of the place, but more significantly, they were pleased with the amenities that made the HPMC seem like something other than a hospital. At every turn, staff greeted the visitors with heartfelt smiles, the rooms were more like fine hotel suites than hospital rooms, the food they sampled at one of the three "galleys" was well cooked and tasty. The old woman kept exclaiming, "Why, it's just like being sick in your own home." The old man teased her. "Better," he said.

By the time the tour was winding down, Gretchen was confused. Though she didn't want to, she could now see that the HPMC was a pleasant place, which was more than could be said for some hospitals. After they toured the operating suite, she was also convinced that the equipment and probably the care were first rate. The fears that the old couple might have had about impending medical procedures had been neatly assuaged by the confident impression created by the staff of HPMC. The value of that sort of reassurance was obvious. And by the time they came to the administrative offices, Gretchen was beginning to wonder if the benefit to the community of a facility like HPMC might not be worth the cost. Betty Bechtold was leading them down a corridor that branched off into different office pods as she was explaining the computerized accounting system, which doesn't bother the patients with bills but deals directly with their insurance companies as patient advocates. It was down a side corridor that Gretchen saw an office with Dr. Cring's name on the door.

The door was heavy oak with a beveled glass window above the nameplate and she couldn't help slipping over and glancing inside. A secretary wearing tiny earphones and typing sixty miles an hour sat at a massive desk. Behind her, the door to Dr. Cring's actual office stood ajar, and by ducking down and leaning far to her right, Gretchen caught a glimpse of a tall, silver-headed man wearing half glasses and pondering a book that lay open on his desk. He didn't look as she had imagined him. He looked more like a grandfather than a man who would refuse to treat a patient because he couldn't pay the fee. The rest of the tour was still moving, so Gretchen took one more second to study Cring. She squinted to focus on his eyes, and when she did, he looked up and caught her peeking past the secretary and into his office. Gretchen was embarrassed, jerked her head out of sight, and hurried after the tour.

They were heading back for the lounge where they had begun. Betty Bechtold made a gesture toward an office pod. "That's our medical records department," she said as she moved along. "Everything is kept electronically and stored on CD-ROM."

Now Gretchen stood staring into the office of medical records. Two trimly dressed women sat at computer terminals. Behind them were rows and rows of very modern-looking filing cabinets. The handwritten notes would be stored there, Gretchen thought. She wondered if somewhere in that maze was a scrawled memo about sending Tad Bordeaux to Denver via airplane. It was unlikely that Annie Simmons was mentioned at all. She stood at the door and watched the women type until a hand touched her shoulder. She jumped and spun to find Betty Bechtold's concerned face. "Are you all right?"

"Yes," Gretchen said. "Sure." She could see then that the rest of the tour was far down the hall.

"Do you have any questions?" Betty asked. "Is there anything else I could show you?"

Gretchen shook her head. "No," she said, "not now." She pulled herself away from the door of medical records, and Betty Bechtold steered her down the hall in the wake of the tour group, which had turned back into the lounge and was again sipping coffee.

"Step right in," Betty said. But Gretchen raised her hand and shook her head.

"No," she said, "I should be going." They stood just outside the lounge and Betty moved to shield their conversation from the others.

"This is for an article," she said with a pleasant smile. It was not a question but Gretchen treated it like one.

"Maybe. I'll have to see what I've got."

"Well, I'd be glad to answer any questions you might have. Facts, figures, numbers, that kind of thing. You know, as you write." She produced a card and handed it over. "You call anytime."

Gretchen took the card and thrust out her hand. "I may be calling," she said. She smiled. "Facts, figures, that kind of thing."

❧ 22 ❧

It was hard to say why Steve Thurston never got married. There were always women around. Girls first, then women. He liked some of them a lot, but he could never flip the switch, and never had considered it seriously until Gretchen.

Like all places, Lakota County had a few old bachelors. It was hard to say about any of them either, but they had always been around. Steve saw them in the cafés and the gas stations. They were out in the sorry grainfields on their beat-up, ancient tractors. A few spent their time chasing cows from horseback. In Steve's heart he felt that they might as well have been riding dinosaurs across the pages of some history book. It was funny: most of the really old guys like his father had wives. They had ranches, jobs that might not make them rich, but jobs they could live with, and families. The new guys, the young kids who worked with Steve, had that same thing. It was the middle ground that slipped. Guys like Bob and Steve never seemed to settle down. But for a while it had felt like Steve would. There was a time when he thought he might marry Gretchen, thought he might be a father to Jake. But that feeling didn't last. It started to fade on the day his father called Bob and him into the kitchen to discuss John Tully's offer to buy the ranch. There hadn't been much real discussion. The figures spoke for themselves: sell the ranch to Tully or give the place to the bank. From that day on, the world had slid back to the way the seventies had felt.

Of course he shouldn't complain. In a lot of ways it was an easy life. At least Steve believed his was easy. Never missed a meal out of want, had a nice pickup to drive and plenty of spending money. It wasn't perfect but he shouldn't complain. Bob, on the other hand, had some room to bitch, although he didn't. He had had a couple of girlfriends but they never took. He said a humorous thing one time that Steve always remembered. He was just out of high school, heading for the war, leaving a puppy-love girlfriend at home, and he didn't know shit. The draft had made him a man by default and somewhere he'd picked up this joke: "Women," he said. "You can't live with 'em and you can't shoot 'em." Steve supposed he wanted to get a little nooky before he took off for Saigon and she was holding back. Steve didn't suppose his brother ever got any of that because the next time they saw each other she was married and Bob was a different guy altogether.

It wasn't long after he came back that Steve asked him if he ever had killed a man. He was keeping to himself, but tough and stringy like no one around McDermot ever had seen. Steve was the little brother who didn't go, in some ways the little brother that Bob went in the place of, and Steve was curious about what his brother had done in his stead. "Maybe," Bob said. "But only the weirdos talk about it and I'm trying not to be a weirdo."

He didn't seem weird to Steve. He seemed like a hero, though there were people in town who thought otherwise. Steve nodded like he understood what Bob was talking about. "I get it."

"You might," Bob said in response. "If not now, someday. Killing people in a war is like any nasty chore. Something you have to do, but not something you want to talk about. Just a job that falls to some of us and not to others." And that's about all he ever said about Vietnam.

The only real story he ever told Steve about the war was the flying cat story. He was with the armored cavalry, a foot soldier who walked along beside the tanks and half-tracks as they crashed through the jungle and over rice paddies. "Shit," he said. "Cavalry?

Sounded good to me. I was so dumb I thought they had horses."
He laughed. "Thought we might be riding through wavy grass
like out home. But hell no. Either tangled-up vines and bushes or,
later on, hillsides cooked to nothing by Agent Orange. Maybe the
saddest part was that I got to loving those Agent Orange'd hills.
At least you knew you weren't getting sneaked up on."

They were always moving and every night they set up a perimeter maybe a couple hundred yards in diameter. They dug holes
around the top of a bare hill and parked their vehicles inside. It
was a lot of work. There was a bunch of soldiers, fifty or sixty.
The night of the flying cat story they had been at work to clear
the perimeter for maybe an hour. "We'd been out for over a week,
chasing invisible gooks, taking some fire, but finding nothing to
shoot back at. The hill was tall and mostly bare; the closest cover thick enough to hide a gook was a mile down the hill. We had
a good spot, safe enough, and we were trying to relax."

They were working to make the perimeter secure, chopping out
withered trees, digging battlements, setting out listening devic-
es. "Guys had their shirts off, lots of them were smoking dope,
trying to shake the tension of it all, when all of a sudden there
was a commotion at the west end. People started yelling and running around, and in a minute the whole place was in turmoil. A
half-dozen guys are chasing something through our camp. Other guys are hustling to get their weapons. Jesus, I thought, what
the hell. And I jumped on a Bradley armored car where I could
see whatever it was.

"Well, fifty guys are running around, half of them chasing something and half of them being chased by something. Lots of rifles
are getting loaded up and suddenly I see what it is. It looked like
a cat to me. A good-sized black fucker that was in the wrong place
at the wrong time. But it wasn't giving up. It was running under
jeeps and leaping here and there and trying to figure out how to
get away from these damned Americans. I figured it was a gook
cat, some son of a bitch that escaped the cook pot long enough to
find itself in this mess. But this was no ordinary gook cat.

"It made another lap of the perimeter and finally spied a lone tree that had been left in the dead center of things. The tree was a charred snag, maybe even burned by napalm. Just a thirty-foot-high scrawny pole with a few bare branches, right in the middle of our perimeter, and the cat headed for it. Blam, he was at the top in no time and a couple dozen excited GIs were circling below. Don't know why, maybe it was the week of nothing to shoot at, or just the frustration of it all, but one guy takes a shot at the cat. He misses and another guy tries. Pretty soon the cat's dodging and ducking, and half the guys below are emptying clips but nobody's hit him yet. It's an ugly scene for someone like me, raised in the country and liking all animals, and everyone knew it was about to get uglier. Finally the cat is out on a tiny branch, swaying at the top of a tree on the top of bare hill. I figure he's totally fucked and so do all the guys shooting. But the cat's got one more trick up his furry sleeve. The shooting has kind of stopped and the sound of fresh clips being slapped into place is filling the air when the cat pushes off with a hell of a leap. Some of the guys even start to laugh, thinking the cat is going to fall in among them. But the cat doesn't fall. It flies."

Steve loved that story and every time Bob got to this part, he said, "Flies, shit." He'd have to laugh. "Cats can't fly."

Bob would shrug. "Well, there it is! This cat could fly. Just took off and left us with our dicks in our hands and our mouths open. Sailed right out of the shithole perimeter and all the way to the trees on another hill."

Steve has always been able to picture what it must have been like for those boys, most of them barely twenty, standing silent, with the finest guns in the world, loaded and ready to shoot, looking up at nothing and wondering if they had imagined it all. Sometimes Steve thought about what it was like for the cat, too. Maybe he understood the cat better. Fuck it, just leap out of that bare, lonely tree and fly to someplace safe. Sail on home.

☙ 23 ❧

On the way to the *Gazette* after her tour of the HPMC office, Gretchen made herself think of Annie Simmons and how Dr. Arnold Cring and his medical business cheated her. She wanted to dwell on this injustice, to focus on what she would have to say to convince Ryan Hooper to let her write the story. Ryan Hooper was in his office when she came into the *Gazette*, and since she had to pick up Jake after school, she didn't take the chance that he'd dash off. She bypassed her own cubicle, walked right in on Hooper, and shut the door. "I want to do this story," she said without sitting down.

Ryan was studying wire-service stories on the computer screen and looked up, a little dazed. "Story?"

"The Cring story. The HPMC story. Refusing care. Selecting patients according to their ability to pay. The whole for-profit, private clinic thing."

He stared over his shoulder at Gretchen until he was sure she was serious. Then he swiveled away from the computer and gestured toward a chair. Gretchen obliged but didn't let herself get comfortable. "Tad Bordeaux died," she said. "There's a young woman on the north end of town who's pretty lonely today."

"You're thinking that this Bordeaux kid didn't get the right care."

"I don't know yet. That's one of the things that I have to find out. He might have gotten the right care, maybe just not soon enough."

Ryan swiveled back and forth in his chair. It was a tic he had when he was thinking. He began to nod before he spoke. "You'd have to go easy. The editorial board wouldn't like it much."

"Would you have to tell them?"

"Sure, the people who own this paper would have to know. I wouldn't need to tell them everything yet but eventually they've got to know. And even now they're going to want to know that one of our own reporters is asking questions about the medical community. Clinics, doctors, and hospitals do a lot of advertising in local newspapers. Nobody is more powerful."

"I can write the story?"

"Don't let anyone see a word until I've had my look."

With that tacit endorsement Gretchen reeled from Ryan's office, suddenly overwhelmed and happy with the responsibility she'd brought to herself. Now the other stories she'd been working on didn't seem very important and she decided to take off work even earlier than she had planned. Gretchen was at Jake's school twenty minutes sooner than normal. She didn't spend the time constructively. She didn't think about the story. She just waited in the car outside the gymnasium until the boys started wandering out in twos and threes. When she saw Jake, dressed in sweat clothes, with the battered gym bag slung casually over his shoulder, she was suddenly struck again by the fact that, though he was still thin and boyish, he was only a few years younger than Tad Bordeaux. It didn't seem possible, but this skinny kid would soon grow up to be a man. She wanted to think that he would get a fair shake from the world, a better shake than Tad Bordeaux. But talking with Annie had rattled her faith. Gretchen possessed a naive belief in justice, but as she watched Jake waving and fooling with his friends, she realized that justice didn't just happen.

"Hi, Mom."

The twenty-pound gym bag was tossed over the Jeep seat like a bag of potato chips. Gretchen marveled at the strength of this

149

boy who only a few years before had been a tiny baby. She shook a smile off her face, knowing that Jake would think she was sappy if she tried to explain. "How was practice?"

"Fine. Let's go for an ice cream cone. I'm starving."

"We should go eat something good."

"Yeah, but . . . " Jake gestured toward the warm sun and blue sky, "it's an ice cream kind of day."

"So it is. Where would like to go, Ashcroft's?"

Ashcroft's had been a fixture in McDermot since Gretchen was a little girl. It was the hometown soda fountain, famous for its homemade ice cream. "Mom. Ashcroft's is so not cool. Everyone goes to TCBY."

Gretchen was about to tell her son for the hundredth time that Ashcroft's was special for her. Dipping homemade Ashcroft's ice cream to her friends had been her first job. But just then a tall, dark-haired girl with a gym bag identical to Jake's walked past the front of the Jeep and waved shyly. Jake waved quickly back but didn't look at her. "Who's that?"

"Nobody."

"No, that was somebody."

"Mom."

"Come on. Come on." She had started to back the Jeep out of its parking place but now she stopped. "I'll blow the horn, call her back here, and ask her name."

"Oh God, Mom. You're so queer." She started to blow the horn. "Okay, okay, okay. Just go."

"What's her name?"

"Mom." Jake looked at his mother with pleading eyes. "Okay. Amy Gunther. Let's go."

Gretchen pulled out onto the street and headed for TCBY. "Gunther. Is her father Ed Gunther the electrician?"

Jake shrugged. "I don't know. What difference does it make?"

Gretchen found herself thinking again about Tad Bordeaux and Annie Simmons. They'd driven another block before she realized that she hadn't answered Jake. When she looked, he was staring at her, wondering where her attention had been. "You're right, honey," she said, "it doesn't make any difference. It shouldn't matter at all."

❧ 24 ❧

Steve had a strong conviction that whoever invented mobile homes should be taken out on the prairie and shot. The one he and Bob lived in was made with two-by-two studs—just two little inches of insulation between the Thurston boys and the wind. Steve tried not to think about it, but he knew that come winter the little electric stove would be running full bore and it would always be cold around the windows where things didn't fit right. Everything was built cheap. The cupboards didn't close right and the appliances were low power all the way around. It was built exactly the opposite of the way Steve tried to build houses. He supposed it worked all right for guys like Bob and him. But think of kids. Think of a batch of kids living in something like that—a bunch of mice in a stovepipe.

On the inside the place looked okay. Gretchen came over once in a while and went through it like a dirt weasel. Jake came along and the three of them worked the place over. Bob was never there to help and Jake and Steve were mostly just furniture movers. Gretchen supervised and, because of her impossibly high standards of cleanliness, did most of the real cleaning. She had a knack for it and a desire to see it done in a way that was difficult for Steve to understand. She concentrated on making a house homey like some guys concentrate on making a perfect cabinet: just like those finish carpenters, it could make a guy a little crazy to work around her. Half the time Jake and Steve just stood back and took orders. Jake would roll his eyes but not when Gretchen could see him. But, except for the cleaning sessions and the feeling that it was all very temporary, Steve got along all right in the tin-can trailer home. It would have been nice to have one of the houses like he worked on every day but he figured that the mobile home, just then, suited him all right. Jake called it the pad and Steve was never sure if he meant it was a place to take off from or something to keep him from getting too bruised up. It could work both ways.

But it sure wasn't a bachelor pad. For a couple years, since Gretchen, he'd been on the straight and narrow, just working, coming home at night, seeing Gretchen a couple nights a week. Sometimes it felt good and he found himself craving the touch of her. Sometimes he longed for her, but other times it wasn't enough and he felt wired and hollow. She constantly pressured him for more commitment. They say it's natural and sometimes it even made him feel good that she cared that much, but it sometimes got out of hand. She wasn't above glancing through his mail, listening to phone messages, or going through the closets looking for who knows what. That kind of stuff was something that was way off limits growing up on the ranch. Privacy was a rule at the Thurston house but maybe not at Gretchen's. Of course, when he asked her what she was doing or shook his head, she said he had something to hide. He didn't think he had, until he realized that it didn't take much to amount to incriminating evidence in Gretchen's mind. A book of matches from a bar, a pair of concert ticket stubs dropped into his trashcan by a friend, junky old sunglasses behind the seat of his pickup, not that she didn't have some cause to wonder. He'd lived his whole life free to do pretty much what he wanted and had probably gotten so he didn't think much about others.

Her mind jumped to wild conclusions—so wild sometimes that for most of a year he thought she might be kidding. By that time, there was a look in her eyes when she questioned him that made him feel like some sort of insect. He was scared to death that he'd say the wrong thing and set her off. Being scared always makes a guy look like he has something to hide. Then he figured she was thinking he was a liar and that made him mad, like some guy had called him a liar, and everything blew up. Then they'd be off, and on occasion, he'd try to get back into the life he'd had before her. But in the meantime the ranch had disappeared and so had his life before Gretchen. They ended up acting like kids. They tried to say it was over, that it had been a good run but was destined not to be. Sometimes it would go on like that for weeks, but eventually they couldn't stand it and after a while he'd find a way to forget the insults and they would get back together. But like a damned elephant, she never forgot. She remembered everything—even dreams and other things that never happened. Those were hard times, but there were other times when he remembered feeling so close to her that it actually hurt in his chest. He never wanted to come off sappy so he never said it, but sometimes he felt like he was part of her life and she was part of his. Like they were in it together and didn't have a chance without each other.

Of course there were normal, good nights too. Like the night Jake was at an out-of-town basketball game. It was a Friday night after a long week. The crew had finished off the roof and moved inside to start on sheetrock as soon as the electricians and plumbers finished up. Gretchen was working on her doctor story—going after it the way she went after dirt behind a couch, and they both wanted something easy. There was a new Mexican restaurant on the east side of town out by the mall, so they gave it a try and took in a movie. Typical deal—he liked the restaurant and didn't like the movie. She saw it the other way around. But that was fine. They joked about it and were feeling content when they stopped by his trailer. His charge card was near maxing out and he'd forgotten his checkbook, so they meant to only run in, grab it, and then go out for a drink. But once they got inside, the week caught up with them and they wilted onto the couch and flicked on the TV. It was just some old movie they'd both seen, but it felt good, so they settled in.

Steve was sliding lower on the couch, letting his eyes narrow down, but then he felt something coming from Gretchen. At first he thought it might be one of her quiet spells that meant something was wrong and he panicked, not having any idea what it was going to be. But the feeling didn't have that knifing edge and he relaxed, knowing it would be something reasonable. Still he had to wait. He knew enough not to ask what was wrong. Asking made her take longer to get it out and was always a bad beginning.

"He really is a son of a bitch," she said, and Steve knew she was thinking about her story.

"Who's a son of a bitch?"

"Cring."

"The doc."

"The dick."

"Did he do something else?"

"Not really."

"So why's he a son of a bitch?"

"Just is." Steve knew there was more to come. She was thinking. "It's like he figures our lives and his business is some kind of poker game, and he holds all the cards."

"Probably not as simple as it looks."

"His life?"

"That and running HPMC. Getting where he is. Staying there. You should talk to him."

"You sound like you're on his side."

"I didn't know we had to take sides. You're the one that keeps talking about remaining professional." Steve didn't intend to be lecturing her, but he could see that she was listening to what he was saying. "I mean, you're dealing with the guy's life." She tilted her head the way she did when she was seriously considering something. Steve would almost hear a little humming noise as she was thinking.

"That's easy to say when you're not personally involved. I'm thinking about the kid that died."

Steve nodded. "Yeah, but it's a tough world out there for all of us."

She tilted her head again. "Okay. I get that." Suddenly she turned to him and smiled, and he was as confused as when she spun around with that look of accusation in her eyes. She reached out and touched his face, and he couldn't believe the tenderness in the fingertips.

"What?" he said.

"You're just so good sometimes. You think I should give him a chance, don't you? A chance to address my charges."

"Well, yeah. He might be a dick, but even a dick should have a chance to defend himself." That came out of him without even thinking, and she responded by bringing a second hand up to his face. A tear rolled down her face.

"Oh God," she said, "I love you so much."

She snuggled into him and he felt her breasts firm against his chest and her breath warm at his neck. He moved against her because he knew that was what she wanted, but he was clueless as to why.

☙ 25 ❧

The Lakota County Courthouse was grand, but old, and Erwin Benson remembers when it was built. He recalls the first time he ever climbed the granite steps leading up to the gothic pillars, the huge leaded-glass doors that had been shipped from Chicago. For thirty years he thought the building was far too auspicious for a nearly broke, humble cattle county. This perception had been correct to the extent that there were austere years when the offices at the periphery of the building—the register of deeds and the auditor—were inhabited in winter by cranky middle-aged women forced to wear heavy sweaters because the thermostats had to be set at sixty degrees to save money. Now, as Erwin slowly mounted the steps, it occurred to him that the world had caught up with the Lakota County Courthouse. Already there were temporary buildings out back that housed the overflow from Motor Vehicles and the sheriff's office. The rail where Erwin's hand rested as he paused halfway up was painted shiny black, but he could feel the rust beneath. He looked up at the carved Greek figure of justice above the pillars and knew that the days of this courthouse were numbered. He had already heard it described around town as "quaint".

There were twenty-one steps from the street to the front door, and Erwin usually stopped to rest on step twelve. Some days he took the time to turn and look back over the town, but today he only rested and glanced at his watch. He was due in municipal court in seven minutes and he guessed that he would make it by the skin of his teeth. His briefcase was filled with the cases for the day, everything from DWIs to possession of drugs with the intent to distribute. Nothing really violent today, he thought, unless he was late to court and Judge Current was in a bad mood. He hiked the briefcase up under his arm and trudged toward the top of the stairs. From behind him he heard the snappy click of shoe leather on granite. He didn't turn to see who was running up the stairs behind him, but he had a good idea. The first case was the drug charge and John Tully was the defense attorney. He was just the type to take the courthouse steps two at a time.

Erwin reached for the brass door handle but Tully beat him to it. "Morning, Mr. Prosecutor."

Erwin turned and looked over his glasses at Tully's too cheerful face. He let his eyes slide down to the rich, red tie beneath the blue suit coat. He couldn't help a subtle smile. It was like turning to find the captain of the high school football team headed for the senior prom. "Morning yourself," Erwin said. They were inside the courthouse now but the courtroom was still the length of the corridor away. Erwin was too winded from climbing those last nine steps. "You go on ahead," he said.

"Ahh," Tully said and waved his hand. "Current is usually late herself."

"But you have a client."

"Just talked to him. They're bringing him over from the jail." They were already walking. But they walked slowly, at Erwin's pace. The corridor was empty.

"I see you're going to say the search was improper."

"I believe it was." The two men moved steadily.

"It's Iron Cloud isn't it?" Erwin asked.

"Yes, Andrew Iron Cloud."

"The officer asked if he could come in and look around, and Iron Cloud said yes. What's improper about that?"

"It's true that he might have said that," Tully said, "but it wasn't his apartment. It was rented by his girlfriend."

"Boissenet."

"Correct."

"They've been living together for three years."

"On and off."

Erwin nodded his head. They were nearly at the courtroom door. "You got the documentation on the rent payments?"

"Cancelled checks."

"Iron Cloud might have been giving her cash."

"Possible," Tully said. They were at the courtroom door and they paused to look at each other. "He says he never gave her a dime."

Erwin nodded again before he put his hand on the door to push it open. "Sad," he said. "He might be telling the truth."

Erwin prosecuted the case all right. He did what the state had a right to expect. But all the time a parallel line of thought was running through his brain. It must have been Tully sitting there at the defense table that got that second line of thought going. Tully had bought the Thurston place and Erwin wasn't sure what he thought about that. Hard to say what sort of deal they had. Erwin knew that Arvid Thurston was still living at the house. He'd known Arvid a little, he could point out the boy who went to Vietnam, and he'd had an insignificant run-in with the one who never left town but maybe should have. He'd known them all since when the mother was alive. Lucy had known Mary Thurston fairly well, and by all accounts, she was a good wife and mother. Something about the Iron Cloud case got Erwin thinking about how everything started going downhill for the Thurstons when Mary died. But that was hard to say. There had been a lot of water under the Thurston bridge. The families of Lakota County knew hard times, always had.

He was walking back to his office when it came to him that the women who stayed didn't have much of a chance. Even if he went to jail, Iron Cloud should be giving that woman a little money for the rent. He should admit it and be proud of it, even if he went to jail as a result. Iron Cloud wasn't much but he'd be less without Boissenet. Sometimes the women simply stayed. The stores were too far away, the roads too long, the company too scarce, the men too rough. It was changing, but it was too late for so many. Better roads, better communication, more money. It was all coming. At least for some, for now. He'd heard it said that when a man sold his cattle the ranch would follow soon enough. But it wasn't losing the cattle. It was the women. God, he missed his Lucy.

❧ 26 ❧

What Steve told Gretchen sank in. The fire had not yet gone out of her campaign for justice, but it was not burning quite as hot. She planned to take one more pass at the story, but Steve was right, she couldn't finish it without talking to Cring. She was feeling exhausted by the weight of the story, frightened by the public conflict to come. In fact, she was ready to be done with it; if getting in to speak with Cring took as long as getting a regular doctor's appointment, it might be months before she could get the interview that would ease her mind. But when she mentioned to the receptionist that she was doing an article about the new medical clinic for the newspaper, she was put on hold for less than a minute, then told to come in at the end of the day. Dr. Cring would be glad to see her around four thirty, the woman said. That was a little too fast. As she hung up the phone Gretchen felt unprepared and slightly dishonest. If Cring knew she was writing an article that was critical of HPMC, she wouldn't have gotten an interview until sometime the next year.

All day long she worried about what she'd ask Cring. The draft of the article on her desk was not as scathing as she had originally envisioned. There were no direct accusations of high-grading patients for maximum reimbursement. She didn't mention any doctors by name and made no attempt to follow the money trail to those who finally benefited the most. Tad Bordeaux's case was given as an example only of a possible abuse of trust, or poor judgment. She had heard about a lot of other examples that she could have brought up in the article, but she blinked when it came to anything that smacked of hearsay against the sacred cow of the medical profession. Basically, the article left any conclusions up to the reader, and though it was decent journalism, it was certainly not hard-hitting. Still, even as it was, a lot of powerful people would be mad; and when she thought of their reaction, she felt sick. She told herself it was her overdeveloped respect for authority that made her feel that way, and she kept telling herself that her responsibility as a reporter had to take precedence. But all the time there was an unsettled feeling that she simply wasn't sure about any of it.

No matter, she dreaded the interview with Dr. Cring. All afternoon she tried to imagine what it would be like, built scenarios in her mind, and prepared answers for Cring's angry questions. Although the only time she'd ever seen the man was in that instant through the office door at HPMC, she'd come to have a sense of him as the story took shape. He was fifty-three years old, a graduate of Stanford medical school, and a board-certified neurosurgeon. By all accounts he was a good surgeon and came to McDermot highly recommended. But a few years after he arrived he became very politically involved in the medical community. He got the entrepreneurial disease and organized a group of young specialists who first tried to take over the administration of the nonprofit hospital. The hospital board resisted but could not control the doctors. Finally the young Turks built their own hospital where they took call only when it was convenient and divided the increased profits like the owners of any business. Though Cring still did a lot of surgery, he spent more and more time administering HPMC.

All that went through Gretchen's mind as she drove through the streets of McDermot on her way to HPMC. It was like being back in high school, when facts and figures run like a movie through your head on the way to take a test. And, as in high school, she sat in the Jeep outside the building and told herself to calm down. The trick that sometimes helped her was to tell herself that she could perform the task in front of her. "I can do this. I can do this," she told herself.

The waiting room was still lined with patients wanting to see one of the clinic's doctors. It would be seven o'clock before it was cleared. Another late night for everyone. But as soon as she told the receptionist who she was, the smartly dressed young woman showed her into a plush little lounge with leather furniture and a breathtaking view of the Pawnee River. She asked Gretchen if she wanted something to drink and Gretchen declined. The receptionist smiled and said Dr. Cring would be right with her. From years of experience waiting for doctors she assumed it would be a half hour at least. But in less than five minutes, the door opened and in swept Dr. Arnold Cring.

He was a larger man than she had thought, with longish gray hair and piercing blue eyes. His handshake was warm and firm, and he started out the conversation with a compliment. "Gretchen Harris. I so enjoy your features." But behind the sincere and practiced smile was a hint of fatigue, and Gretchen wondered if he had ever found the time to read one of her articles, let alone enjoy it.

"Thank you."

Cring waved her into his office, but once the door was shut they both remained standing. "I understand that you're doing an article about the new facility."

"Partly," she said, "mostly I'm exploring HPMC's role in the community." Her palms were sweating, and she had to still a tremor in the index finger of her right hand by grasping it with her left.

Cring smiled, trying hard to hide the weariness that gathered around his eyes. "That's wonderful. We're proud to be bringing world-class care to the community. Have you had a tour?"

"Yes, I've had the tour," Gretchen said. Something in her wanted to talk about the tour, how she had actually been quite impressed. But she forced herself to focus on what Cring had said about the quality of HPMC's care. "Do you mean to say that McDermot did not have world-class medical care before you built the clinic?" It was like jumping off the high diving board. If she could have closed her eyes, she would have.

"Well," Cring instantly was watching her closely, sizing her up, gauging the intent of what she had just said. "The clinic is state of the art."

"But all the doctors that practice here used to work at the regional hospital."

"Many did. And they still do." Suspicion had crept into Cring's voice. "We all have privileges at both facilities."

"And responsibilities?"

Cring nodded. "Of course."

Now Gretchen found herself in the unwanted roll of the aggressor. It was not what she had had in mind. She realized now that she wanted Cring to lose his temper. So far, the grand doctor did not seem to have any trouble remaining pleasant. Yet she felt certain he was not the kind of man who liked to be badgered by anyone, certainly not a woman a dozen years his junior. What was clear to Gretchen was that Cring was no stranger to conflict. His even expression seemed calculated to make her want to back up, knuckle under, and placate him with some deferential comment. But she heard Steve in her mind: "Hard as it is, you owe the guy a chance."

"Doctors always have immense community responsibilities," Cring said, and she got the nauseating impression he felt she was just another misinformed misanthrope taking a crack at rich doctors. It was as if he pitied her.

"Of course," she said. Her voice was quavering and she wanted to stop, but this was the part she owed Cring a chance to answer.

"I was just curious how the doctors at HPMC juggle those responsibilities when they are stockholders of a for-profit corporation? Isn't there some pressure to sacrifice care for profit?"

"No," Cring said flatly. He had been standing all this time, but now he moved around his desk and sat down. The fatigue became even more apparent. He waved Gretchen toward a chair out of habit, but Gretchen didn't sit down. "We can offer better service because we are not hamstrung with government red tape."

"Red tape like Medicare?" It came out more venomous than Gretchen had intended.

"We accept Medicare."

"But much more seldom than the public hospital." Again, she snapped it out too fast and it didn't even sound like Gretchen Harris.

Cring's grandfatherly patience wavered but he forced himself to remain calm. "Is this what your article is about?"

Gretchen had surprised herself and now forced her voice to become more professional. "It's part of what is in the article, yes."

Cring sat quietly for an instant. He held an index finger to his lips and tapped them gently. He curled the finger into a fist and supported his chin with the knuckles. "Would you sit down, Miss Harris?"

Gretchen sat without answering Cring's question. "Then I'm to understand that you have already written your article?" he asked.

"I have a draft."

"And the draft includes these accusations?"

"They are not accusations."

"They sound like accusations." The finger was up, tapping at the lips again. "It sounds like you pretty much have your mind made up and that this interview is mostly pro forma." Cring let that sink in. "I have nothing against you, Miss Harris, but I want you to listen to me."

Gretchen nodded. "But I'm not here for a lecture."

Now the finger moved from the lips and pointed across the desk at her. His voice rose only slightly. "Call it what you like. But if you start printing accusations you better have your facts straight. My board of directors will sue you and your paper into the poorhouse."

This was, at once, the response Gretchen had wanted and her worst nightmare: that she was completely off base and would suffer for it. There was also the specter that she might be hurting people because of her own shortcomings. But she held her chin high. "I'm being thorough," she said. She wanted to get back on equal footing with Cring.

"That's imperative, Miss Harris. For all of us," Cring said with confidence. Something in Gretchen wanted to get out of the conversation, to simply apologize and leave Cring's office. But if she did, she knew she would never be able to report a story again. In an instant all the people she would be letting down tumbled through her mind: Ryan, Annie, Tad, Steve, Jake, herself. She couldn't stop and so clasped her hands tighter to keep them from shaking. Hold your ground. Hold your ground, she thought.

"I have my facts," she said, as much to reassure herself as to answer Cring. "For instance, it's a fact that a young man came into the hospital emergency room three weeks ago with severe neurological problems, and without being examined, he was sent to Denver instead of coming here, to this world-class facility."

Cring stared at her for a moment, then sat back in his chair and looked out the window. Her eyes followed his lead and found a bend of the river that she knew well from her childhood. Suddenly Gretchen wished she were ten years old again. She could almost feel what it had been like, one day of play following the last. A safe place to go. Love. But the tiny sound of Cring tapping his lips brought her back in time to watch the fingers raise up and run through his gray hair. "I don't think you understand what you're getting into. There are many factors that figure into a medical decision. I don't recall the incident you are referring to, but if in your draft you're pitting your judgment against mine, you are on shaky ground. You might want to consider some revisions."

"I don't pretend to be a doctor."

Cring's smile was sardonic. "That is good, Miss Harris, because I don't think you have much notion of what it's like to be a doctor. I don't think you have any idea how hard a fellow like me has worked." Now he looked straight into Gretchen's eyes. "Harder than you can imagine, through medical school, internship, residency, years of seventy-hour weeks. I've spent my whole life with jealous jackals at my throat." He nodded, as if agreeing with himself. "You seem like a perfectly nice young woman. But you may well be an unsuspecting agent of those jackals." He made no attempt to hide the fact that he was exhausted inside and out.

"I'm not judging you," Gretchen said. "I'm reporting on how this facility serves the community of McDermot. The costs."

"And the benefits?"

"And the benefits."

Cring put both hands on his desk and smiled a weary smile. "Then there will be no problem. I will look forward to reading your draft."

"The public is not usually able to read drafts of articles."

His hands were still on the desk and now they made small circles on the smooth hardwood. "Of course," Cring said. He stood up and surprised Gretchen by thrusting out his hand.

She stood and took his hand. The pressure was still even and the hand still warm. "I'm doing good here in this little town of ours," he said. "I'm not doing anything that those jackals wouldn't do if they had the chance." She thought he would release her hand then, but he did not. "It's a constant fight," he said, "and I've learned to save my energy for when it's needed. Even if your article is actually published, I'll survive it—no matter what it says. I will thrive." He exhaled with what seemed to be real concern for Gretchen. "I'm not so sure about you."

That night, on her word processor at home, Gretchen put the final touches on the HPMC story. She tried not to be her usual wishy-washy self. She made it a little tougher, a little more suggestive of wrongdoing, but there was something in her that wanted to collapse from remembering Cring's steely eyes. His aggressive stance and threats had brought out in her the desire to fight, but at the end he let down his guard and let her see how tired, how normal, and perhaps how decent he was. If she let herself forget what he'd done, she felt some compassion for him. The facts, after all, were disputable. There were medical considerations that she might not understand. It could very well be that all the doctors in McDermot were engaged in the same medical practices. It could be that doctors everywhere were taking advantage of the merger of medicine and business. But that didn't alter the fact that Cring and his cohorts refused to treat Tad Bordeaux because he couldn't pay their price. Or did it?

Finally she couldn't pull the trigger either way and ended up e-mailing a story to Ryan Hooper that she wasn't proud of. She felt like she wasn't doing what Annie Simmons or Ida Miller deserved, yet she couldn't forget what Steve said about threatening a person's livelihood. It actually scared her a little. She turned off the computer, then the overhead light, and walked out into the tiny living room. It was a Saturday night and Jake was at a friend's house. She hadn't spoken with Steve since the evening at his trailer.

It was the night at Clyde's bar before that. She hadn't come out with her jealousy of Carolina Riggins and it had festered. The house felt quiet, big, and empty. Suddenly she felt sure that Steve and Carolina had been together in the days since that night.

All at once she felt like she was being taken for a fool, but at the same time, in contradiction to those feelings, it struck her that it was silly for Steve and her to be apart. Jake was safe at a friend's house—probably curled up on a couch watching videos. Steve should be with her. It seemed prophetic that he was not; it had been coming to this ever since he had moved from the ranch house. But maybe it was just her and that empty house. Maybe a postpartum reaction connected with finishing the HPMC story. She tried to put a positive spin on the evening ahead. Occasionally he just showed up on Saturday nights. She hoped he'd at least call, hoped she wouldn't break down and start calling around for him.

It was after nine o'clock when she went to the kitchen to make something to eat. The HPMC story kept rolling over in her mind. Now, when she thought of the interview with Cring, she recalled the undertone of anger and frustration in his voice. She remembered what he said about the superhuman effort it took to put together an institution like HPMC, what it took to keep it together. As she spread yesterday's tuna salad on a piece of bread, she couldn't help feeling that there was a hint of desperation in the way Cring expressed himself. When a car's lights shone through the kitchen window, a chill tumbled down her spine. Could Cring be that desperate? She moved to the side of the window and peeked out from behind the curtain. The car turned down the alley and moved slowly along the side of her house. Crazy. The car proceeded down the alley and she shifted to the back window to watch it turn again and disappear.

The television was in the living room, and though she was not a great fan of TV, she was lonely and it helped pass the time. Juggling a glass of milk and the plate with the tuna salad sandwich, she reached down to turn on the set. But there were car lights again in the alley. She left the television off, put the sandwich on the coffee table, and turned off the overhead. The car, or perhaps it was another car, moved down the alley behind the house. It was impossible to get a license number or even to tell for sure what kind of car it was. She was being silly. It was just a neighbor. The car was a half block past her house when the brake lights flashed. Yes, a neighbor coming home. She stood at the window and thought she could discern the figure of a man moving from the car. The neighbor walking to his house.

She waited to see if the house lights would come on, but if they did, they must have been on the other side of the house. The view out her window was murky yellow from a distant streetlight. With her own lights turned off, she felt like the stalker. "God, this is ridiculous." The light switch was on the other side of the room and she was halfway there when there was a sound at the back of the house. It was just a muffled scrape, but it froze Gretchen in the center of her own living room.

If her mind was not playing tricks on her, then someone or something was just outside her back door. She wanted to turn on the light but knew that if someone was at a window it would give them all the advantage. The telephone—but that would have forced her to move through the whole house. She was safer where she was, against the back wall where her silhouette couldn't be seen from the outside. It was nothing but her imagination, but she waited for a minute to see if there was another sound.

The sound came again. First the same scraping noise, then a single dull thud. Her heartbeat doubled. Now she was sure. Someone was in her driveway, near the basketball backboard Steve had erected for Jake. She wanted to stay against the back wall but the doors were not locked. Two options: walk quietly to the telephone in the kitchen or run for the front door. But how could she be sure whoever was out there was still on the basketball court? He could be waiting just outside the front door.

She edged along the wall toward the kitchen, listening for any sound, and trying to make none herself. As she got to the kitchen door another thud came from behind the house. She moved the last five feet to the telephone and grasped the receiver. Another thud, just outside the kitchen door, and she picked up the phone. It was her intention to call 911, but before she could dial, she heard a series of thumps and the faint sound of a human voice. She kept the phone in her hand but leaned close enough to the back door to look out into the night. In the yellow glow from the streetlight, when her eyes adjusted, she could make out the silhouette of a man. He stood fifteen feet from the backboard and dropped the basketball twice in succession.

She leaned back and replaced the receiver, then opened the back door just a crack. It was Steve, cowboy boots and canvas coat, dribbling the basketball with his right hand and holding up his left as if asking the crowd for silence. "Score's eighty-five to eighty-three," he was saying to himself and to the imaginary fans. "Thurston needs a three-pointer."

She watched him dribble back behind the key. He spun silently in the half-light. "One second to go." He leaped gracefully into the air and released a jump shot that soared in slow motion through the night air. The ball floated light as a balloon until it swished through the net.

"Score!" Steve raised both fists in triumph and stood for a long moment with his head bowed.

27

Since Carl Lindquist needed to teach for a living, he never had as much time to hunt birds as he would have liked. But for a working guy, he did pretty well. By juggling his class schedule and utilizing strategic sabbaticals, he managed some wonderful hunts: bobwhite quail in Georgia, ruffed grouse in Ontario, partridge in the Prairie Provinces, pheasants in the Dakotas, and woodcock in Vermont. He loved them all, but his favorite game bird was the one he grew up with. For him, sharp-tailed grouse were the finest of them all. They were intricately beautiful and hearty birds, about the size of a large Cornish game hen, but unlike Cornish game hens, they did not adapt well to alien landscapes. They seemed to Carl to be the essence of wildness. To a sharp-tailed grouse home is home, the only place they can survive. That is all there is to it. Only life in pristine prairie satisfied them. They ate only the purest foods and seemed to need constant wind and long sunsets. Their plumage was mottled gray, brown, and white. Their feathers grew down their legs and were one of the unique, evolutionary adaptations protecting them from the worst winters on the continent. The meat of their breasts was dark red, and Carl loved to serve them medium rare to guests of discriminating taste. Eleanor Stiener seemed just that sort of person. Like the grouse, she was really quite beautiful—tall but full-figured, with lovely skin and a shy but devilish smile. She had apparently already fallen in love with the sharp-tailed grouse's habitat. Carl's hope was that she would fall in love with the rich, sweet flavor of their flesh and, in the bargain, give an old grouse hunter a little of the joy that only the company of a woman could provide.

Cooking elaborate meals was a favorite pastime, but Carl was a believer in heavy sauces only when there was something to hide. He had been fussing in the kitchen all day long: slicing vegetables for ratatouille, carefully mixing the dough for puff pastries, baking the wild plums he had spent the afternoon before picking from the same brushy draws from which he had gathered the grouse. But the side dishes were mostly garnish for the main course. He had done nothing to the grouse breasts except cover them in a light marinade of olive oil, salt, and pepper.

It was already after five o'clock and Eleanor was due at six. She said she was interested in watching the sunset from Carl's front porch—a telling and tantalizing desire. The sunset would occur about seven o'clock. Sitting in the two rockers he had just installed on the porch, sipping cocktails, and watching the sunset sounded marvelous indeed. It was part of what he had in mind when he finally retired to this place. For years he had longed to return, but he knew it would be difficult to survive without either renting the pasture to someone who would overgraze it, or plowing the flat spots in an attempt to grow winter wheat. Both activities would ruin the habitat for his grouse and he would not do that. As a result he had to teach longer than he wanted to so he could qualify for full retirement.

Now, like the grouse, he was at home. He had what he had always longed for—peace, quiet, a lovely house, his dog, and his grouse. Eleanor was a surprise bonus. Though there were interesting women everywhere, he had not dared to dream of running into someone quite as lovely and sophisticated as Eleanor. There was a sense that a momentous evening was in the offing and everything had to be perfect. The sign of a truly good cook and entertainer is to do it all fabulously without the guest suspecting it is a chore. Carl didn't want to be jumping up and down all night, so he took special care to be sure that everything would be ready in sequence. The table had been set for hours, but he smoothed the linen and rechecked the crystal for water spots. He put a pair of highball glasses in the freezer, stepped over Tolstoy, who was sleeping sprawled out to full length on the kitchen floor, and replaced the burned-down candles on the end tables. He straightened the bouquet of wild flowers he'd picked that morning, and returned to the kitchen to separate the eggs for the soufflé. At exactly six o'clock the sound of crushing gravel came through the window from the driveway. He looked out to confirm that it was Eleanor's car, and glanced down to realize that he was still stark naked.

Tolstoy stood up, disoriented and not sure if there was a car in the driveway or if he had been dreaming of a car in the driveway. He barked once but was wagging his tail, so Carl shot up the stairs and began to wrestle himself into a white shirt as he watched Eleanor out the bedroom window. She was already out of the car, and he could see that she was dressed in a tasteful yellow western blouse, blue jeans, and boots. He was pulling on clothes as fast as he could but couldn't help watching as she dove into the back seat of her car and emerged with a bottle of wine in each hand. Her hair was perhaps a bit too curly for Carl's taste, but the way she reached out with a booted foot and slammed the car door was charming. He was still dressing when she knocked on the back door. Tolstoy barked again with friendly excitement and Carl called down to reassure him and to tell Eleanor it was all right to come inside. He rushed the best he could, cursing himself for not being at the door to welcome her.

She was standing in the living room petting Tolstoy's head and looking down at the newly finished hardwood floor when he stepped out onto the top landing. Again he viewed her from above and this time was close enough to feel her radiance and grace as her eyes inspected his handiwork in the restored maple and hickory parquet. He remained silent and let her sense him watching. When she looked up, her smile deepened, "What . . . ," she said, "are you wearing?"

Carl looked down at himself, then back up to Eleanor's laughing eyes. "It's a kilt," he said as her hand came up to her lips. "I see that." She was shaking her head in disbelief. "It's wonderful." She couldn't help letting her eyes run down to the tasseled, tall stockings and then up to the starched and ruffled white shirt.

"Thank you." Carl was halfway down the stairs, close enough to see that she meant it. "Comfortable."

"I'll bet," she smiled but avoided the obvious intrigue. From their first meeting, she had taken Carl for an iconoclast, but a kilt? She needed to change the subject, so she turned back to face the main floor of the house. "And the house is wonderful." She spun around to take it all in. "I only ever saw it peeking through the windows, but you've been busy."

"Only a start, I'm afraid."

"It's marvelous." She circled the room, letting her fingers trail on the leaded glass of the front windows, the stone fireplace, and the hardwood banister. She sighed and looked at him. "Really," she said, "quite incredible."

He smiled but repeated, "Just a start."

Then she sniffed the air. "What about those heavenly smells coming from the kitchen?"

"The meal is beyond the start stage. It's due to be finished ten minutes after the sun sinks below the ridge on the other side of the river." Carl was beside her then and leaned to kiss her lightly on the cheek. "It's good to see you."

She allowed the kiss, but he could feel her tenseness and so he made it quite crisp and proper. She pulled back slightly and looked at him with contemplation. Then, "Yes, it's good to see you, too."

Carl turned and ducked down to glance out the west window. "We have to hurry to our seats. Don't want to miss the first act. Could I pour you a cocktail?"

"Certainly. It's a nice warm evening. Do you have gin and tonic?"

"A civilized choice," Carl said. "By far the best choice for September sunset watching."

The color had not yet begun to bleed back into the prairie sky when they stepped out onto the porch, but there was a thin cloud bank in the west that assured something grand was about to begin. Tolstoy came out with them and sat thoughtfully at the top of the front steps. He looked out over the prairie, and Carl was sure his dog mind was considering the grouse that he knew hid in the swaying grass. Carl lit the grill at the end of the porch then took one of the rockers and gestured toward the second. But Eleanor opted for the porch rail where she sat sidesaddle as capriciously as a woman half her age. When the first pinks began to ripple among the scalloped clouds her silhouette reminded Carl of Penelope, how she must have looked as she waited, watching the ocean for Odysseus.

They tried some conversation, but as gold began to shoot under the clouds and the light on the porch turned to ocher they fell silent, sipped their drinks, and didn't think about much of anything until night began to slide blue-black up the cottonwoods along the river. "Greatest show on Earth," Eleanor said quietly.

"Possibly," Carl said, rising slowly to his feet. "But I wish you would withhold judgment until you've tried my dinner." He was standing beside her with his shoulder close to hers. At the western horizon was a narrow strip of an incredible yellow gray. There was a pulse of anticipation where his body was closest to hers. He liked to think that she felt the charge longing to leap between them. At any rate, she smiled up at him, then looked back out to the west, and they took another few seconds to stare after the fallen sun.

The briquettes were the red of horseshoes in a forge when Carl laid the grouse breasts on the grill. Olive oil flared and the smell of it wafted thick and rich across the porch. Two and a half minutes on a side. No more. Then the meat was laid on a platter and whisked into the kitchen where Carl nestled it down on the garlic mashed potatoes and adorned it with fresh basil sprigs.

The '97 Terra Valentine cabernet had been breathing the cool prairie air for an hour when Eleanor filled the glasses for the first time. They sat across from each other and swirled the wine in their glasses. Carl leaned forward and extended his glass. "To a wonderful new friendship and to whatever it may bring." Again there was that tiny hesitation. But Eleanor raised her glass to the toast and the glasses touched lightly. The perfect ring of crystal pierced the still spaces of the dining room.

They did not talk much during the main course—the food and wine took most of their concentration—but when the wild plum tart came out they began to probe each other for background. Carl supposed it was Eleanor's interest in his life that caused her, out of a sense of fairness, to offer up details of her own. Her shyness faded with the wine and she talked about her life back in Chicago, her divorce, the long, ongoing period of recovery after the betrayal. She had been completely blindsided and now knew that she had been naive and inattentive to life. After the divorce she found that her courage was gone. Once, she said, she had not been afraid of change. She talked of a repressed passion for action, of her desire to now fulfill that passion and to take brave positions for unpopular causes. She smiled, hoping she didn't sound too silly.

"But happiness is what we are all after," Carl said. "No?"

She glanced wistfully in Carl's direction but he knew that her thoughts were about her own life, perhaps her own mistakes. "Small as our lives may be, on a worldly scale," she said, "I suspect that, if the happiness you speak of exists at all, it resides in something even less." It came out personal but guarded and, from Carl's point of view, profound—as if she was speaking of him.

He nodded. "Sometimes I wonder if that place may not be empty of expectation and dreams."

"But still filled with those unpopular causes." They looked at each other and silently agreed that that was personal enough for the first night.

Eleanor changed the pitch. "I've been doing some research," she said. "I figured out on my own why they call this the Butler place."

"Let me see," Carl said with a humoring smile. "I'm related?"

"Great-grandfather. He was also the great-grandfather of the Thurstons, too. Next ranch over."

"The Thurston boys and I have called each other cousin since I can remember. But I never thought much about it." In the middle of their lovely evening Carl was suddenly struck by how little importance was placed on people's true roots out here. It was his home and all he really knew were the generic western myths. Personal connections had been bowled over by those myths and had become as fuzzy as his blood relationship to the Thurstons: real, of course, but vague and undervalued. He brought himself back to the conversation. "Old Edward Butler and his wife, Alice, are buried in the family plot." He indicated with his head. "On the knoll just behind the house."

"No. You have a family graveyard?"

"Certainly." Carl spoke with affected haughtiness. "Every proper ranch family buries its dead on the place."

"And your parents?

"Planted there too."

"My God," Eleanor said. "I'd love to see it."

"Then see it you shall. But not tonight. Too creepy."

Their gazes hung on each other's eyes, then drifted to the fireplace. They watched the flaming fingers massage the logs until Eleanor spoke. "I found out a little about your predecessors in the library but not much about you."

"What were you looking for?"

"Oh, little things. If you were ever married, for instance." Her smile began as wily, and then went full-blown. She was being daring and had surprised herself.

"Well," Carl said. "I'm glad you're interested, and the answer is yes. But how did you know it was amusing?"

"Was it now?" The wine was catching up to them both and it smoothed the evening sounds and made the house familiar.

"Well," Carl said, "yes. But I don't think I know you well enough to regale you with the details."

"Come on. I told you my whole life story." She leaned over and filled his wineglass.

"A bare outline, I should think. And besides, your life has no seedy underbelly."

"Seedy underbelly?" She laughed. "Does this story have anything to do with that kilt you wear?"

He smiled and sipped his wine. "Not directly."

"My," Eleanor said. "Sounds steamy, at least. Now you have to tell me." The ice was melting and she was having fun. She raised her eyebrows. "I want details."

"Well," Carl began with a transparent hint of obfuscation. "I'm addicted to salami, onion, and jalapeño sandwiches. One of the reasons I live alone."

"I'll remember that," Eleanor said, "but I'm more interested in the details of the marriage."

Carl sighed. "Diagrams and all?"

"Save the diagrams. Tell me what was so amusing about your marriage."

"Okay, we're adults." Carl stood up and leaned against the mantel with his wine in hand. Eleanor wondered how the fire felt, radiating up under the kilt. Carl rolled his wineglass and looked at the color against the flames. It was wonderful wine, hollow on the tongue, with a finish as real as well water. He stepped over Tolstoy, who was completely passed out in front of the fire, no doubt dreaming doggie dreams of pastel and subtle scents drifting through native grasses. One log needed to be moved to increase the airflow over the top of another. When Carl touched it with his shoe both logs sprang into flames. He watched the blaze for a moment and considered making another attempt at turning the conversation away from his marriage, but the wine was warm and wonderful in his head, and he knew that he'd tell the story. He turned and looked hard at Eleanor over his glasses. "I hope you won't be shocked. Responsibility has never been my strong suit. I've lived in a Bohemian world for most of my life."

Eleanor clapped her hands. "Bohemian is good. It's something I've always thought I'd be good at."

"All right, then." He rested one arm on the mantel, assuming a position suitable for a Greek bard about to begin the *Iliad*. "In the midsixties I was a serious graduate student of literature at the University of Denver, a nineteenth-century man. The Romantics: Shelley, Keats, Byron, that sort of thing. The sexual revolution had struck and I took advantage of it the best I could, given my obvious shortcomings in the area of attractiveness."

Eleanor graciously pooh-poohed him with a wave. "I want the truth."

"The truth," he said with studied contemplation. "The truth is a slippery beast, and now I see that what I thought was true probably was not. But I thought I fell in love with another graduate student. Lilly Kessler by name, a PhD student in the relatively new and burgeoning field of women's studies."

"Beautiful?"

"Quite. And smart and daring. And extremely Bohemian. We dated very seriously all during graduate school, and when it came time for us to graduate and apply for jobs we found a university that needed both a nineteenth-century man and a twentieth-century woman. That turned out to be Emory University in Georgia. It was really quite a coup and we were feeling so good about ourselves that we got married in the summer before our contracts began. I was thrilled to get to Georgia because I figured I'd have at least a few students whose families owned good quail hunting ground and I could extort invitations for grades."

"Did that work?"

"Very well. I got my first really good bird dog. The great-grandmother of Tolstoy."

The weary dog raised his big head at the sound of his name but could see it was only silly human palaver and let his head nearly slam back down onto the hooked rug.

"Is that the amusing part?"

"No. The amusing part is that a year into our jobs there at Emory I became attracted to a student."

"Ah ha!"

"Not that simple. I'm a liberated man but a forthright man too. I told Lilly about my attraction, and Lilly, who knew the woman, understood how I could be attracted. In fact, Lilly found the woman attractive too."

Eleanor sat back in her chair and Carl hesitated. Hard to say what she was thinking. It was not too late to foreshorten the story, but hell, why begin a relationship with a falsehood. "We conspired to get the young woman into bed."

"The three of you?"

"The three of us."

"And how was that?" Her voice had cooled but there was a new flutter of interest that was beguiling.

"I'd be a liar if I said anything other than marvelous."

"But in the morning light you both realized that the trust between you was shattered."

"Not exactly. It actually seemed to work out well. Six weeks later the woman moved into our house." He hesitated and again considered the color of the cabernet. "But two months after that, I was asked to leave." His eyes narrowed ever so slightly and his voice lowered as if in an aside to himself. "It was a tumultuous time," he said. "I moved to Canada—for a combination of reasons." He looked at Eleanor and shrugged his shoulders.

"You're shitting me?" she said with a laugh.

"I am not shitting you. I think they are still together."

There was enough wine left to fill both their glasses and they took them outside to sit together on the top step with Tolstoy lying behind them, his back touching Carl's. Nighthawks boomed the sky in their diving search for moths. They looked up at the cold starry sky but the birds were invisible. After a minute Eleanor asked how long ago he'd been divorced. "Over twenty years," he said.

"Other women since then?"

"Some, but nothing serious." He reached around behind her and rubbed Tolstoy's head. "All in all," he said, "it's been lonely for a long time."

⚜ **28** ⚜

Perhaps the greatest quality of life is its capacity to surprise, and Carl Lindquist was one of those surprises. He seemed so comfortable that Eleanor didn't trust herself to be reading him accurately. When the sky had gone as dark as it would get, and the stars intently white, Carl disappeared into the house and reappeared with bagpipes under his arm. He said nothing and neither did Eleanor. Carl stood facing the night and steadily inflated the bagpipes. Then the night was filled with a sound so piercing and sad that Eleanor thought she might cry. Her mind did not recognize the tune, but it was no stranger to her soul.

She did not stay at his house that night, though the thought crossed her mind and scared her so much that she left in a bit of rush. It had been too long, and even though she was feeling safe and right, or perhaps because she was feeling safe and right, she knew she had to get out of that house. She drove slowly back to McDermot with the dark band of Pawnee River cottonwoods constantly on her left. She was surprised with the sudden possibility that her life could become rich and full again. She didn't credit the feeling. After all, she had had a similar feeling once before and it turned out to be false.

Could this time be different? The dark ribbon of trees just outside the driver's side window did not seem foreboding, though she knew it to be filled with shadowy, wild animals and cold, moving water. Instead, it seemed a guide for the car and she imagined it to be a track to take her back and forth from her city condo to Carl Lindquist's house. And the land that had before seemed to cascade down on her from the ridges on each side of the river now rose up to the highlands and gave her a hint of the access and connection that she longed for. But Eleanor fought those feelings, and by the time she was home and in her own bed she tried to convince herself that she was just a foolish old woman who had had too much wine. Really, she did not feel that she had drunk too much or that she was the least bit old. Foolish? Perhaps.

She couldn't shake the new connection she felt to the Pawnee River valley. The next day her mind still wandered to the history of this little corner of the northern Great Plains, to the reasons things were the way they were, and the origins of the people and rules that governed them. She had to fight the girlish feeling that there was something new afoot. It was silly and she wouldn't have told a soul, but for the first time in memory she felt less like an observer of the history taking place constantly around her and more like a participant. Maybe it was that old, defiant house of Carl's, the way it was lodged in the landscape, at once part of it and standing in opposition to it. She had no right to feel any of that. She was usurping Carl's heritage. And though he didn't seem to need that heritage or even know much about it, it was still his. She had never been an unhappy person, but never thoroughly engaged with life either. In the days after her first evening with Carl Lindquist she sensed a shift and savored the feeling of well-being she received from that subtle movement.

Yes, life's greatest quality is its ability to surprise. How could she have known she would ever feel at home in the middle of the continent, surrounded by a million miles of grass? Who could have guessed?

🦚 **29** 🦚

The telephone woke Gretchen, and when she rolled over to reach for it, she found Steve just pulling on his boots. She pointed at him, "Don't leave yet." Struggling across the bed to pick up the phone she felt the cool sheets against her naked thighs and realized she was still sexed up from the night before. He was such a gentle, thoughtful lover. She flashed on how nice it would be to simply let the phone ring, pull Steve back into bed and suck him back to life. Almost before the thought had run through her mind she was ashamed. Knowing that she had thought such a thing, nearly acted on the thought, rocked her, and she sat back on the bed, rubbed her face, and looked at the phone. She still wanted to let it ring, but of course she couldn't do that because the caller might be Jake.

But it wasn't Jake. It was Ryan Hooper. "Your story is dead in the water."

Gretchen sat up in bed. "You hated it."

"I didn't hate it. The decision to kill it came from above."

"The editorial board?"

"Higher. I don't know but I imagine your buddy Cring got to someone in the main office in San Francisco. I got a call last night—on a weekend—and a message from a local attorney representing Cring waiting on the machine this morning. It's Sunday morning, Gretchen. The story is dead as hell."

"For God's sake, Ryan. And nobody's even read the thing?"

"I warned you."

"Yeah, but Jesus. Talk about a story, a guy with enough power over the media to stop a story that no one has read. Now that is a story."

"It would be at the *New York Times*. It isn't at the *Gazette*."

"It should be."

"But it isn't."

Gretchen was sitting up in bed with the sheet wrapped to her waist. Steve was watching her and she straightened up. "Well, what the hell's the use, Ryan." She knew that would silence Ryan and she was right. He hadn't wanted to make this call any more than she had wanted to receive it.

"Sometimes I'm not sure," Ryan finally said. "It's just the way it is. You gotta drop this thing, Gretchen. They aren't above firing you."

"Now *that* is against the law."

"Doesn't matter, so is refusing medical service. Just the way it is."

"Right," Gretchen said. She exhaled and glanced at Steve. "Well, I'm going to think about this."

"Don't think too much. It will make you nuts."

"Thanks, I'm already nuts." She hung up and stared straight ahead.

"What's happening?" Steve asked. He moved over and put both hands on her shoulders and massaged them. His big hands felt like they could gather all her muscles and wring out the soreness to the depth of the soul.

"My story just went out the window."

"About the HPMC docs breaking it off in us?"

"That's the one." She looked up at Steve. "I wanted to talk to you. Now I have to worry about my job."

"What did you want to talk about?"

"Us."

Steve continued to rub her shoulders. The roughness of his skin felt good, and combined with the disappointment from Ryan's call, it made her want to just shut up and go back to sleep. The sexy feel of the sheets was gone. She just wanted to sleep. "What about us?" he asked.

"Oh, I don't know." She reached up and caught his hands in her own. "What are we doing, Steve?" His hands went rigid and she knew he would construe anything more as pressure for him to make some sort of commitment. She didn't care.

"I don't know either," he said. He moved his hands away and they looked at each other.

"I want more than this, Steve."

He nodded. "That I know."

She fought the anger that rose up inside. It was not a time to trust emotions, but he made it sound like she was asking for something unreasonable. The longer they stared at each other the less power she had over her anger. "Jesus," she said, "why can't you just step up to the plate. Do you love me or not?"

Now he exhaled in the way she so hated. "Look," he said, "I love you. Okay. I love you. But that doesn't mean I'm ready to take on the whole thing."

"The whole thing? You mean me and Jake?"

"Yeah, the whole thing."

As if his name had cued Jake's entrance, they heard a car door slam and the sound of voices. Her son was home early from Randy's. He'd have already noticed Steve's pickup in the alley. Gretchen hustled to get up. "I don't even deserve you," Steve said.

"That is so weak, Steve." She was naked and moving around the bed to find a robe. Her comment pushed him to sarcasm.

"I'm a weak guy," he said and turned away.

They heard Jake's footfall on the porch. "I guess you are," she said and immediately wanted the words back. Steve started from the room and she reached to catch his hand, but he jerked it away.

Gretchen was still naked, searching for her damned robe, and just as Jake came through the back door the phone rang again. Steve was already into the kitchen. "Oh, shit," she hissed.

Gretchen heard Steve saying something to Jake and heard the hesitation in her son's laugh. The phone rang again. "Shit, shit, shit." She wanted to go out into the kitchen and joke with them, like a real family, but she was naked, and besides, Steve would only shut her out. Tears welled in her eyes but she fought them back. The phone rang again and Jake answered it.

"Mom? It's for you."

She groaned as she pulled on a pair of sweatpants. Her breasts were still bare and she felt old and ugly as she picked up the phone beside her bed. It was Ida Miller. "What the heck's going on?" Ida asked.

"A lot, Ida, and none of it's good."

"This have anything to do with the crackdown over at HPMC?"

Gretchen could hear Jake and Steve talking in the kitchen as she wrestled with a sweatshirt. "I don't know anything about any crackdown."

"Just talked with a nurse over at HPMC and there was a memo waiting for everyone when they got to work this morning. No talking to any reporters. It also said that the memo was not to be mentioned. My friend put her job on the line to tell me about it."

"Seems to be a lot of jobs on the line this morning."

"What?"

"Never mind." Steve and Jake were still talking. It sounded like Steve was saying good-bye. She didn't want him to leave but still hadn't managed to cover her ugly nakedness. "I got to go, Ida."

"Yeah, yeah, go on. Just thought you should know."

"Thanks." She was going to hang up but suddenly she was angry again. "It's a shitty deal," she said.

"Shitty is the word for it," Ida said.

Just as the sweatshirt came fully over her head, she heard the back door slam. The whole house felt instantly hollow and all urgency drained out of her. She pulled the sweatshirt off. Might as well get properly dressed.

By the time Gretchen changed into blue jeans and a blouse, Jake had toasted a couple pieces of bread and poured himself a tall glass of orange juice. He sat at the kitchen table and his body language told his mother that he was perturbed about something. Gretchen suspected it was the fact that he had found Steve coming from her bedroom, but she knew enough not to ask. It might not be that at all. It could be anything: something that happened in school, a snit over something a friend said. It was better to let it come out by itself. So Gretchen offered an acceptably cheery "Good morning," put her own piece of bread into the toaster, and waited.

She felt put upon to have to contend with Jake's mood. She had her own problems in spades, but when the toast was ready she put it on a plate, poured herself a glass of juice, and went to sit with Jake. He still hadn't spoken and Gretchen didn't push him. They sat chewing in silence until Jake was finished and took his plate to the sink. He stood with his back to his mother, and while he washed his plate, it came out. "I'm not stupid, you know." The fury of the statement took Gretchen by surprise. Once the shock subsided, it angered her. Jake was being theatrical and she didn't want to deal with it. "You lecture me all the time," Jake said.

"Honey . . ."

"No." Jake spun around. "You're always telling me about girls and you do all sorts of things."

"Honey, it's different."

"Right!"

Gretchen sat paralyzed by injustice. Maybe it wasn't different. She wanted to put a stop to this with strong words but when she spoke she sounded pitiful. "But it's Steve. You like Steve."

"I like Steve. But you always say it's wrong."

Gretchen stood up. "Baby, I've known Steve for a long time."

"But you're not married, Mom. You're not 'sposed to sleep together if you're not married." He stood up to his mother with his back against the sink and his arms folded across his young chest. He was trying to be the man of the family, simply doing what he had been taught.

"Jake." She reached out for him but he moved away. He paused only long enough to shoot her a look of contempt. Then he stomped out of the room and Gretchen felt behind her for the edge of the table. She steadied herself first with one hand, then with both.

There was no point in even trying to get Jake to go to Mass with her. It was often a battle to get him to forego shooting baskets with his friends, and after their fight she simply didn't have the heart for it. Attending Mass was mostly for her anyway, and so she dressed and slipped out of the house without even saying good-bye. Jake would know where she went and be glad to be off the hook.

Mass was at ten o'clock and Gretchen always tried to be there in time for the rosary but seldom made it until just before the processional. Today was no exception and she hurried to dip her hand in the holy water and get down the aisle before the music began. She knelt quickly and slid into her seat beside two old ladies whom she had seen many times before but whose names she did not know. She nodded and smiled but wanted to pray before the Mass began and so she knelt and held her eyes tightly shut. She wanted to say something about what had happened that morning but she didn't know how to begin. She had to take solace in knowing that God knew what she had been thinking, what she had said, and how she had acted, because the music began before she had a chance to put it into words. She shut her eyes that much tighter and simply asked to be forgiven.

By the time she was standing, the priest was halfway down the aisle and the altar boys were fanning out at the front. The two old ladies glanced at her and made her feel that they knew what was in her mind and in her soul. She looked straight ahead and only then noticed that the priest was not Father Hittle. She glanced at the bulletin and found that this new priest was a visitor from Croatia, Father Donavitch. By then he had reached the altar, turned around, and spread his arms. Gretchen knew that what he said was the welcome but his accent was too thick to understand. He smiled, showing poor teeth, and nodded his head. Gretchen tried to follow the gospel reading but the words were unintelligible. She began to lose focus and wondered why they hadn't stuck with Latin.

She decided to think about God and how to live her life in his service, but the droning combination of English and Croatian was distracting, and she found herself surreptitiously glancing around the church. It was about half full and seriously skewed toward old people, women, and children. But two rows ahead of her and ten feet to the left was a middle-aged man sitting by himself. He sat straight with ebony black hair and a strong jawline that Gretchen could just barely make out. He wore a crisp polo shirt that stretched at his biceps. Father Donavitch was still reading and his English had not improved. She thought she should pray and tried again to put words to the uneasy feeling she had brought to Mass with her. She failed again to find the words for her own life but found a few to say for Anne Simmons and Tad Bordeaux. She tried not to feel sorry for herself by comparing her life to that of those innocent kids. The story of that night on the dark road outside of McDermot began to play in her mind. The stolen car, the young lovers, the sudden deer. She sat paralyzed by the thought of it, but she was still able to slide forward to a kneeling position when the two old ladies cued her. She thought of the emergency room and the airplane flight to Denver. And suddenly the old lady nearest to her was touching her shoulder. "Peace be with you," she said, and shook Gretchen's hand.

"Peace be with you." She shook the hand of the second old lady and turned to shake the hand of the woman in the row in front of her. It was then that she felt the eyes of the man in the polo shirt. She turned and found that the man was indeed looking at her. They smiled and nodded but Gretchen could not stare. He was handsome and seemed very alone. She did not want to look at him. It was certainly not what she had come to Mass to do, but once she was seated again and listening to the last reading the man was stuck in her mind. "My God," she thought. "What is wrong with me?"

When the Mass was finished she raced to leave the church but found herself in the greeting line with Father Donavitch taking his time shaking the hands of the parishioners. There was a pressure at her back and when the time came to shake the priest's hand she did not linger. Father Donavitch smiled with his poor teeth. He nodded and said what sounded like "God be with you."

"God be with you too," Gretchen said and hurried for her Jeep.

✽ 30 ✽

Steve planned to leave work an hour early. His father had called the night before and asked him to come out and help get the water tanks ready for winter. Since he was fifteen years old the water tanks had been Steve's job, ever since they got electricity at the corrals. The tank heating elements kept the water from freezing when the temperature began to fall. Getting the tank in good shape wasn't a plumbing job or a job for a real electrician. It was a job for someone who knew a little about electricity. Certainly not a job for Arvid Thurston. He never understood electricity and was fond of saying, "I don't work with nothing I can't see. 'Specially if it can kill ya."

The electricity in the tank heaters wasn't going to kill anyone but you couldn't tell that to Arvid. He didn't even like watching Steve check the current. Someone told Arvid once that water was a great conductor of electricity and he knew damned well that the tanks were full of water. That was all he knew. All he wanted to know. He'd lived the first twenty-five years of his life without electricity and never had learned to trust it. "Don't fool with that shit when you're wet" was about all he ever said about electricity. He was of the last generation to be more comfortable with animals than he was with a light switch.

Arvid's skill with animals, especially horses, was one of the reasons Jake liked spending time with him. Watching his father teach Jake the same lessons he had taught his own children touched

Steve in ways that nothing else could. It was like looking back to the best times of his life. For that reason, and a few others, he loved to take Jake to the ranch when Jake could get away from his busy twelve-year-old's schedule.

As soon as his father called him for help Steve called Gretchen at work. "Can you two come out and play?"

"Just what do you have in mind?"

"Dad needs some help. I'm going to the ranch about three thirty. Thought maybe you and Jake might want to come along."

"Three thirty?" she said, as if that was the silliest time she'd ever heard of.

"It's getting dark earlier every day. I don't know what I'll get into fixing the tanks. Might need a couple hours of light."

"Well, Jake doesn't have practice tonight, but I'd have to sneak out of work."

"That's what I'm doing. Let's take a walk on the wild side."

"Right."

"Do you want me to write a note to Hooper?"

"Okay, I'll slip away about a quarter after three. Jake and I will be at the house."

"Wear your old clothes."

"All my clothes are old."

"See ya at three thirty."

Since he met her, Steve had known that Gretchen was something special. He didn't know exactly why she was special, but he knew she was. Her energy was endless, but the ups and downs that seemed to come with their relationship were tough. Strong as she was, sometimes Steve felt like he was trying to take care of a baby bird. All this ran through his mind as he hurried to finish his last job of the day. It really wasn't his job, but the boss had asked him to cut down a cottonwood tree that grew at the side of the garage they had just finished roofing. The tree was perfectly good and Steve didn't like the job. When he protested, the boss shrugged. "Owner wants it cut down," he said. "Says his wife wants an ornamental planted there."

"Ornamental?" Steve shook his head. "Cut down a perfectly good, mature tree and plant a froufrou tree?"

Another shrug. "That's what he wants."

A laborer should have been given the job, certainly not the job foreman, but Steve was available and so he dug out the chain saw from the back of the company pickup. "Shit," he thought as he choked the engine. He pulled the starting rope with all his might and the engine popped to life as if frightened into it.

As Steve put the spinning chain to the soft cottonwood he winced. "Perfectly good tree," he thought. A ribbon of chips streamed into the air and in a minute the old cottonwood tipped, then toppled, to the ground. As he cut the tree into lengths that could be picked up by one man, he couldn't help thinking that working for someone else was the hardest kind of work. He looked forward to fixing the tank heaters. At least he could imagine doing that for himself.

They rode three in the front seat of his pickup, Steve driving, Jake tuning the radio from one teenybopper rap station to the next, and Gretchen watching the dried browns of the grass roll by like a movie. They passed Carl Lindquist's place and Gretchen commented on the new paint job. "I didn't think anyone would ever live there again."

"Me either. Thought cousin Carl was gone for good. Took off like a wild goose."

"Looks like he's come back home to roost."

It made Steve smile to imagine big, stout Carl balanced on a branch like an old goose trying to roost. "He never really fit in around here when we were growing up. But things are different now. All this," Steve swung his hand to indicate the prairie and the river bottom, "was a way of life back then. Now they're poor-boy estates." He laughed to think of the ranch he grew up on as an estate.

He thought Gretchen would say something but she just kept staring out the window. When she did speak it wasn't about the land but a question about Carl. "How did he not fit in?"

They turned into the driveway of the old place. "I don't know. Smarter. Knew from the beginning that there wasn't a living out here. He was older than me but Bob says he was a rebel in high school, always in trouble with the teachers." Steve smiled and turned his gaze to Gretchen as he pulled the pickup to a stop. "He's always said he was ahead of his time. The sixties hadn't really gotten here yet but he claims to have had a healthy disrespect for authority."

"Healthy?"

Steve shrugged. "That's what he says."

Arvid was standing in the corral, staring at the water tank from ten feet away like it might be full of snakes. When he heard the pickup he turned and waved in a way that he never did when it was just Steve. Behind him, tied at the hitching rail, stood Jack and Elsa. They weren't saddled yet. He liked to have Jake saddle his own horse.

He nodded a hello to Gretchen and Jake but his first words were for Steve. "You bring that tester thing?"

"Right there in the toolbox." He pointed into the bed of the truck.

"You going to need some help?" That was what he always said but he had no intention of getting close to the tank heaters or the voltage meter and they both knew it.

"That's okay." Steve winked at Gretchen. "I brought an assistant."

"Well, heck," Arvid said. "If Gretchen's going to help you, maybe Jake would want to go for a ride."

"You bet," Jake said. "I get Elsa." He was already running toward the shed where the tack was kept.

Arvid lingered for a moment, but he was leaning. "Okay then," he said. "I guess I'd better go with him. Sure you don't need me?"

"I can handle it," Gretchen said. "If I can't we'll holler."

"Okay, then. We'll check back."

Gretchen and Steve sat on the tailgate of the pickup and watched Arvid limp toward where Jake was wrestling saddles from the tack room. "This is so good for him," Gretchen said. "Horses, fresh air, and an old, solid man to play with."

Steve heard what she was getting at—her emphasis seemed to be on "solid man." He didn't want to get into that just then. Instead he tried for a little joke. "I don't know how solid he is, but it'll keep Jake out of trouble." Steve turned, reached into the pickup bed, and dragged the toolbox to the tailgate. "Look what happened to you."

"Horses and sports keep kids out of trouble," Gretchen said. "Isn't that an old saying or something?"

"Should be. Here, take this." He handed her a small box and several hand tools that she didn't recognize but hefted as if she loved the feel of them. It was the first time since he'd picked her up that she seemed to be enjoying herself. Steve filled his own arms with larger tools, pry bars and such. "Follow me."

They walked through the gate and across the dusty corral to the first water tank. The ornery Hereford bull stared at them from the bull pasture, just on the other side of the corral fence. Steve frowned and shook his head. "Put everything right here." They laid the tools down on the concrete pad where the cattle stood to drink. "We need to take the top and part of the back off to get at the heating units, but let me shut the gate so that bull stays out. Dad says he's interested in the horse grain." He pointed toward the old barrel beside the corral. "The son of a bitch."

Gretchen watched him cross the corral and shut the bull out, then recross the corral and begin unscrewing the row of screws holding the wooden cover that protected three-quarters of the water surface from freezing. He used a battery-powered screw gun. "That looks like fun," she said. "Let me try." The tank was steel but surrounded by wooden walls filled with insulation to help the heater keep the water warm. Behind the boards, where Steve had to reach in and check the heater fuse, was a nasty place where only mice, insects, and the occasional snake was comfortable.

Gretchen liked to help with physical stuff so Steve handed her the screw gun. "Just back all those screws out." He pointed to the ring of still-silver screws that held the top to the walls. Then he lay down on his back in the mud and dirt to begin on the backboards with a hand screwdriver.

Gretchen was working on the screws and surprised him by saying, "He actually didn't seem like such a bad guy." Steve was lying in the corral crud trying to concentrate on what he was doing, and she was talking away like they were having coffee. It was something she did—like she's been thinking of something completely different than whatever's been going on.

Steve grunted from behind the tank. He had one board off and was peeking in to see if there was a rattlesnake between the fuse box and where he lay helpless on his back. It was hard to say if she even meant to speak out loud. But she went on like they were in the middle of a conversation. "I mean the story should come out, but he was sort of a gentleman."

Gretchen couldn't see Steve shake his head in amazement. There she goes again. Never knew where she stood on a subject. He considered pointing out to her that they'd been through this. One minute she was trying to bust this Cring and the next she was defending him. But Steve couldn't talk. Half the time he wasn't sure what he thought either. Besides, what happened at that clinic was not his business.

The light was going dim by the time they got everything checked out. Steve was just coiling up the electrical leads when he heard the sound of a pickup. By the sound of it, the pickup had to be Tully's diesel Dodge. "They're everywhere," he said as he stood up.

Gretchen was getting ready to fasten the lid back on the tank and stood with the screw gun in her hand and a mouthful of screws. Her ponytail had come loose and her skin was rosy from the cool, fresh air. She looked great. "Who's everywhere?" she said.

"Outlanders." Steve smiled, reached out, and wiped a smear of dirt from her cheek. "You know, if you want to quit that reporter job, I might be able to get you a job building houses." She just looked at him, and he couldn't tell what she was thinking.

❧ 31 ☙

As soon as he stepped from the spanking-new pickup truck, John Tully reached out and took Gretchen's hand. His eyes told her that he recognized her from Sunday-morning Mass, but neither of them acknowledged that meeting as Steve introduced them. Of course, though she had never had a face to put with the name, she knew all about him, the way he'd set up the purchase of the ranch so Arvid would always have a place to live, how he seemed to be sensitive to the brothers' relationship to the land they had grown up on. What Steve never said was that Tully was nice-looking and young—younger than Steve by maybe a half dozen years. She had expected someone older. But Tully couldn't be much older than she was, with a good handshake and interested eyes that she had not forgotten since she'd noticed him in Mass. It all confused her and she stood slightly dumbfounded. He seemed confident and energetic but there was tiredness around the eyes like the tiredness she saw in everyone these days. Right away she realized that Tully could never be a real friend of someone like Steve. The relationship would always be something other than equal. She could see, by the way Tully walked to the water tank with genuine curiosity, that his vast abilities would never extend far enough to understand that some people would see him as cocky.

But perhaps the cockiness was earned. He wore a leather bomber jacket and a ball cap with COLORADO ROCKIES printed on the front. "So," he said. "What are we doing here?"

"Making sure the heaters are working." Steve said.

"Ahh. Heating coils? Hundred and twenty volts?"

"Yeah. We got 'em checked out and turned on. Working good."

Gretchen was screwing the last boards on the back of the frame that surrounded the tank and understood what Tully meant when he spoke. "I enjoy working in the open air," he said. "Been cooped up inside all day." She let the screw gun drive another screw into the wood. She had learned that if you hold it just right, it was like pushing a toothpick into a piece of cheese. The sensation felt good. The sun was going down and the air was cooling and still. When she looked up to show Tully that she understood about being cooped up all day, his eyes met hers and he smiled. It made her touch her forehead self-consciously, and when she did, she found that the ponytail had gone wild. She laid the screw gun on the lid of the tank and expertly refastened the tie. "Clients," Tully laughed. "The practice of law would be pleasant without them."

He smiled, and suddenly, standing in the coolness of the coming night Gretchen's confidence collapsed. She turned away from the men and looked out to the prairie. Jake and Arvid were unsaddling the horses at the hitching rail. Steve and Tully were talking about the water tanks and she felt invisible. She turned back and picked up the screw gun from the tank lid. There were still a half-dozen long silver screws to put into the backboards, and they still rolled in their elliptical pattern on the wooden top where she had laid them down.

That movement drew Tully's eyes. He watched the screws sloshing back and forth, then looked up at her face. Again their eyes caught for an instant and in that time he could see that Gretchen was not going to finish her job. He reached and took the screw gun from her and their hands grazed each other. Gretchen could not look at him, but pulled her hand away as if his was red hot. The conversation about the water tanks continued without a pause, and she stepped back to let Tully move around to the back. He looked over the situation and understood how the boards went up to seal the crypt behind the tank. He knelt down and peered into the darkness. He was still talking to Steve as if he did this sort of work every day. She watched Tully from the corner of her eye and saw him raise the screw gun, then pause. He reached into the pocket of his bomber jacket and pulled out a crumpled paper bag. It was obviously trash he had carried for a while, and now he had found a perfect place to deposit it. With a neatness that most of the men in her life did not possess, he tossed the trash into the void and joyfully began sinking the screws deep into the wood. She watched his hands move without wasted movement.

On the way home Jake jabbered about his ride. Arvid and he had ridden the trail to the top of the main ridge that cut the ranch in half. Gretchen had been there herself and knew that from the top of that ridge you could see south to the river and north to the high flats at the back of the ranch. Jake told them about seeing the roof of Carl Lindquist's house two and a half miles east and, way far off to the west, the band of trees where the river broadens into what eventually becomes Bluffs Park at the edge of McDermot. He sat between them and bubbled after the afternoon in the open air. Jake's love for days like that was the most painful part about Steve's and her inability to draw their two lives into one. What was right about this relationship was so obvious sometimes, but so impossibly difficult.

Jake laughed at the things Arvid told him: the apocryphal story of "Moby Coyote," the white coyote he claimed to see periodically, the days when Bob and Steve were his age and skipped school on horseback, the story of the famous hailstorm of 1981. He'd told Jake about the horses that had brought his grandfather to settle the ranch in the first place. It was a story that Gretchen had heard a half-dozen times, but this was the first time Jake had heard it and he insisted on retelling it to Steve and his mother as they wound their way back along the river toward town.

Arvid claimed that the ancestor that the Thurstons shared with Carl Lindquist had ducked the Civil War. He had the story all mixed with a gold rush, buffalo, and the wrong Indian tribe. But Arvid was right about the lack of law and order in the Pawnee Valley when Edward Butler arrived. He was also right about Butler's desire to "make a little cash."

"So they just took the Indians' horses and got rich," Jake said.

Gretchen looked across to where Steve sat driving, looking straight ahead. His head was moving slowly up and down. He might have been nodding or it might have been the waves in the road below. Gretchen offered a weak explanation to her son. "It was a crazy place back then." She wanted Steve to say something but nothing came, and she felt let down.

❧ 32 ❧

Steve had never been much of a hunter. He liked to ride and walk the ranch. In his youth he had shot a few deer. Later, he had made the occasional bird-hunting trip for pheasants in the cornfields in the middle of the state. But those trips had been mostly to get away with some of the men he worked with, and they spent a great deal of the time in bars. Oddly, he had never hunted the sharp-tailed grouse that inhabited the ranch where he had grown up and that had so thoroughly won the heart of cousin Carl. Bob had not touched a firearm since Vietnam. But after Carl's return, they were badgered by their cousin to come out and at least walk with him while he hunted. Neither Thurston was too interested in walking, but Carl had spoken with such passion about the joys and benefits of following his dog up and down the hills that they decided to humor him.

They left their trailer home just after noon and stopped by the ranch house to see if their father still had the old shotgun that had leaned against the wall behind the door of the porch since they could remember. "My skunk gun? Hell yes. Always good to keep it handy for varmints." Arvid stepped onto the cluttered back porch and produced a long-barreled Mossberg, bolt action, twelve gauge, with adjustable choke. "She's a sweetheart," he said as he rubbed the dust away.

Bob looked at the gun with barely disguised disgust, then up at his father with something like pity in his eyes. "Take care of a gun like that, they'd have run you out of boot camp."

Arvid looked at the gun, scratched at a crust of rust on the top of the barrel, and frowned. "She's a goddamned sweetheart," he said. Then he reached out to the adjustable choke and twisted it. "You just dial her in for distance. If the son of a bitch is at the corral I like number six. If it's on the porch, crank 'er right on up to one."

Steve accepted the gun from his father. "Is the sweetheart loaded?"

"Well, hell yes. If it ain't loaded it's just a piece of pipe screwed to a stick."

Steve pointed it to the ceiling and pulled the bolt back. A live twelve-gauge shell cartwheeled out and landed on the floor.

"Jesus," Bob said.

"You boys go ahead and recreate with cousin Carl. I got work to do." Arvid disappeared back into the kitchen where Steve and Bob knew he was refilling his coffee cup with Black Velvet.

"Let's get out of here," Bob said, "before he decides he wants to go with us."

Four hours later Steve, Bob, and Carl were making their way back toward Carl's house. The sun was touching the western horizon, and Leo was still running out in front. They topped the ridge that eventually ran back to the house. Purples and reds shot over their heads and fanned out toward the east. The air was dead calm, and the world was as quiet as it can be. There had been a great deal of joking at first. They teased Carl about wasting all his energy chasing birds. "You're going to need all the energy you got for that new gal."

Carl smiled and retaliated by making fun of the old shotgun that Steve carried. "Gun like that creates the wrong impression of the man carrying it," he said.

"That snazzy job of yours makes you fancy?" Bob shook his head.

"No, not like that. It's more like what your dad says," Carl mimicked Arvid to a tee. "Finest lady or the saltiest cowboy looks ridiculous on a pissin' horse."

"Dad said that?"

"I heard him."

But as the afternoon wore on, they stopped talking, and the rhythm of the walking and the feel of the autumn air conspired to mesmerize them. The dog found birds and Carl shot two. To his amazement, Steve killed one with the old Mossberg. Bob had stood far behind the hunters as they shot, but when the birds jolted in a puff of feathers, he smiled. They wanted to make fun of the way Carl caressed the dead birds but they couldn't. When he held them out for the brothers to touch the feathers, they did not hesitate. "They are as nifty as a pocket-sized dictionary," Carl said. And though they weren't exactly sure what he meant, they nodded because they could see what he was getting at.

From the ridge they saw that Eleanor's car was parked at the back of the house, and Carl's smile provoked a comment by Bob that his pace seemed to pick up. But no amount of ribbing had enough power to break the spell of the afternoon. They walked on, past the little graveyard that held their ancestors, and each man in his turn glanced toward the headstones. But no one bothered to speak. Steve was thinking back on the afternoon, engrossed in the details of memory, when a trio of grouse winged overhead. He wouldn't have known the grouse were anywhere near if Leo hadn't heard them and looked up. When he followed the dog's stare, he saw the birds flying high above just as their intermittent chuckles and the whir of their wings reached his ears. Steve was walking twenty yards from his brother and Carl, and they did not notice when he stopped to watch and listen. The birds cut the watercolor sky like tiny turbo-powered footballs, and it was clear that they had a destination in mind. Leo perked up his ears and twisted his head, first at them, then at Steve. He wanted Steve to shoot but Steve had no desire. Their day was done, and instead of focusing his attention for a shot Steve let his mind wander at where the grouse might be going.

He fantasized that the locus of their flight might not be linear but temporal. What if they are flying backward in time? he thought. Leo's lip puffed out with exasperation. They continued to walk the ridgeline, but Steve's thoughts stayed with the departed grouse and the idea that they could fly back through the decades. It was impossible to say what the grouse were seeing once they topped the next hill. The old, forgotten stories tumbled in on Steve. Perhaps the grouse were now looking down on the original line shack that great-grandfather Butler built when he broke with McDermot, and on the little herd of thin longhorns he took as his last paycheck. Maybe they watched Arlo Abrahamson, the poor Swedish emigrant who tried to farm the bench above the river, as he sank his new, mortgaged plow into the native sod. Steve imagined the next fall and the grouse searching that field less desperately than Arlo for the grain that never grew. Were the grouse now witnessing the tearful aftermath of the daughter, Angela, sneaking away in search of opportunity on the morning of her seventeenth birthday? The grouse must have flown over the desolate pastures of the thirties when almost none of their kind had habitat enough to survive. They saw the rest of the Abrahamsons leave in the battered pickup. And the Hansons, and the O'Learys, and the Gialotties.

Maybe, Steve thought, as the three of them and Tolstoy descended the hill to Carl's back yard, at that very moment the grouse were seeing floods and devastating winter storms. Migrating swans and buffalo. Perhaps they were flying to the eternal mating ground that was now paved under the new highway north of McDermot. From his youth onward, Steve had been told that grouse did not usually fly far. But who really knew. Perhaps some grouse, like the family group that had careened over their heads, never came to Earth. Perhaps they had been flying over the Pawnee River valley forever and knew the ephemeral nature of it all.

❦ 33 ❦

Gretchen set her alarm for five o'clock with the intention of getting into work early and catching Ryan Hooper in his office and alone. She was surprised to find that the very early morning was as cold as it was; she had to take an extra couple of minutes stretching up the canvas top of the Jeep and levering it down tight. The Jeep had been in the garage, protected from the coldest part of the night, but as she drove through town, she noticed windshields covered with frost. It struck her that winter was nearly upon them and she wondered, as she did every year, where the summer had gone.

She parked right beside Hooper's Toyota. As she stepped out of the Jeep she looked into Hooper's car and noticed the child seat strapped in the back and the mountain of junk that went along with children: toys, baby wipes, an extra coat, food wrappers, a tattered blanket. The chaos of the back seat brought back memories and Gretchen was surprised to find herself at the edge of tears. She didn't usually think of Ryan as a father, but he was. He was probably a good one: provider, dad, and faithful husband. She put her hand on the glass of the rear window and took another moment to look at the mess. How did he keep all the balls in the air?

When she found him, he was exactly where she knew he would be. Hunched over his computer in his tiny cluttered office. They were alone in the newsroom, a full half hour ahead of the earliest arrivers. Ryan's eyes shifted from the screen for an instant. "Hey." Then back to finish what he was working on. "What's happening?"

Gretchen stepped in and set her bag on the floor beside the extra chair. "Came in to see if I still have a job."

Ryan made a few final keystrokes and swiveled to read Gretchen's mood. He motioned to the chair. " 'Course you have a job."

Gretchen took the chair. "It's just the story that vanished?"

Ryan nodded and exhaled. "Happens. Don't get your dorker down."

"What?"

He waved Gretchen's question away. "Just something my dad used to say. Don't let it discourage you."

"Discourage? Jesus. Am I an idiot? Was I way off base to think that Cring needed to be outed?"

Ryan shrugged. "Not really our job to out people. If it happens along the way, fine. But we're not the morality police."

"But the story was quashed."

"Maybe it was reckless."

"Nobody read it."

"I read it."

"Oh, well, then you'd know if it was reckless. Was it?"

Ryan shrugged again. "I didn't think so."

"Did you fight for it?"

"A little."

"But not much."

"I came to see that it was a lawsuit waiting to happen. The *Gazette* couldn't take it."

Gretchen was nodding, listening. "Yeah?"

"We live in the real world here. I have to weigh the consequences against the benefits."

"And?"

"It was no contest, Gretchen. Interfering with a person's right to make a living is a slam-dunk, big-money lawsuit. I had that explained to me by Cring's attorney. If a story in our paper makes Cring lose one patient he's into us for thousands. He loses ten—we cease to exist. And what was really to gain?" He paused and Gretchen realized this was not coming easily for Ryan. He threw his hands in the air and held them with the palms pointing to the sky. "Real world."

Gretchen pursed her lips. She felt herself crumbling and suddenly wanted to get to her own office. Now her confidence was destroyed and she felt foolish. But she didn't want Ryan to know. She reached down and grasped her bag, then stood slowly, trying desperately to think of what could be said that would salvage some self-esteem. "That attorney frightened you," she said.

Ryan heard the challenge in her voice but decided to ignore it. "Not really. He was nice enough. Doing his job."

Now Gretchen was standing. "He came down here?"

"No, just a phone call."

"Maybe someone should meet him face to face." She turned to the door.

"Maybe."

"What's his name?"

"Tully," Ryan said. "Guy named John Tully."

❦ 34 ❦

Carl Lindquist invited Steve, Bob, and Gretchen over to see the remodel job on his house and to spend an evening with his new lady friend. Gretchen had met Eleanor Stiener when she interviewed her for the paper about an area art show, but she didn't know her well. Steve had only met her briefly, and Bob wasn't sure he wanted to know her. But Carl was so excited about having them as guests to see the sprucing up he'd done that declining the invitation was out of the question. Ordinarily Bob would have simply failed to show up, but both Steve and Gretchen insisted. They told Bob what he already knew, that the food was always good at Carl's house.

The days were getting shorter and the evenings getting cool, so they planned to eat inside. Eleanor Stiener took her drink out on the front porch to chat with Bob, who was leaning against one of the big posts that held up the porch. Steve didn't think his brother would stand for it and eased over to the window while Carl and Gretchen were in the kitchen talking about some little hot peppers that looked like tomatoes that hadn't matured right. Steve wanted to give Eleanor a chance but he also wanted to be close enough to step outside if Bob got sullen. The tops of the two front windows were cut glass leaded in like the stained glass in a church. But the glass was clear. It looked a little like the glass in heavy, fancy drinking glasses. The main pane of the window was big, maybe four feet by five feet, and there were imperfections in it that made Bob and Eleanor wavy and distorted. It was the kind of glass that would get sent back if it showed up in one of the houses Steve worked on, but it looked good in Carl's old house. It made sense in a house like that.

Eleanor Stiener was dressed in a long, green skirt and white blouse with dangling copper-colored earrings, and she simply walked up to Bob and started talking. Had she approached him too strongly he would have clammed up, but her manner was somehow subtle, and Steve could hear that she began by asking him about his childhood on the ranch. It was cold out there, and Steve knew they weren't going to stay long. He hoped they'd come back in and join the conversation indoors when they got chilled. What he didn't want was for her to spook Bob and have him just drift off into the night. He felt protective of his big brother because he had always felt protected by him. It didn't matter what Bob knew or what he really might be. He was still Steve's big brother and always would be. No matter how old he got, Steve needed Bob. Not because Bob knew more or was more capable, but simply because he was Steve's big brother. Never mind that he may be a failure. Bob might be mediocre in a million ways but just the thought of him still had the power to get Steve past a particular night and into the next day. For his big brother, Steve thinks, he would fight to a grisly death, and he didn't want some fancy Chicagoan to make him feel less than he was.

So Steve leaned casually against the window where he could catch the odd word, and to his surprise they appeared to be having a normal conversation. They were talking about what it was like growing up on the Pawnee River. Satisfied, Steve wandered back into the kitchen and listened to Carl telling Gretchen about the dinner he was cooking. It was a leg of lamb—something Steve had never eaten and, to be honest, had never missed. But Carl was talking it up like it was God's gift to mankind. Steve was pretty sure Gretchen had never eaten lamb before either and knew damned well that Carl hadn't learned to eat it until he left home. There were mashed potatoes and brussels sprouts, for crying out loud. Gretchen was talking to Carl like he was a long lost pal and sipping her wine at a pretty good rate.

On the porch, Bob was chatting up an older lady, and in the kitchen, Gretchen was drinking wine and discussing recipes like she was a chef. In some way it all seemed pretentious to Steve. But as he watched and listened, it occurred to him that it might not be pretension on the other people's part but stubbornness on his. He was on the edge of one of the moods that sometimes gripped him and made him pull away. If he wasn't careful he might find himself driving alone through the night, ending up who knew where? He felt very alone, and as he took another beer from the refrigerator, he admitted that happiness had always come hard for him. He was not a contented guy. Gretchen said he found the negative in every situation. He thought he simply found what was there. Like the way Gretchen was scurrying around that kitchen pretending to be interested in cooking. It made him crazy. Just the way she smiled and leaned forward to listen to what Carl was saying. The way she threw in tidbits of knowledge that he was pretty sure she was making up.

But Steve pulled himself together and forced himself to help her take the food out to the table, and then he called Bob and Eleanor to come inside. There was a fire going in the fireplace and Carl's dog was stretched out flat in front of it. Once everyone was sitting down, Steve's attitude began to shift. It was calm and warm there in Carl's dining room and the sound of the glasses ringing as they were moved jarred him. For just an instant it reminded him of the time before his mother died, before Vietnam and before the ranch began to slip away. It was civilized. People passed the food and they drank Carl's wine and even the lamb was good. It was damned good, and Steve found himself grimacing at his outlook of only minutes before. The wine bottle went around again, and when it was found to be empty, Eleanor jumped up and brought another one to the table. The fourth bottle arrived just as the homemade ice cream was dished out family style.

Gretchen passed on the ice cream but took another full glass of wine. She was thinking about Annie Simmons and Arnold Cring, but she surprised herself when she took advantage of a comment Eleanor made to turn the conversation to what was bothering her. When Eleanor mentioned that she had not met many Native Americans, Gretchen leaped. "Maybe that's because they're kept in the shadows." It wasn't exactly what she wanted to talk about, but it was the step that allowed her to tell the story of Cring and the HPMC. It poured out of her in a sort of purging, and once she began, she could not stop. She talked about her belief that HPMC withheld treatment from those who could not pay top rates. The table quieted and others listened as she went on to say that she understood how business worked and that maybe she was being naive. She felt tears gather in her eyes but would not let them fall. Although she felt she was making a fool of herself, she couldn't stop until it was all out. When she looked up, it was clear that everyone at the table was shocked. But were they shocked at what Cring had done or at how silly she had been? She ended with a smile and a wave of apology. "I think maybe I've been foolish," she said and hoped that the conversation would take up where she had interrupted it.

No one spoke for what seemed to be a long time. Carl and Bob looked down at their hands, Steve stared straight ahead, and Eleanor looked kindly at Gretchen. They were as confused about what to think as Gretchen was and the moment threatened to slide into embarrassment for all. But Eleanor and Carl were expert conversationalists; they had a way of putting their own emotions on hold and working together to salvage any situation. "There is no limit to injustice," Carl said.

After the perfect amount of time had lapsed, Eleanor spoke.

"And heartbreak is never far behind." Another pause, and then the segue into another subject. "I came across a photograph," Eleanor said. "It's not a good picture and it might not even be from around here, but it is clearly a man standing in front of a partly finished stone house. The house is small, and the picture is sad. I was told it was built somewhere along the Pawnee River for the man's sweetheart." Her voice was full of concern, and she shook her head when she mentioned the part about the sweetheart.

The others at the table rushed to help swing the conversation to something more comfortable. "I know where that is." Carl, Bob, and Steve spoke at the same time.

Gretchen exhaled a sigh of relief and Eleanor completed the change of subject. "Where?"

"It's up in the breaks," Bob said.

Carl nodded. "Right on the border between our two places." He pointed at Bob and Steve, then back at himself.

"I've never seen it," Gretchen jumped in to cover her embarrassment and because she was genuinely interested.

"It's up there," Steve said. "Falling into the basement, but still up there."

Eleanor was really excited now. "Off which road?"

"No road," Carl said. He was up, taking away plates and bringing coffee and brandy.

" 'Course there *was* a road," Steve said. "You can still see the track. Hell, there's even a couple of culverts in the worst draws."

"Can you get back to it?" Eleanor said as she took her coffee from Carl. "I'd love to see it."

"Not a problem," Bob said. "Take you back there tonight." Steve was amazed. He had never seen Bob so relaxed. He checked to be sure that he hadn't gotten into the wine or brandy. All he had in front of him was a cup of coffee and a glass of water.

"What about the sweetheart?" Gretchen put in. It was like her to think about the romance. She had certainly gotten into the wine. Steve thought she might have had more than was wise. She was upset about the story that had been cancelled, and when she was upset, she sometimes drank too much. She'd never admit it but Steve had known her long enough to know it was true. It was one of those nights.

"And the old guy?" Eleanor said. "What happened to the sweetheart and the old guy?"

Bob still had the floor. "What were their names, Carl? Your folks must have known them."

"The old man was German. Swartz? Swinden? Something like that. I'll bet it was originally one of those 160-acre homesteads. Granddad must have bought it when whatever-his-name-was went broke."

It came to Steve. "Swiegert!"

"Swiegert! That's it! Rudy Swiegert."

"But you don't know the girl's name?" It was Gretchen again.

"Hell," Steve said. "They were both dead and gone long before we were born. Ask Arvid."

Eleanor could see that Gretchen and Steve were getting on each other's nerves. "That's your father?" she asked of Steve.

"Yea, Arvid. You know Arvid."

"I'm afraid not."

"Well," Carl said as he lifted his brandy glass. "You shall meet Arvid. A fixture of this place. A pleasant fixture."

They drank to Arvid, and Steve thought the conversation would move on to another subject, but the women were stuck on the stone house. They were fascinated by the legend that old Rudy Swiegert tried to lure a woman out to the windy knob he called his homestead. "I want to see it," Gretchen said.

Eleanor seconded the motion. "Me too."

"Not tonight," Steve said. "Probably couldn't even find it in the dark."

Gretchen looked at him and smiled. "There's a moon."

Carl finished his brandy. "We could do it. Might be just the perfect romantic finale to a fine evening."

"We could get out there in a pickup." Even Bob seemed interested in the idea. He stood up and took a deck of cards from the mantel. "Need to figure out who's going to risk their outfit driving through the dark." Steve wanted to protest but it was no use. Bob was already dealing out the cards. A single card spun to a stop in front of everyone who owned a pickup. Steve rolled up the corner of his card. Jack of hearts. Shit.

ꙮ 35 ꙮ

Steve didn't even like driving his good pickup down gravel roads, and there he was, creeping out into a midnight pasture with four drinks in him and a load of party animals in the back. It was cold but only Bob got into the front of the pickup with him. "They're nuts," Steve said and pointed to the pickup bed.

"There it is," Bob said. "Squirrel bait. The whole bunch of them."

"You know how to get where we're going?"

Bob nodded straight ahead. "Through that gate. Over the ridge."

They crawled out into the pasture, and Steve couldn't help glancing into the rearview mirror at the three in the back. Carl had brought his bagpipes and a pewter flask full of brandy. He was waving the flask as he quoted from Yeats. The women were listening like kids, and it struck Steve that this was the sort of thing Gretchen wanted: moonlight rides through the pastures of her man. She wanted to feel part of something. Maybe even a little poetry. He'd been edgy all night, and thinking about all these things that he couldn't give her made him worse. He resented the fact that they seemed not to notice the cold. Only people who work inside feel they can pass up a chance to be warm in the cab of a pickup. They rolled over the land that Carl had held on to by going away and toward the land that the Thurstons had lost because they had stayed. Steve didn't want to be where he was. He didn't have an alternative in mind; he just wanted to be somewhere else. The ruins of a man who had lost his land generations before did not interest Steve. He didn't want to look at the wreckage of another man's dreams.

But that is where they ended up: a quarter section of land that Arvid had always called the Swiegert place. Steve didn't know the story, just that the house was mostly gone. A few handcut stones like the ones in Carl's house, fallen into a hole that must have been the basement. When Bob and Steve and Carl were young they used to ride horses out to play among the scattered cut sandstone blocks. They found lizards and rattlesnakes sunning themselves on the stones. Steve liked the place then, but by the time he was grown it only made him mad. He was often angry when he was young. He thought that was behind him, but as he drove, the feeling of it came back as real as if the thirty years hadn't passed. The first time it bubbled over was in his junior year of high school. It was spring and they were in the process of signing up for senior classes. There was a boy named Berry Andrews who would go on to become valedictorian. He was smart, very popular with the socially adept crowd. His girlfriend was the best-looking girl in the school. Cindy Crawly was a long-legged brunette who was as sophisticated as Berry Andrews. They were both destined for East Coast universities and it was understood that they were in a strata above the rest of the students at McDermot High School.

Steve was helping put up hay on the ranch and Bob was getting ready for boot camp. Berry Andrews and Cindy Crawly were no concern of Steve's and their paths seldom crossed. But in a line for signing up for senior physics Berry made the mistake of looking at Steve and shaking his head. To taunt Steve Thurston was a daring act for Berry and it was done mostly for Cindy's benefit. "Thurston," Berry said, "you must be in the wrong line." He glanced at Cindy to be sure she was listening. "Physics is a collage prep course." They both suppressed giggles.

Steve was instantly embarrassed but he was surprised to find that he was also angry. "I like physics," was all he could find to say.

"This is physics," Berry said, "not phys. ed." He chuckled at his own joke, and when he looked to gauge Cindy's response, Steve hit him a piston blow to the side of his head.

If he had stopped with that one punch, Steve might never have met Erwin Benson. But he did not stop, and as a result Berry Andrews's parents wanted him arrested. But the closest he came to jail was a stern talking-to from the county prosecutor. "I know your family," Benson said. He pointed his finger across the desk at a frightened Steve Thurston. "You were stupid to do what you did."

"He was asking for it," Steve mumbled.

"He was manipulating you, son. He was trying to see if you were stupid enough to react the way you did." They looked at each other across the desk and Steve was surprised to see that the man was trying to help him.

"Was I supposed to let him make fun of me?"

Benson narrowed one eye and thought. "No," he finally said. "But unless you want to end up in jail, you better find another way."

They stared at each other a few moments longer before Benson let Steve go. And in those few moments Steve recalled the fight. It had not been much of fight, just Berry Andrews trying to cover his head as he went down. Benson was right, it was stupid. Then Steve remembered one thing more—the way Cindy Crawly looked at him as he stood over Berry. Her lips were slightly parted and her eyes were wide but soft with a look he would never forget. Those scenes of anger and realization from his youth mixed with the clutching feeling he had had all evening, and he knew there was nothing left for him in the night to come.

The moon was low in the west but bright in a cloudless sky.

The shadows of the ruined stones fell over other shadows and the ground was different shades of black. The grass grew up from the basement like the headdresses of the Indians who died trying to protect the horses his great-grandfather stole. To Steve it was like a graveyard, but everyone else seemed to find something cheerful in the wasted fruit trees and lilacs that were nearly choked out by their wild cousins. They said old Swiegert planted a garden for the gal he was after. Those lilacs were probably the last of it. Another few winters and they'd be gone too, finally defeated by the landscape they were intended to transform. Steve could feel the coming winter lurking out there in the cold night, ready to hit those poor alien plants one more blow.

Carl went to the truck and brought out his bagpipes. He played an eerie song that made them all quiet until Bob spoke up. "Jesus," he said. "That gives me the creeps."

Carl laughed. "It was meant to. It's what the bagpipes are for."

"They invented bagpipes to give people the creeps?"

"For sad occasions." Carl said. "For rallying the troops and giving them heart. The pipers would march with blood on their faces once the battle was joined."

"Joined?" Eleanor asked. "Where does that come from, joined?"

"The battle is joined," Carl said. "The battle is begun."

"We know that," Gretchen said. "But joined is an odd word. The armies join, the combatants join. But why does a battle join?"

"I don't know," Bob said, "but that's what they say. Joined."

"Okay, okay," Carl said. "Let's get back to sad. Let me play one for poor old Rudy Swiegert."

Steve listened to the song but all he wanted to do was just walk away and into the hills. He wanted to get away from it all, but of course he couldn't. Now the others were talking in low voices about what it must have been like to be Swiegert. Steve felt he knew what happened here, but he didn't try to tell them. There were no words that would work. Just let them talk about how much the old man must have loved the girl and how sad it was.

When Carl reached out and took Eleanor's hand, the movement caught Steve's eye and he stared at those hands cradled one in the other. It made him uncomfortable, and when he looked up, his eyes met Gretchen's. They were cold as the tumbled stones that surrounded them and Steve knew that they could not go on. The world beyond what surrounded them demanded something more.

They'd planned to spend the night together but they both knew it was a waste of time. It was somehow easy to be grown up about it. When Steve pulled up in front of Gretchen's house he left the engine running and that didn't surprise her or even disappoint her. This time it was truly finished and they knew it. There was ample opportunity to be mean and cutting and they had learned to be good at it. But that night they did not see the use in any of that. They sat in the pickup with the yellow of the streetlight slanting in on them and for maybe the first time, in a very long time, they communicated—though they didn't say a word. Steve didn't want to talk because it would make things worse. He thought she might want to say something, but as if to prove that they were hopeless, she simply shrugged and let herself out.

3

☙ 36 ❧

They'd had terrible arguments before. They'd decided to call it quits several times. But that night after the dinner at Carl Lindquist's was different. Gretchen was so exhausted by the relationship—the insecurity, the bickering, the pressure of Jake, the suspicions—that it actually felt good to have it over. Of course, the first mornings were difficult. She stayed in bed too long each morning for nearly a week and she knew that Jake wondered what was wrong. Kids are so sensitive to their surroundings but have no way of understanding or articulating what they are feeling. She felt sorry for her son when he came to her bedroom door and knocked softly and asked if she wanted some toast. It broke her heart that she couldn't pop out of bed and be cheery and set a good example. When she tried, she failed.

Gretchen told him to come in but she hesitated, and that hesitation sounded like she didn't care, or worse, like she was lying about wanting Jake around. It was another thing that he felt but couldn't understand and that made him even more worried about his mother. He knew that Steve hadn't been around, and Gretchen supposed he was old enough to put two and two together, but he still didn't get it. Gretchen didn't get it. For twenty minutes after Jake's knock she lay in bed and felt nothing. But finally, like a sleepwalker, she forced herself up and into the shower. By the time she got into the kitchen Jake was almost ready to leave for school and there was no time for anything except a quick rundown of his schedule and the transfer of a little lunch money. When the door went closed on him the house felt hollow as a steel drum: a layer of recrimination settled on top of Gretchen's already dismal mood. It was not until her third cup of coffee that any balance returned. By then she was running late and feeling that only immersion in work could save her.

She could not get Annie Simmons, Tad Bordeaux, or Dr. Arnold Cring out of her mind. Gretchen wondered what Annie was doing with her shattered young life. She wondered if she had made it to college yet. Thinking of that made Gretchen work listlessly, and at intervals she found herself staring and sitting for long hours, thinking about what had happened. Occasionally she was angry, but usually it felt more like embarrassment. There was no more of the crusader left in her. Now all she wanted was to understand. It was in one of these dark moments, just after she had reached her office in the morning, that she decided to call John Tully.

"I had no idea that you were the reporter on the story in question," he said.

"Would it have mattered who wrote the story? Did you even read it?"

"No, on both counts. I was only making a call to the editor of the paper, trying to avoid the hassle of a restraining order. I was bound to make that call. I was working on behalf of a client."

"Arnold Cring." Gretchen regretted a touch of venom in her voice and repeated herself to expunge the peevishness. "Arnold Cring."

"Yes, Dr. Cring is a client and something of a friend."

"A friend?"

Gretchen could feel Tully's smile through the phone. "Yes. He's not the monster you might think."

She liked it that Tully could drop his professional façade. "I don't think he's a monster."

"Well, good. He's really quite a guy."

"A control freak, maybe?" She tried to say it with a lilt in her voice that would tell Tully she was not hung up on professionalism either.

"He does like to be in charge."

"Well, he's a doctor."

"Hmmm." Tully needed to be careful not to go too far with his casual banter about a client. "He is, indeed." He paused, and Gretchen could tell that he was preparing to change the subject. "I don't know quite how to ask this," he said. There was a longer pause and Gretchen was suddenly paralyzed with the irrational dread that something was wrong with Jake. It was crazy, an effect of her mood since her breakup with Steve, but in the split second that Tully fumbled for words she scrolled through the list of possible problems with Jake. She had started on the list of things that she might have done wrong when Tully finally came out with what he wanted to ask. "I don't suppose you could get free for dinner one of these nights."

"Dinner?"

"Yeah."

"With you?"

"Well, yeah, I eat dinner. I sort of like the Vietnamese place."

"The Saigon," Gretchen said flatly. She was misfiring, trying to understand what was happening. "The Saigon. What's this about?"

Tully laughed. "Well, it's about you and me getting some dinner."

❧ 37 ❧

Carl was such a sweetheart. It was the old boy-girl game to be sure, but Eleanor wondered if it might not be more. There was the house, of course, but she was realizing that this house did not stand alone, its existence depended more directly on the landscape that surrounded it than any other house she had ever known. And there was the matrix of Carl. From the very beginning Eleanor had been attracted to the sense of Carl having a private life that he only hinted at. There was something missing in his story that she could not put her finger on. But there was another thing about Carl that, irrational as it seemed, she was quite sure of: she was attracted to him like she had never been attracted to a man before. That made it sound like she had been attracted to many men, which certainly was not true. There were really just the two: her ex-husband and Carl. The sad thing was that because of that first romance, she couldn't bring herself to trust the second. In some ways she felt sorry for Carl for having to endure her uncertainty. He was chivalrous in his attention to her feelings, though she couldn't imagine how. On their second date he leaned to kiss her. What he had in mind was a real kiss. Nothing inappropriate—he was dropping her off at her condo after a wonderfully simple evening of dinner and a movie. There was no reason not to accept the kiss. Indeed, no reason not to return it. But Carl was a passionate man, and naturally the kiss he planned might well have led to more intimacy, and she was afraid. The truth was, for all her years and worldly appearance, she had had little experience with intimacy. Only with her husband, and in that she had been betrayed.

She didn't want to make kind Carl suffer for another man's cruelty, and passion was definitely stirring inside her. But it had been a very long time and she wasn't sure she could do what they both wanted. Carl did not complain or pressure her unfairly. On the night that the boys took Gretchen and her out to see the stone house he was particularly wonderful. Even though it embarrassed Bob and made Steve and Gretchen uncomfortable, he held her hand every chance he got. She was so moved by the remains of the old German's house that Carl's hand in hers took on special meaning. That cold, still night with the shadows cast by the moon somehow made things come into focus. They were with a man, Bob, whose life had been difficult and was now complicated by loneliness. The other couple, Steve and Gretchen, oozed with tension. On that night, and every night since, Eleanor couldn't help thinking that she was fortunate indeed to have the hand of a good man wrapped tightly around hers.

She was driven to find out more about Rudy Swiegert and fascinated to learn that Arvid Thurston had actually known him. By the time she actually got to meet Arvid it was almost winter. Carl was nice enough to drive her out on a windy, gray November day. Though she didn't know it at the time, it was not the best sort of day to visit Arvid. He was an outside man, and when weather drives a man like that inside he is caught like a nocturnal animal flushed out in the light of day—the proverbial bull in a china shop, a hog on ice. That was the way Arvid was in the kitchen of the rickety old Thurston house.

Carl assured her that he was usually quite at ease in a kitchen. "Great coffee drinker," he said. Then he laughed. "Arvid is a great drinker of all kinds." But somehow Arvid thought it was necessary to feed them. He'd known about their coming for a couple of days and had evidently decided that it was his opportunity to entertain. There was the coffee of course, but there was more. From the back door they heard a flurry of activity and Eleanor caught a glimpse of Arvid scurrying across the kitchen with a towel over one shoulder and juggling an obviously hot baking pan as he hollered over his shoulder that he'd be right with them. There was a pause, and even over the wind, they heard the bang of an oven door and a string of indecipherable expletives.

Carl smiled and shrugged. They were both cold and so Carl went ahead and pushed the door open and called in. "Arvid?"

"Yeah, yeah." He came around the corner holding the index finger of his left hand with his right. "There you are. Come on in." He released the finger and gave it a good shake before he reached out to take Eleanor's hand. "So you're the gal, huh?" He stood back and appraised her. His eyes went up and down in a way that would have incensed her if it had been another person. "Well, hell, you don't look so bad. No wooden leg. What you doing with this galoot?"

Carl had his hands on his hips and a large smile on his face. He was still in his heavy coat, and Eleanor ran her arm inside his. "He may be a galoot," she said. "But he's my galoot." The statement was quite spontaneous, and she was instantly afraid it took Carl by surprise. It took her by surprise, but she stuck to her guns and held onto Carl's arm. Carl's smile grew and Arvid smiled back through two-day's growth of gray stubble.

"I don't get it." He threw up his hands in mock disgust. " 'Course you didn't even know me when you got mixed up with him. Things might turn around for you yet. You guys want a cup of coffee?"

"Please," Carl said.

"Got some cinnamon rolls in the oven. They weren't quite done, but should be ready pretty soon."

Eleanor looked at Carl and raised her eyebrows as Arvid turned back to the stove. She had not envisioned Arvid Thurston as a baker. "The kids' mom used to cook these little beauties. Sometimes I'd help her. Haven't tried it for year and years." He was sipping from a glass of caramel-colored water and held it high. "You want a drink instead of coffee?"

Eleanor and Carl looked at each other again and Eleanor shrugged. "Sure."

"All I got's Black Velvet."

"That will be fine," Carl said. "Maybe a little water."

"Yes," Eleanor said. "Water."

"Two Velvet and waters, coming up. Ice?"

"Everybody gets ice," Carl quoted. "Rich folks get it in the summer. Poor folks get it in the winter."

Arvid looked at him and shook his head. "It's November. You want ice or not?"

"No ice for me," Carl said.

Eleanor wasn't sure. "I guess just water."

"Good."

They watched as Arvid dug into the cupboard for two more glasses and held them up to the light. They were jelly jars. He rubbed one on his shirt as he reached for the whiskey on the shelf above the stove. Just two fingers of Velvet and a splash of water. He brought the drinks to them with a broad smile. He winked at Eleanor. "Rolls will be ready any second."

In fact, both Carl and Eleanor could smell the first twinge of burning sugar, but Arvid took the time to offer a toast. "To Lord Lindquist and his lady."

They raised their glasses, but Eleanor could stand it no longer and sidled to the oven and turned it off before she drank. Then she opened the door and faked surprise. "Oh my God, they're burning."

Arvid rushed forward with a towel in hand. "Stand back. I'll handle 'er." He flung the oven door fully open and reached in with the towel. The rolls came out smoking but not on fire. The towel was not thick enough to protect Arvid's hands for long and he tossed the cookie sheet toward the table. "Jumping Jesus," he said. "She's a hot one."

He stood over the steaming cinnamon rolls shaking his right hand and peering closely at his creation. They were not individual rolls but a solid chunk a foot square. Half the mass was charred black, but the other half appeared salvageable. He poked with his left index finger, swore, and began shaking the left hand like he had been shaking the right. "Hot, hot," he said as he stuck the finger in his mouth. "Oh, oh." He tasted and thought. "But not bad." He tasted some more. "Burned hell out of that end, but I believe we can still have rolls." He looked up and smiled as if he just realized that he was being watched. "Going to be all right," he said.

Eleanor could not stand to watch Arvid as he sawed away at the burnt end of the rolls with a large knife, and when Carl offered to help, she became frightened. The knife looked sharp. They both set their drinks down. "Here," she said, "let me try." She took over the job of cutting away the burned parts.

Arvid handed over the knife. "Just quarter it into three equal halves," he said.

Arvid freshened all the glasses while Eleanor found plates in the cupboard. Finally they were seated around the kitchen table and they took a moment to savor the rolls. In fact, they were really quite good. It only took a minute for Eleanor to understand that cinnamon and whiskey were really not too bad of an idea.

"So Eleanor was curious about the Swiegert place." Carl was trying to keep their visit on track.

"Oh God. Rudy Swiegert. Haven't thought of him for thirty years."

"I never knew him," Carl said. "When did he die?"

"Oh, hell. Right after the war. Forty-six maybe." Arvid was shaking his head, trying to remember. "You were still shitting your pants." He winced. "Damn, I'm sorry." He turned to Eleanor. "Not used to having a lady around."

"Quite all right. You just tell your story."

"Well," Arvid leaned back in his chair. "He was an old bastard when I was a kid. He lived in the barn loft over to your place." Arvid pointed at Carl. "Let's see. My grandma Butler, that'd be your great-grandmother, used to get me over there to sort of help the old guy gather up his dirty clothes. Kind of pick up a little. But he died when I was a teenager."

"He lived in your grandmother's barn?" Eleanor was suddenly leaning forward, looking hard into Arvid's eyes. "What about the stone house?"

"Oh hell, that stone shack was always a ruin in my lifetime."

"But Swiegert built it."

"Hell, yes. Built it with his own hands. Drove a wagon into the bluffs and sawed stones out of those hills for a year. Moved them around with rolling logs, gin poles, mules. Christ almighty. Hand work. Never get it done today. Even with a crane." Arvid took another sip of whiskey and shook his head. He had some idea of what that kind of work would be like.

"But there was a woman," Eleanor took a sip of her own whiskey. "In the story I heard, he was building it to lure a girl."

"I never knew her."

"But you knew of her."

"There was that story." Arvid squinted his eyes, trying to remember.

Now Carl was leaning across the table, too. "Mail-order bride? Something like that?"

"No. No, I don't think so. Think it was one of them Bohunks lived down around where Horse Creek runs into the Pawnee. Kolda, Hersman, Bocheck, one of them maybe. There was still a little bunch of them when I was a kid. But that girl must have been gone. Dead, or just gone. I don't remember old Rudy saying much about her. Lot of them went to California, Oregon. Everybody moved out in the thirties."

"But he talked about her. She did exist."

"Oh, I think she did. I mean, hell, he built that house for her."

"But she rejected him."

"Shit. Like a crumpled dollar bill at the car wash."

"Never," Carl said, "was the tragedy of unrequited love described with such succinctness." Eleanor smiled at him and reached to find his leg under the table.

"Well, maybe," Arvid said. "I don't know what you said."

"I think Carl was saying that it is a sad story. Was Rudy sad?"

Arvid sipped and thought. "Sad?" He sipped again. "Yeah, we're all sad."

Eleanor squeezed Carl's thigh under the table. Carl looked at her and asked the question he knew she was thinking. "But she said no and the house just deteriorated?"

"Guess he never really finished it. Grandma said he lived in it without a front door. Said Granddad found him up there sitting by a potbellied stove, wrapped in a blanket, wind whipping right on through."

"And they moved him into the barn?"

"That wasn't uncommon then. Lots of people lived in barns."

Now Eleanor's hand was moving up and down Carl's thigh. Warm. Comforting. "And the stone blocks just fell apart?"

"Yeah," Arvid said. "They left the broken ones. Good ones went to build your porch."

The table fell silent. Contemplation, sipping, rubbing of chins. Finally Arvid spoke. "Grandma loved that porch."

"So did my mother," Carl said.

Eleanor knew she had to tell the truth. "So do I," she said.

As soon as they got into Carl's pickup for the ride back to his house, Eleanor scooted over beside him and put her head on his shoulder. "Do you mind?"

Carl smiled and started the pickup. "I don't mind." It had gotten dark. The headlights came on and slowly swept Arvid's yard until they straightened out on the long driveway.

"I wonder why she left. What sort of a life she ended up with."

"Impossible to say."

"Sad."

"Oh, yes."

They fell silent then, and rode for several miles drenched in their own thoughts. They were turning into Carl's driveway and the mercury vapor light could be seen down the lane of gnarled trees. "I brought you the makings for your favorite sandwich."

"No."

"I did. A Vidalia onion, salami, and jalapeños."

"Ambrosia. Should we try one tonight?"

"I think that particular sandwich should be a private experience. And besides," as she spoke the headlights fell on the cream-colored stone blocks that anchored the front porch. "I think it is time I spent the night."

Now the pickup was parked and they looked at each other. Carl chose not to speak. He only nodded and with his thick arm drew her tight against his chest.

❧ 38 ❧

Steve and Gretchen had gone all week without talking to each other. Steve had done nothing but work and lie on the couch of his trailer watching television. He bought a case of beer on Tuesday, but now it was Saturday and he had drunk only three bottles. Bob had been in his bed most mornings when Steve left for work but never was home at night. The major evidence that his brother still lived there was the mess in the kitchen that Steve woke up to every morning. The mess made him think of Gretchen and the way she insisted on an insanely clean kitchen. He recalled one morning when they were in her kitchen, waking up and talking about nothing. There was coffee and Gretchen absent-mindedly cleaned the already spotless sink and counters. She talked and cleaned like a machine, and he moved to the cupboard and took out a bowl and a box of cereal. When he went to the refrigerator for the carton of milk, Gretchen moved in behind him, and by the time he turned around she had replaced the cereal in the cupboard and was washing his never-used bowl in the sink. It made him smile to think how crazy she was, but he didn't miss it.

He knew what it was like to clean up after someone. He didn't mind cleaning up after Bob, and now, as he waited for a college football game to begin, he stood at the sink and ran very hot water onto the dirty dishes that were not his own. Despite what Gretchen thought, he actually enjoyed washing dishes. There was something about the feel of the hot water that relaxed him.

The slipperiness of the soap, and the way that slipperiness dissipated as he rubbed the glasses with his bare hands, let him daydream. When he washed dishes, the daydreams were kind and light. They often took him to the time before things went bad. He thought about his mother and it occurred to him that it might be the dishes that awakened those memories. She was forever washing dishes too, standing straight at the sink, looking out the window that faced south so that the winter sun slanted in and across her sandy hair. He remembers her hands, large and strong and rough. She was a Lindquist, a big-framed Scandinavian with pale blue eyes. She and Arvid were the same height, and though his father had been a strong and solid man when Steve was young, his mother might well have weighed more than the diminished man who now lived alone with his bottles of Black Velvet.

Mary Thurston did not coddle her children. When the boys were growing up, she demanded hard work and respect. But until the boys were well into their teens, she always came into their rooms and woke them slowly with soft words and back rubs. Those warm mornings and those loving caresses are what Steve remembers as he stacks his brother's dishes in the drying rack. His face is in the down pillow and his mother's warm, strong hands move gently up and down his back. "You need to get up, son."

"Hmmm."

"Your breakfast is waiting." And as she moves to rise from his bed, Steve rolls over and smiles. She leans to kiss his forehead, and standing there at his own kitchen sink, he thinks he might cry. When the bright, ruddy face of his mother begins to go pale and gray with the cancer that killed her, Steve fights the daydream and brings himself back to the trailer house with the tattered couch positioned like a church pew in front of the jabbering television. The game was finally on, and Steve dried his hands on his jeans, took a beer from the refrigerator, and made his way to a seat.

But the game couldn't hold his attention and he found himself simply sitting and staring. He was competing in a rodeo, in Montana, on the day his mother died. He rode a big, sorrel, bareback horse that threw him hard, and he landed on his shoulder and dislocated it. His friends found him in the emergency room in a lot of pain and told him about his mother.

It was another two hours before the doctors set him free and he wandered, dazed by painkillers, into a bar in downtown Lewistown. He was searching for his friends, but what he found was a fan who had seen him come off the horse and watched him drag himself to the corral rail.

"Are you all right?" she asked with wonder in her eyes and voice.

The bad arm was in a sling, but with the good one he reached into his shirt pocket and pulled out the bottle of pills. He shook the bottle like a dice cup. "I am now."

"Oh, I was going to buy you a beer for the afternoon's entertainment."

Steve looked once more around the bar for his friends. Finding nothing but strangers, he sat down beside the rodeo fan. She was obviously a tourist and knew almost nothing about men like Steve. "Well," he said, "what's stopping you?"

Now, with the football game dancing without meaning in front of his eyes, he remembers the motel room and the pain of the shoulder as they rolled in the bed. But it was the pain of the next morning that was too much for him. He shook his head as if to erase the memory. He finished the first beer and wanted to go for another but he didn't want to move. He sat until the phone rang. But even then he was slow going to it and didn't pick it up until the fourth ring.

It was Gretchen, and though he was glad for the familiarity of her voice, he thought of hanging up. In some way he believed that he had made it over a hump and his life was moving onward through the fog as it always had. "Look," she said, "I don't want to hassle you but I need to get something squared away."

"What's that?"

"It's about Jake. So you and I have our problems, but I don't think it's fair that Jake should suffer more than necessary."

"You're right."

"He wants to keep seeing your dad. He wants to keep going out to the ranch and riding the horses. I think he needs it but I don't want anyone to get stuck in the middle. I want you to know that this is about Jake and Arvid."

"I don't have a say about any of that."

Gretchen thought about pointing out how typically evasive his comment was but didn't bother. "Then you don't mind."

" 'Course not. Dad's his own man and that place doesn't belong to us anyway. Belongs to John Tully."

Tully's name stopped the conversation. In fact, Gretchen was getting ready to meet John Tully for dinner. It was thinking about that meeting that made Gretchen want to come to an understanding with Steve. "Well," she said, "all right then."

Steve felt her getting ready to say good-bye. He wasn't sure he wanted her to hang up, but he had nothing to say. "Yeah, okay then."

There was another pause. "We don't have to be strangers."

Steve thought about that. "No," he said. But he knew it wasn't true.

"Well, good-bye then."

"Yeah." He let the phone slip back into its cradle and went to the refrigerator for another beer. When he turned back to the television the game had lost all its appeal. He stood looking at the telephone book on the counter beside the phone and sipped his beer. Finally he picked up the book, turned to the R's, and ran his finger down the column until he found the number for Carolina Riggins.

🌿 **39** 🌿

The Butler family graveyard held a dozen graves and was cordoned off from the pasture by a rusted wrought-iron fence. Carl and Eleanor had walked up to have a look, but Carl stood back, thinking, while Eleanor examined the headstones carefully. He had been in a pensive mood all morning, and standing there on that hill with his forebears at his feet made him feel small and insignificant. They had been at the graveyard for nearly an hour. Carl was still staring out at the pastures that rolled down to the river when he felt Eleanor's hand snake in under his elbow. "What are you thinking about?"

The touch of her felt good, and he smiled, though he could not pull himself away from the view of the Pawnee. "Steve, and Bob, and Gretchen, and Arvid." He paused and his head began to bob up and down slowly. "And us."

"I know what you are thinking."

"You do?"

"Yes. You're thinking that you and I have it easy. That our neighbors have a very tenuous hold on their lives."

Now Carl grinned but still watched the valley. "You're a pretty fair mind reader. We're all in peril," he said, "but some more than others."

"Peril. It is always out there, isn't it."

"Some are born with it, some achieve it, some have it thrust upon them."

"Poor Shakespeare. It is Shakespeare, right?"

"Not quite."

"But close enough." Eleanor squeezed his arm tight. "Where do we fit into that?"

"And some spend great quantities of their life avoiding peril."

"Maybe we're just careful."

"Or cowardly."

"Or just not very interesting."

Carl pulled his eyes away from the river and looked down at her. "We're interesting enough, but perhaps not tragic."

"Like Steve, and Bob, and Gretchen, and Arvid?"

"And those kids in the car, and the High Plains Medical Clinic."

"Gretchen has given up," Eleanor said. "Given up on Tad Bordeaux and Arnold Cring." She paused and exhaled. "And Steve Thurston."

"You think so."

"Can you blame her?"

"No," Carl said. "He's not what a woman needs, is he?"

"No. But he's hard for a woman to resist."

"Oh?"

"All that woundedness. All the stuff he's taken onto his shoulders."

"All the stuff that men like me have managed to let slide off."

"What are you getting at, Mr. Lindquist? All what stuff?"

Carl pulled his arm out of Eleanor's and draped it over her shoulder. He held her tight and turned her away from the graveyard. They began to walk back toward the house. "There is something about me," Carl said, "that you might want to know."

At first, Eleanor thought this might be one of Carl's jokes, but after only a few steps, feeling the tension in his grip, she knew that he was serious. "Go on," she said.

"Did you ever wonder why I taught at the University of New

Brunswick? Why I seldom made it back to this place where I was born?" She shook her head, but already the pieces were falling in line.

They took a few more steps, then stopped, and Carl turned her so he could see her face clearly. "For many years it was illegal for me to come back. If I came home at all it was like a thief in the night." He tried a smile but it failed. "I ran to Canada to avoid the draft. I suppose I chose my exile." She touched his face, amazed that he was so upset by something she saw as heroic. "It has bothered me for nearly forty years," he said.

"Well," Eleanor said without hesitation, "it doesn't bother me." She held the big bearded face in both hands and her eyes filled with tears. She could feel her head shaking and wasn't sure she could speak.

"My God, Carl." She finally said. "You made a very hard decision. Had I been a man I only hope that I could have done the same." She shook her head. "You did nothing wrong."

He nodded and sighed. "Perhaps not," he said. "But growing up, I never imagined that I would be one to stand by and let others suffer for my sins."

"Sins?"

He smiled sadly. "My good fortune, then."

"Why do you speak in the past tense?" Eleanor said. "We're not dead yet."

Carl nodded. "I see. Still time for redemption."

"No redemption needed. It's just that neither of us believed in that war. If the threat were real I would step up to the plate and so would you."

He gathered her up in his arms and they stood like that for several minutes. "I certainly like to think so," he whispered. "I like to think that I would."

❦ 40 ❦

Gretchen had eaten Vietnamese food only twice before. Some of it seemed good to her but some of it was far too hot. For that reason, and the fact that he was clearly anxious to help her, she let John Tully do the ordering. "Now, you don't like hot, right?"

"Hot's okay," Gretchen said. She did not want to sound unsophisticated. "But some of this Asian food can be a little too much."

Tully raised his eyebrows. "I understand," he said. "I've had a bad experience or two myself." He took a pair of half glasses from his jacket pocket, held them up for her to see, and shook his head. "Creeping old age."

"Oh, old age. What are you? Thirty-five?"

"That was bald-faced flattery."

He was right. She could not tell how old he was but didn't want to guess him too old. "Okay, forty."

"You're closer but still a flatterer. I'm forty-two."

She looked hard at him. He seemed older. "Forty-two? We're pretty close."

"Now you're trying to make me feel good." He held the glasses up again. "Let's see your bifocals. Can't be close without this token of passage."

Gretchen laughed. "Okay, I fudged a decade or so. But I've got glasses too. I'm just too vain to bring them out in public."

"Ah ha. That's why you wanted me to order." He slid the glasses on and peered down at the menu.

She took an instant to study his features: a full head of ebony hair, a square, clean-shaven face, the trace of a jowliness that would soon give him an even more judicial bearing. "I have trouble with the Vietnamese words," she laughed.

"Me too. How the heck do you pronounce n-u-o-c-c-h-a-m?"

"Just point." Gretchen nodded to the waiter who was approaching. "Or order by the numbers."

Tully looked up and smiled. "Brilliant." He closed the menu. "Greetings," he said to the waiter. "We'll have a number four for the lady and I'll go with twenty-two."

"Good choice," the waiter said. "Cocktails?"

Gretchen and Tully looked at each other and shrugged. "I guess not for me," Tully said.

Gretchen nodded. "Yeah." It seemed strange to pass. "Not for me either."

"Tea," Tully said.

"Yes, tea."

After the waiter left, there was a moment of silence. "Do you eat here often?" Gretchen asked.

Tully nodded. "Quite a bit. When I go out, that is. There are really only two places in town, don't you think? This place and the Bluffs Bistro."

"They're pretty new." The Saigon was only a year old, and the Bluffs Bistro had been in existence less than a month. Gretchen had not been to the Bluffs Bistro, and this was her first visit to the Saigon. They were places that depended on the new people. "I'm afraid I'm not experienced. I love it, but my experience is a little limited. I was raised on pot roast and potatoes."

"Nothing wrong with that. I was raised the same way." He looked full on at her and raised his eyebrows. "And Catholic."

She laughed. "That's a good start." Although Gretchen doubted that they were raised the same way, she was curious. "Over by Omaha."

Tully smiled. "How did you know that?"

In fact, she'd heard it from Steve or Carl. "Oh, the word's out on you."

"Is that so?"

"That's so. Handsome young attorney from Omaha."

"There you go with the flattery again. But the 'over around Omaha' part is right. My dad had a little dairy farm when I was growing up. He worked in town but we lived in the country." He grinned and corrected himself. "Not country like you have out here. There was a shopping mall on the other side of the road."

"But you had cows."

Tully nodded back. "A few. My father actually owned the Ford dealership in a little town that is now part of Omaha.

Gretchen nodded thoughtfully. "Good business. And you went to college and law school."

"The University of Nebraska."

"Good school."

"Good school," he agreed. "Where the N stands for 'knowledge.'"

They both laughed at the old joke, and as the laughter faded, they looked at each other. In the silence they both became aware that Gretchen was going to speak. She shook her head first. "So what the hell," she said, "are you doing out here?"

They both began to nod and chuckle. The waiter was coming but Gretchen held his eyes. It was a real question. Tully shrugged. "Same reason we're all here."

Gretchen tilted her head. "Why is that?"

"American as apple pie," Tully said as the platters were laid in front of them. He shrugged. "I like places where cows live."

Tully looked down at his meal but Gretchen continued to look at him. Steam was rising from the dishes. "Good answer," she said.

He looked up and smiled. "You want chopsticks?"

She shook her head. "No, I'm kind of a fork girl."

❦ 41 ❦

Tully dropped Gretchen off just after ten. They sat in the car for only an instant before Gretchen popped her door handle. The short, awkward moment took her back to college days, when she was so self-conscious that she could hardly stand to be alone with a boy. There had been a few dates before Jake's father and a few dates after. Those dates had seemed in the ancient past, but suddenly the dilemma of the good-night kiss was as real and immediate as it had been in the eighties. Mercifully it only lasted for that instant and evaporated when the door popped open. But that odd tension stayed with her as she walked to the back door of her house. She smiled at the way it made her feel.

Jake's bedroom light was on and she could hear the radio rhythm and the rapping voice blending with the bass vibrations. She shook her head as she touched the doorknob. She didn't like Jake's music much and knew that her dislike was not that different from the dislikes of her own parents. They found Bruce Springsteen borderline subversive. They had long ago retired and moved to a cramped condo in Phoenix, but Gretchen shook her head to think what they would make of their grandson's music. She shook her head at the feeling of being somehow caught in the jumble of generations: from an understanding of what her parents went through with her to the giddiness she had experienced in John Tully's car. Not once in all this did she think of Steve Thurston, and she was surprised how good that felt.

At that very moment Steve was lying back on Carolina Riggins's bed watching her unbutton her silk blouse. The room was dark except for the candle Carolina had lit. Steve was still fully dressed, and when he realized that fact he jerked in a start to take them off. His boots were clean. They weren't hurting anything, so he relaxed, dragged another scented pillow under his head, and watched how the candlelight flickered on Carolina's skin and her long blond hair. He liked her boldness, the way she stood upright with her breasts bulging from the lacey bra. They had been drinking and dancing, and as he watched her, he could again feel those breasts rubbing heavy against his chest. He felt the tight blue-jeaned thighs against his own thighs, the subtle grinding in sync with the bass guitar.

He had never been in the room before, but somehow it felt familiar to him. The corners near the ceiling swayed from the alcohol but it didn't frighten him. The bed was comfortable and the exotic smells made perfect sense. The stereo played Van Morrison. It was tuned low but the words and music were comforting. Steve could have sung along, but he wanted Carolina to believe that all his attention was on her. She stood sultry in front of him and unfastened her rhinestone belt and the top button of her jeans. A ballet dancer could not have toed her boots off with more ease. Then she moved to the dresser and opened the top drawer. She pulled out a bag of marijuana and cigarette papers, but before she began building a joint she came to Steve, leaned over him, and kissed him deep and wet. At the same time her hand slid down his shirt and her thumb popped the buttons until she came to the growing bulge in his own blue jeans. She held him firmly the way a person might test a grapefruit. Again she kissed him deep and let her tongue linger. Steve let his eyes close but did not reach up for her. There was lots of time and he was fine just where he was.

The paper was curled around her index finger and made a perfect trough for the marijuana. The shadows of her breasts flickered with the candlelight and the movement of her hands held Steve's attention. Two pinches, then a crease and a roll with both hands. Carolina's lips were parted with concentration and she looked up and smiled at him just before she leaned to touch the paper with her tongue. Steve felt himself growing again and reached down to adjust his jeans to make room. He felt meaty but not hard. It was just the way he liked to feel. He knew he could stay like that for a long time. Before she lit the joint, Carolina unfastened her bra and let it slip to the floor. Her nipples were large and lightly colored. They were not the breasts of a girl but curved up gracefully. The fact that she was aware of how they moved made Steve aware. He watched them come to his face and took one in his mouth. When Carolina pulled away she replaced her breast with the lighted joint.

Almost instantly the room went distant and the music wrapped around and pressed down on Steve like a blanket—like the blanket he had had as a child. He suppressed the thoughts of his mother, the way she had tucked him in and the way she had awakened him as a child. He watched Carolina stand back and finish unbuttoning her pants. She wiggled free to expose a thin, shaved line of pubic hair that she covered with her hand and rubbed slowly as she took the joint from his hand. It glowed red above her breasts and she handed it back to him before she slid one of his legs out from the bed and swung her leg over it to pull off his boot. Facing away, she held his left boot up firm between her legs and he gently put his right foot against her buttocks and pushed. His foot slid out smoothly and Carolina took up the other boot. She let the second boot fall to the floor, then turned to his belt buckle.

It was the buckle he had won calf roping, with Blacky, in Belle Fourche, South Dakota. As she worked the buckle free he remembered the calves that he had drawn that day. They were big, red calves and they ran hard. They were the kind he used to like.

They were the kind Blacky had always liked. As she moved his jeans down he thought of Blacky—how he loved that horse and how everything had to do with everything else. He let himself sink into the bed and felt his naked body move on the satin bedspread. When Carolina's long hair first touched his hips he felt at ease except for the gnawing sensation that it was all temporary but might never change.

❧ 42 ❧

Linda Anderson worked in little more than a cubical. It was not much of an office for someone who had worked as Erwin Benson's assistant for most of her life. She called it her lair, but it was really just the corner of the waiting room with a hastily built wall along one side. The wall was meant to be temporary but had stood now for seventeen years, and though they were starting to hear comments about its shabby appearance, it had avoided criticism for most of that time. From the day she was moved up from filing clerk to Erwin's assistant, Linda sat behind a partition wall and typed—first on a manual typewriter, then an electric, then an electric with some memory. Unlike many in the courthouse, she moved into rudimentary computers easily. Now she sat surrounded by what seemed to Erwin to be an unfathomable maze of humming boxes, screens, wires, and mouses. Or would that be mice? he wondered.

"Jesus, Linda," Erwin would say periodically, "you could run the space shuttle from here."

She would invariably smile up at him and say, "I'd like to try it, but I think we're short of RAM."

RAM? Never mind. He'd smile back at her and move on into his dark inner sanctum.

Sometimes, if there had been messages while he was gone, she would hand them to him on his way past. But that day in early winter, when he returned from a pretrial hearing concerning a stolen car, she did not hand the pink message notes to him but followed him into his office and laid them on his desk.

"Messages," she said.

Erwin looked down at the three slips of paper and spread them out with his index finger. None were pressing, and Erwin knew that Linda had something else on her mind. "Thank you," he said and sat down. "What's up?"

They were old friends who respected each other immensely and had long ago given up on dancing around topics. "They're going to run someone against you."

"They?"

"The Republicans."

"Ah yes, the Republicans. What makes you think that?"

"I heard it at the Zonta meeting."

"Good source."

Linda was a stout woman with dyed blonde hair done up in a permanent. She had worn glasses all the years that Erwin had known her and she was always dressed as if going to court. Before she was born her father had been state chairman for the election of Eugene Debs. She grew up in a home that hosted clandestine meetings of the Farm-Labor Party, and though she was now in her late fifties, she was as feisty as ever. "We can't let them drive us further underground."

Erwin smiled. "We're so far underground now we should be carrying a canary."

"Well, that's exactly right. That's why we have to get to work."

"Who we talking about here? John Tully?"

"That's what I hear."

Despite his age, Erwin could feel a rush of combative adrenaline surge through him. "Is Tully a done deal?"

"That's the word."

Erwin smiled and laid his hands flat on his desk. "Well, Miss Anderson, we have a lot of friends in this county, and I think we can beat Mr. Tully."

Linda nodded but wouldn't let herself smile back at her boss. "I don't want you to simply beat this guy. I want you to annihilate him. I want this to be the election that turns the worm."

That made Erwin laugh. "Goddamn," he said, "you're a tough old war-horse."

Now Linda smiled. "I am," she said. "And you are the last gallant knight in the county."

"You spelling that with a *K* or an *N*?" They grinned like two teenagers. "We'll kick some ass," Erwin said. "Going to be great fun."

☙ **43** ❧

Carl Lindquist was more of a literary man than a philosopher, but
he did have his theories. One theory he held particularly dear,
and remained completely silent about, was his belief that, at least
for the male of the species, urinating under the open sky imparted untold health benefits. In fact, during the restoration of his
family home, the architectural change that he relished perhaps
more than any other was the lowering of the back porch railing
by two inches. As a child, relieving himself from the porch was
strictly verboten and could only be enjoyed surreptitiously, but
now, as a man, it could be relished at any time of day or night.
Indeed, there were many times that he stood smugly against his
newly lowered railing for long minutes, letting his prostate play
its silly game, secure in his belief that the longer he stood under
the prairie sky the healthier he would become.

It was the Friday before the last weekend of the grouse season
and Carl sat reading in his living room in the year's last warm
sunlight that came full force through the front window. He was
rereading *The Old Man and the Sea* and thinking how Hemingway's
descriptions of the sea were not unlike what he saw from his front
window. He was contemplating the power of simple declarative
sentences, and Tolstoy was stretched out at his feet. They were
taking a day off in preparation for the hunt he had promised his
new neighbor, John Tully. He had put it off as long as possible
and had secretly hoped that Tully had forgotten about the deal

they had made. But Tully was not the kind to forget a deal. He had called on Wednesday to confirm that he and Dr. Cring would be out on Sunday morning. His voice was genuinely excited and that gave Carl the lift he needed to be enthusiastic himself. At first, Carl had been taken aback to hear that Dr. Cring was coming. Gretchen's story about Cring had shaken him and he had reservations about spending a day walking the draws with a man of questionable character. But fairness was a matter of character too, and hearsay, after all, was only hearsay. He made up his mind that he would not let rumor hamper his enjoyment of the last day of grouse season. They would have a fine, civilized hunt and that would end the season. It would be anticlimactic, as he and Eleanor were planning to hunt a few hours on Saturday afternoon and he hoped Eleanor would be staying over. Those hours would have been a more a fitting end to the best season he had ever known. A shame. Sunday would be more like politics: securing hunting rights for the coming years.

In fact, it was Eleanor whom he waited for. She had promised to sneak off from the Arts Council to meet him and Bob Thurston just after lunch. Bob had been so intrigued by Eleanor's interest in old homestead ruins that he had volunteered to take them out to look at a much more obscure ruin in the far corner of John Tully's ranch. Bob could not bring himself to call the ranch "the Tully place" and referred to the homestead ruin as "the dugout in Dad's northeast eighty." Carl knew the place and could have guided Eleanor to it easily, but Bob had found a rare friend in Eleanor, and she seemed to enjoy his company too. It would be a lovely afternoon. He would leave Leo and the Parker shotgun at home and simply walk. On a day like this one, it would be grand. He laid the book down on the carved end table. It was nearly time for lunch, and for several days he had been thinking about the sandwich makings that Eleanor had brought him. It would be the perfect time for an onion, salami, and jalapeño sandwich. Leo raised his head slightly as Carl moved toward the kitchen, but the sunlight was strong on his belton coat and the energy of rising with his master was simply too much for him. His head eased to the hardwood floor, and he drifted back to canine Valhalla where the breeze is always in your face and the rabbits are slow.

A certain pageantry was necessary to indulge in an onion, salami, and jalapeño sandwich. First, a person had to be sure he had all the fixin's. Carl laid them out on the counter in order: sourdough bread—excellent. The Vidalia onion—sublime. Salami—divine. Jalapeño—bueno! He took the chopping board from the cupboard and found his sharpest knife. He checked to make sure there was Dijon mustard and milk in the refrigerator. He had learned over the years that, because of the fire in the jalapeños, a glass of milk could be vital. He likened it to the precaution of keeping a bucket of water handy while burning autumn leaves.

He had a particular way of chopping the onion—on the bias with long leisurely strokes first one way and then the next. He only needed one good slice but he cut a half dozen so that he could choose the one that was the perfect thickness. The salami too was cut on the bias so that the pieces would be oblong, cover the bread more completely, and fit together like fine masonry work. Then he came to his favorite operation—the slicing of the jalapeños. He took great pride in his ability to shave the pieces off, thin to the point of transparency. He held the peppers tight and pretended to be making sections for a microscope slide. The juices and tiny seeds squeezed out between his fingers, but he remained focused. Long smooth slices and a piling up of perfect, juicy discs to top his perfect sandwich. When he finished, he stepped back and saw that the sandwich elements were good.

He did not want to hurry the assemblage process and stepped back into the light that shot diagonally through the window of the back door. It was such a beautiful Indian summer day, and he was drawn through the door and out onto his newly redesigned back porch. It seemed appropriate to relieve himself at the custom railing, to relax, to take a minute and savor his life. When he was finished, he zipped up and turned his face upward to the warming sun. Then he turned toward the kitchen and with great deliberation entered the house for the long-awaited revelry of the taste buds. But he would not let himself rush. He went to the sink and washed his hands. Then to the refrigerator for the mustard and milk. He poured a large glass of the milk and set it on the counter. He spread the mustard thickly and nestled the salami oblongs with great care. He had not yet laid the onion slice on top when he felt the first tingle in his pubic area.

No, he thought. Some phantom sensation and nothing more. But by the time the jalapeños were laid out on the very top, he knew he was in trouble. Squirming did no good and pulling his pants away from the affected area seemed only to exacerbate the fire. The sandwich lacked only another layer of mustard and the top piece of bread. But his concentration was broken, and he felt a surge of panic. He needed relief and finally broke and ran for the upstairs shower. He tore his clothes off at a full run, and he was naked before the shower curtain was drawn. He plunged into the icy water and moaned in relief.

As Carl toweled off, he continued to feel a tingle, but the thought of the sandwich drew him back down to the kitchen, Now he stood naked in front of the nearly completed sandwich and determined that what had happened was for the best. He would eat his sandwich like the satyr he believed himself to be. With renewed care he spread the final layer of mustard and pressed the top piece of bread down snugly. He tried to ignore the rekindling fire in his groin. My God, had the water reacted with the jalapeño juice? The intensity grew, but Carl forged on. He held the sandwich tight to the cutting board and dissected it laterally. It was a perfect sandwich. But now he wiggled his bare knees together to ease the discomfort. He tore his eyes away from the sandwich and stared at the kitchen cupboards. But finally his eyes fell toward the pain and he grabbed himself. He bent over in pain and thought of running outdoors. But he knew that one should never run while on fire. Still, he was nearly panicked.

Finally he looked up and his eyes fell on the glass of milk. What the hell! He picked up the glass, held it low, and forced himself inside. "Ahhh. God, yes," he moaned.

The fire was suddenly out and relief made him slump where he stood. But the pain was replaced with a different feeling of unease. He kept the glass of milk where it was but began to cautiously move his eyes from side to side. He did not locate the source of the discomfort until he had turned his head enough to see Eleanor and Bob standing with mouths agape at the back door.

When found in a compromising position Carl knew it was best never to apologize or explain. Eleanor and Bob might not have understood what had happened but they were kind enough not to mention it. All the way out to the far corner of John Tully's ranch Carl caught both of them occasionally looking at him, smiling, and shaking their heads.

Luckily, the day had turned out so lovely and the walk was so brisk that they were forced into a mesmerizing concentration and awareness of the landscape. Before they were halfway to the ruined homestead Carl was pointing out to his companions which draws would likely hold grouse, where the mule deer would be, the spots to expect a great horned owl to cruise silently from the ash trees. Bob knew the places, too, and despite his eternal field jacket, long hair, and lunging gait Carl could still see the boy who had grown up as part of those draws.

"So who lived at this homestead?" Eleanor said when they stopped to catch their breath.

Bob shrugged. "I never heard a name."

Carl shrugged too. "No. It's just always been there. I don't suppose they lasted very long."

The three were on the shoulder of a steep draw with plum thickets below them. Most of the leaves had fallen but a few dried plums remained. A trio of robins flitted through the tangle of gray limbs and tut-tut-tutted to each other. "They better get headed south," Bob said. And as if by instinct, the two native men looked to the northwest to see if winter was descending on them. Eleanor took note of this, glancing first at the faces of the men and then in the direction they were looking. The sky was clear and blue, but when she looked back at Carl and Bob she found the reflection of all the winters that they had endured.

"We've been lucky," Carl said.

"Today's unreal. It could just as easy have been zero with a twenty-mile-an-hour wind."

Without saying it, all three thought of the nameless homesteaders whose dugout cabin had once burrowed farther up the draw. They computed that the winter that lay somewhere beyond the blue sky would have been very real to them, indeed. They moved off the shoulder of the draw and up to the ridge where the walking was better. From there they could see the snake of trees that marked the river two miles to the east. In the far distance they could make out the bluffs that towered over the town of McDermot. They were two hundred yards from the indentation that had once sheltered the homesteaders, and since the walking was easier, they were able to speak. "You ever find any sign of water up here? A spring, anything like that?" Bob asked.

Carl shook his head. "Not that amounted to anything. The brush grows pretty well in the draw so I imagine there's water underground somewhere."

"Maybe it flowed back in the old days."

Eleanor had read a little about the end of the nineteenth century in Lakota County. "They say it was a lot wetter then." They were approaching the site of the homestead. Two low, unnatural mounds of grown-over dirt rose up like monuments. A few stones were scattered at the edge of the pit that had once held the dirt. Peering down into the hole they could see three extremely weathered boards lying akimbo at the bottom. "Must have built a roof over it," Bob said. "Just a dirt floor." He laughed. "Not quite as fancy as the house Steve is working on, but a better view."

"How's Steve doing?" Eleanor asked.

"He's doing." They continued to stare down into the hole.

"You're still staying at the trailer, aren't you?"

"Sure."

"That's best."

"But not tonight. Guess I'll just stay out here with Dad."

They still did not raise their heads from the hole. "That's good too," Eleanor said.

Carl nodded to himself. "You're a good son. Arvid must get lonely."

44

The new YMCA in the center of McDermot had three gymnasiums, and early Friday evening all three were in use. Steve Thurston sat in his pickup truck, parked in the Safeway parking lot three blocks down, and watched the parents stream into the building from their jobs. He had just come from his own job. The house they were building was completely closed in, and the Sheetrockers had already finished the lower floor. His crew would be working indoors all winter, no matter what the weather did. He hoped it snowed like hell until spring.

The sun was setting and the streetlights came on to make the gray sky go even darker, but Steve remained in his truck until the glow left the sky and there was little chance of being recognized as he made his way to the YMCA. He had not seen Gretchen go in and didn't want an awkward moment on the street. The paper said that the Storms were playing their last game of the season, and Steve Thurston wanted to catch at least a few minutes of it. He had covered one of the three blocks on his way to the YMCA when a man rose up out of a parked car fifty yards ahead of him. He'd never before seen John Tully in a black overcoat, but without even getting a look at his face he knew it was him. He felt foolish to slow his pace and raise his hand to his face to obscure himself long enough to let Tully hurry into the building a safe distance ahead. The bright lights of the YMCA made him feel even more foolish about his clandestine entrance. Anyone who knew him would recognize him now, no matter how he covered his face.

The game was into the second quarter, and Steve stationed himself at the door where he could watch but where the parents in the stands could not see him. The score was already twelve to twenty in favor of the Storms. He leaned against the door and folded his arms across his chest. In his faded work jeans, canvas coat, and ball cap he felt out of place and belligerent. It was not the way he wanted to appear. All he wanted was to see Jake dribble the ball down the court, to see him happy, and young, and filled with promise. But when a ball skittered out of play and he stepped to see the call, he caught sight of Gretchen sitting with Tully and was unable to pull back until he had watched them for an instant. They sat close, intent on the game, but Gretchen's small fist pounded on Tully's thigh when the referee awarded the ball to the Storms.

At halftime Tully and Gretchen were finally able to speak to each other. "I'm so glad you made it," Gretchen said. "I wasn't sure you would."

"I'd have been here on time but things got busy right at the end of the day." Tully grinned. "Jake looks like he's doing great."

"Six points." She reached out and pounded lightly again on Tully's thigh.

Her touch made him lose his place and it took a beat to start again. "And he brings the ball down."

"Yep." She left her little fist on his leg. It was casual but intimate. "You sound like you played."

"I did. Not very well, but I played. Loved it."

"Jake, too."

"Loves it?"

"Oh God, yes. It's about his favorite."

"Horses and basketball," Tully said. "Pretty good taste."

"No kidding."

"It's set up with Arvid for tomorrow afternoon. He said he'd even bring him back into town."

Gretchen waved away the idea. "We can go get him." Then she looked up, nearly frightened. The wave could be construed as dismissive. "Can't we?"

Tully laughed. "Unless we're out late."

"Out late? Dinner?"

"A nice dinner. I'm afraid I invited a friend."

"Oh? Who's that?"

"Well, the man who brought us together."

"Dr. Cring?" Gretchen was astounded but smiling.

Tully smiled broadly. "You were the one who said you probably hadn't given him a chance."

"I probably didn't." Gretchen heard herself talking and imagined what the two of them must look like, chatting like schoolkids. She could hardly believe the change that had taken place—hardly believe how good it felt to have a relationship that wasn't combative and tense. She wasn't completely sure she would like Arnold Cring, but he was a friend of Tully's and she would try. "Speaking of dinner," she said. "The half is about over and I could use some popcorn."

They rose and made their way to the lobby. Gretchen did not wrap her arm through his but they both felt that it was possible. When they came to the concession stand, Tully pointed to the men's room and excused himself. He felt young and light as he turned into the rest room and saw his reflection in the mirror. He even looked boyish and he couldn't help smiling at himself. But when he came around the corner his grin and buoyancy dissolved. There were two urinals. One was empty and Steve Thurston occupied the other.

Instantly, Tully saw that Steve wanted to see him no more than he wanted to see Steve. But there was no chance to withdraw with any sort of dignity, so Tully stepped up and stood with his shoulder inches from Steve's. "How's it going, Steve?" It was an inane question and hung dead in the pungent air.

"Good," Steve said. "Yourself?"

"I'm good, too."

Then there was nothing but the faint sound of urination and the chill of humiliation that lasted until Steve turned away from the urinal and stepped silently around the corner and out of sight.

After the game, Gretchen talked Jake into coming with her and John Tully for a snack. The negotiation involved a compromise. Jake waved goodbye to his friends, but Gretchen and Tully had to settle for ice cream at TCBY. It turned out to be not much of a sacrifice for Tully because he claimed a secret and deep love of chocolate malts. Gretchen was the only one who had to give up much. Not only was she unsure that ice cream was the right thing to eat at that time of night but also, if it was going to be ice cream, she would have preferred Ashcroft's.

She was clearly not only out of step with her son and new boy-friend but also out of step with half the population of McDermot. TCBY was packed with young and old. The line for ice cream went nearly into the street, but it didn't bother Gretchen. It was fun to stand and watch people enjoying themselves, and though she did not recognize many, she felt as if she was part of the crowd, protected and surrounded by friends. She tried to hold onto Jake but he wouldn't have it, and after leaving his order for a caramel sundae made with strawberry ice cream, he disappeared into a gaggle of young people.

"Well, there goes our time with Jake," Gretchen said.

"He's fine. He's a kid. And he'll be back when we get his caramel strawberry sundae."

"Gawd."

They laughed at the thought of a caramel strawberry sundae until suddenly it was their turn to order. The soda jerks scurried back and forth behind the counter with scoops and dishes in their hands. They were swamped, and when the next available waitress stepped up to help them, she wiped her forehead as gracefully as possible with the sleeve of her white coat. When she looked up—it was Annie Simmons. "May I help you? Oh, hi." She laughed and shrugged her shoulders. "May I help you?"

Gretchen could only nod but John gave her the order. "Medium caramel sundae with strawberry ice cream and a chocolate malt for starters." He turned to Gretchen. "Sweetheart?"

It was the first time he had ever called her sweetheart. Gretchen knew that she should pay attention to it, but she was too stunned by Annie behind the counter. "Just a small vanilla cone. You didn't go to college?"

Annie shook her head. "No. I got this job."

Gretchen nodded, and because she didn't know what to say, she said, "Busy tonight."

"Wow, yeah. I'll be right back." Annie turned and hurried off to the ice cream buckets.

"Gretchen?"

She looked up to Tully. "Yes."

"You all right?" He held a five and a ten dollar bill in his hand and questioned her with his expression.

Her head began to nod before she spoke. "Yeah, I'm fine." She took the bills from him. "You go sit down. Find Jake and get a seat, if you can." He nodded and smiled but was still wondering. "Go on," she said and gave him a playful push.

When Annie came back, Gretchen handed her the money but did not let it go. They tugged over the bills for an instant. "You have to go," Gretchen said.

"Go?"

"To college. You have to go."

Annie took the bills. "It's too late. Classes already started." She would not look at Gretchen. "It's eleven dollars and twenty cents." For a few seconds, neither of them spoke or moved. Other people were clambering for service behind Gretchen. "They probably cancelled my scholarship." Annie turned to the cash register and brought back the change. A man pushed his way in front of Gretchen and began his order, but Annie held the change out to Gretchen.

"You should go," Gretchen said.

"Hey," the man said. "I've been waiting for five minutes."

Annie looked past him. "Your change," she said.

Gretchen shook her head and finally held up her hand to tell Annie to keep it.

❦ 45 ❧

Saturday morning brought the first real taste of winter. The temperature was supposed to warm to the midforties, but by nine o'clock it was still below freezing. Something in the grayness of the sky, the way the black tree limbs divided the sky, made Gretchen consider keeping Jake home. But he was so excited to spend the day with Arvid that there was really no option. They picked up a McMuffin on their way out of town, and to Gretchen's surprise Jake asked if Tully was coming along.

She looked hard at him before she answered. Was he disappointed or relieved? "No sweetheart, he has work to finish up."

"You're not staying, are you?"

"No, I have things to do, too. But we'll pick you up after dark. Around nine."

Jake sat in the passenger's seat looking straight ahead. He nodded his approval but didn't speak until they had cleared the last row of houses and were ready to turn onto the gravel road that ran along the river. "You're going to dinner with Mr. Tully."

"Yes. And with one of his friends." She felt that Jake deserved more of an explanation. "He's going to pick me up about five thirty. I'll be out to get you as soon as I can." She nodded her head toward the back seat of the Jeep. "I've got a casserole for you and Arvid to eat at noon and a frozen pizza for supper. There's a cooler of pop, too."

Jake rolled his eyes and giggled. "Like Arvid drinks pop."

Gretchen smiled with him. "Will you ride today?"

"Sure, when it warms up. For the morning, he'll probably have some chore to do." He lowered his voice to imitate Arvid. "Something to build character."

Gretchen nodded in agreement. "You listen to that old man. He's the last of a breed."

"Breed?"

"Like the last of the old-timers. The last of the cowboy breed."

At this point, Jake disengaged. He shook his head. "No," he said nearly to himself and looked out the side window at the passing grassland. Gretchen didn't speak. She thought she knew what he meant and was touched by it. He meant that Steve too was of that breed. He might even have been thinking about himself.

When they pulled up at the gate in front of Arvid's house they parked beside Bob's pickup. No horses were tied to the rail in front of the tack room, but the two men were outside standing hunkered over an ancient tractor pulled up beside the woodpile. "All right," Jake said. "We're going to cut wood." Just as he opened the Jeep door, a plume of black smoke belched from the tractor's stack and a low, rhythmic popping began to gain speed. The men raised their hands in what looked to be worship and Bob slapped his father on the back. Jake was already running toward them. "They got it going," he called over his shoulder.

Gretchen followed at a walk, with her arms wrapped around herself for warmth. By the time she arrived at the woodpile, Jake was holding a grease gun and looking intently to where Arvid pointed. "Right in there," the old man yelled over the engine noise. "Ought to be a little zerk deal right in there." They stood beside an angle-iron cradle that supported rollers over which a wide leather belt ran for six feet. Gretchen looked down the length of the rickety contraption to where a huge circular blade stood attached to one of the rollers.

She moved up beside Bob who stood at the tractor's flywheel

and shouted over the bass popping of the engine. "What are you guys doing?"

Bob was watching his father for a signal. "Buzz saw," he said. "Cutting a little firewood." He raised his chin toward the saw blade that was attached to the flywheel by the leather belt.

"Give it a little goose," Arvid called out, and nodded his head when he saw Gretchen. "Just a touch."

Bob pushed the long clutch lever forward and the belt tightened enough to turn the saw blade a half revolution. Arvid held up his hand to stop Bob. "Good." He pointed to another place on the drive train and Jake leaned in to apply grease. Gretchen had to look away. Though she knew her son was safe with Arvid, the mysteries of men and danger were incomprehensible to her.

"Give 'er another poke," Arvid called to Bob. The lever went forward and the belt moved easily this time. "Whoopty-doo!" Arvid shouted. "They'll be talkin' about this in Tulsa." He patted Jake on the back. "Leave 'er in, Bob. Me and my assistant are going to cut some firewood."

Bob pushed the clutch lever forward until it clicked into place. The saw blade at the other end of the cradle whined with more power than speed, and Gretchen shook her head. When she felt Bob looking at her she looked up and saw that he had something he wanted to say. They moved away from the popping old tractor and walked slowly toward the front of the house. "So how's Bob?" Gretchen said.

"Bob's pretty good. S-O-S-N-R," he said. Then, in response to Gretchen's quizzical look, "Same old shit. No rain."

"If it rained we wouldn't know what to do with our good fortune."

"Well, there it is," Bob said. He shook his head with disgust. "Right there it is."

They had arrived at their vehicles and they leaned, side by side, against Bob's pickup. "You're out here early," Gretchen said.

"Spent the night."

"A Friday night? Did they shut down the pool tables?"

He smiled at the ground. "No, guess not. I was out at Carl and Eleanor's. Just got this feeling that I ought to spend the night."

The tractor had been running steadily but now the popping slowed and, like a living organism, groaned under the work of cutting its first log in who knew how long. Bob and Gretchen watched the stream of wood chips being spit to the ground as the carriage moved forward and the first piece of firewood tumbled to the side. Jake retrieved it and began a stack as Arvid moved the carriage back and slid the log sideways for another cut. "Is that damned thing safe?" Gretchen asked.

Bob shrugged, "Safe as anything is safe."

"Are you staying out here today?"

"For a while. I'll keep an eye on them."

They remained leaning against the pickup until Bob was ready to speak again. "About Steve," he finally said. "You shouldn't worry too much. It's nobody's fault. Just the way it is."

Gretchen knew Bob well enough to know that was all he had to say. "It wasn't right for a while," she said.

"I know. He's my brother."

It was not exactly what Gretchen meant, but she saw that what Bob said was true. "Is he all right?"

Bob nodded. "Yeah."

Gretchen nodded too. Then she pushed away from the pickup and opened the passenger door of the Jeep. She brought out a brown grocery bag and set it on the hood of Bob's pickup. "Some food for you guys. A casserole and a couple of pizzas." She added the cooler of pop to the pickup hood, then stepped up to Bob and stood on her tiptoes to give him a hug. "You're all good men," she whispered, then pulled away.

Bob was too embarrassed to look her in the eye. But his head nodded. "Well, there it is," he said.

🦅 46 🦅

For two hours Arvid, Bob, and Jake sawed four-foot-long logs into sixteen-inch stove wood. By the time the log pile was gone, the stove woodpile was higher than Jake's head. Arvid shouted for Bob to shut the tractor down, and just as the whine turned into the squeal of metal against metal, the tractor gave one last pop and fell silent. The buzz-saw blade shuddered to a halt and Jake was amazed how quiet it suddenly became. There was a little wind in the treetops but that was all. Not an automobile, a human voice, or a bird's song to be heard.

They broke for lunch and ate the casserole that Gretchen had made for them. After lunch they moved to the porch on the downwind side of the house and Bob smoked a cigarette while Arvid drank a cup of coffee laced with Black Velvet. As predicted, the day had warmed, and after his cigarette, Bob closed his eyes and let the sun's heat penetrate toward his core. He was nearly asleep when Arvid finished his whiskey and stood up. "Burning daylight," he said.

Bob did not open his eyes. "Let 'er burn," he said.

"Let's ride," Jake said.

"Just what I was thinking," Arvid said. "Need to go out and see where that goddamned bull of Tully's is getting in."

"You leave that bull alone," Bob said with eyes still closed.

"Son of a bitch's been coming right up here to the corral. Bashing through fences to get to the oats barrel."

"Leave him alone."

"We'll just see where he's at. Try to figure out how he's getting up here around the house. You coming?"

Bob opened one eye. "Guess not." He turned the eye on Jake. "Long as you two don't go trying to rope that old bull."

Jake was on his feet. "We won't."

"Hell," Arvid said, "We probably won't even find him."

When they stepped off the porch they felt the wind, but it was warm enough to allow them to enjoy the day. As they walked across to the corral, Arvid whistled and was answered by three nickers. Blacky, Elsa, and Jack ambled from around the corner of the shed and lined up along the rail across from the oats barrel. Jake ran to pet them and give them their oats. Arvid cut toward the tack room and called out as he opened the door, "Who you want to ride?" Jake looked up from the oats barrel with surprise. When he and Arvid rode, he always rode Elsa. "How about you ride Blacky," Arvid said.

"But he's Steve's horse."

"Steve ain't here," Arvid called from the shed. Though there was no one to see him, Jake shrugged and tried not to act too excited. "He'd like you to ride him," Arvid yelled.

"Can I handle him?" To Jake, Blacky was the Corvette of horses.

"Hell, yes. He's tame as a chicken. Besides you're—how old are you?"

"Twelve."

"Twelve. Just right." Arvid was dragging saddles out and rolling them up onto their swells. "You're just right."

Jake reached out and caught Blacky by the mane. The horse didn't resist and followed the boy to the hitching rail with the other horses right behind. Arvid tipped the oats barrel back and retrieved his bottle of Velvet. He leaned against the corral and raised the bottle to Jake. "Old enough to saddle those horses by yourself."

They rode along the fence to the southeast and looked for the place that the bull was getting through. The winter bull pasture was on the other side of the fence and when they came to a high place they could see a group of bulls lying on a hillside a quarter mile to the east. "There that Christer is." Arvid pointed to a red spot a hundred yards up the hill from the other bulls. "He's lying up there by himself. Innocent as a cherub. Must be just jumping the fence when he feels like it. Comes down there to the house just to torment me."

Jake smiled. "He just likes to bug you."

"He's damned good at it." They were riding again and Jake was enjoying Blacky's long, smooth gate. "Nice horse, huh."

Jake nodded. "Can I lope him?"

"You're the driver."

Jake touched Blacky's ribs and the horse went directly from the walk into a rocking-horse lope. A smug smile spread across Jake's face and Arvid spurred Jack just enough to keep the profile of that smile in sight. Jake had never felt anything quite like it and Arvid hadn't seen a smile like that for thirty years. They covered ground like the shadows of twin clouds on a windy day. Along the ridge, then down into the draw, and up again. They loped through knee-high grass that moved like water beneath the horses. They followed the cattle trails—or were they buffalo trails? Along the edge of the chokecherries and between the cottonwoods that sucked their lives from the spring that seeped in winter but was absorbed in summer. A kettle of a hundred sandhill cranes circled above, and their cacophony bubbled between the rhythmic grunts and the pounding of hooves. The wind brought tears to their eyes but they didn't think of stopping until the corrals again came into sight.

The day was dimming fast as they peeled the saddles from the horses and gave them their taste of grain. Arvid visited the oats barrel like a horse of a different stripe and Jake replaced the saddles and bridles on their jacks and pegs. Bob's pickup was gone and it felt good to be alone in the open air with the old man. The boy was tired and hungry and happy as they walked shoulder to shoulder toward the house. "Pizza," Jake said, and slowed so Arvid's limp was hardly noticeable.

"Jesus," Arvid said. "Hippie food."

"Hippie?"

"Never mind. Let me cook you up something that'll stick to those skinny bones."

"Like what?"

"Like fried potatoes and Spam."

"Fried potatoes and Spam?"

"Oh, hell yes. Bulk you up. Make you tall." He slapped Jake on the back. "You're the potato slicer."

They didn't bother to wash their hands and Jake felt like he was getting away with something. He started to peel the potatoes, but Arvid stopped him. "Peels are the best part," he said, and Jake felt giddy, like he was robbing a bank. By the time he was done slicing, the oil in the black iron skillet was smoking. "Stand back," Arvid said. "Cover your eyes." He dumped the potatoes in and they popped and splattered and would have caught fire except that Arvid slammed a lid down in time. He cut the Spam in thick slices and added them to the potatoes. "So what do you want to drink?"

"I'll have one of those Mountain Dews Mom brought." He was heading for the refrigerator. "You want one?"

"No. I think I'll dance with the gal that brought me." Arvid went to the cupboard and brought down the bottle of Velvet. They poured their respective glasses full and sat down at the wooden kitchen table. The potatoes and Spam sizzled violently in the skillet. It felt good to sit, and they were silent for several minutes as they sipped their drinks.

"How come you always drink whiskey?" Jake finally said.

Arvid looked at his glass. "Well," he said, as if he had often considered the question. "When I was just a little older than you I had a bad experience with banana cordial." Jake looked up at him with nothing but questions on his face. "No foolin', kid. Whatever you do in your life, stay away from banana cordial."

They drained the oil into a peanut butter jar on the back of the stove and divided the contents of the skillet onto two plates. It was still too hot to eat, and as Arvid dug in the refrigerator for the catsup, Jake looked out the window. The western sky was a darkening cream color and the wind no longer shook the tree branches. He looked to the corral to see if the horses, and especially Blacky, were still in sight. He expected to see three silhouettes standing against the rail, hip-shot and dozing. But instead there was only one, pacing and swinging ivory horns. "The bull!"

Arvid slammed the ketchup down on the table and came to the window. "That dirty bastard." The bull beat at the corral rails with his horns. "That crazy son of a bitch." Arvid was heading for the door. "You stay put," he said to Jake but the boy followed him to the back porch.

Arvid was nearly to the new woodpile when Jake found his voice. "Be careful," he called. But Arvid had already picked up two pieces of stove wood and was heading directly for the swinging horns.

❦ **47** ❧

Gretchen had promised herself that she would give Arnold Cring a chance. It could well be that, since she first heard his name, she had been unfair. The older she got, the more she came to know about herself. She had a tendency toward bossiness, a need to try to change things for the better. She felt great sympathy for underdogs, and as a result was capable of narrow-mindedness. Perhaps all those elements of character had come together when Ida Miller approached her with the Tad Bordeaux story. Maybe Ida had been less than fair-minded. Perhaps she had an ax to grind with the medical community and Gretchen had become her agent. John Tully had never said anything to Gretchen directly, but some of their conversations led Gretchen to ask these questions of herself.

When she got to thinking like this it wasn't long until she moved on to her other faults, and key among them was her belief in a clear differentiation between good and evil and a tendency to be bulldogged by figures of authority. Late on Saturday afternoon, as she got dressed for her dinner date with John Tully and Arnold Cring, she thought about authority figures and her love-hate relationship with them. She wanted to resist their power but, at the same time, wanted to please them. At heart she was a pleaser. As she tried on first one skirt and then the next, she wondered if her rebellious side had not gotten out of control and that now her desire for repentance was pushing her to please Arnold Cring. Or was she interested in pleasing John Tully?

There was not much doubt that she was attracted to John. He was a gentleman in the very best sense. He was thoughtful. He was interesting to her, and he seemed interested in her. It had been a long time since she had felt she could be included in a man's life, and he held her in obvious high regard. Because of the situation with Steve, she feared rebound syndrome and was struggling to go slow. But there was a sense that this was an opportunity to move on with her life and into a different and better world. When was the last time she had taken such care readying herself for a date? When was the last time she had a real date? She laughed at her image in the mirror. Even without her makeup, she looked good. She looked happy.

And with her makeup she looked fabulous. She had settled on a simple white blouse and a long pleated skirt made of a sheer fabric that showed off her legs to anyone who took a moment to look. She wore brown leather sandals with medium heels and a turquoise bracelet and necklace that her mother had sent her from Arizona and that she had never worn. Her hair was up. A picture of Southwest sophisticated. It made her giggle to take one last look in the mirror. If nothing else interesting happened, the night was already a success.

John pulled up in the driveway in a Toyota sedan. She had never seen him in anything but his Dodge pickup. When she saw him step out of the car in a coat and tie, topped by a long black overcoat, she thought at first that he might have come from his office. But when she moved out to meet him she saw that he wore a blue blazer and a red tie. He wore freshly shined loafers with playful red socks. She wrapped her fringed shawl around her shoulders as she came down the steps and without a thought they came together and kissed.

They pulled away only a few inches. "You look tremendous," John said.

She smiled from the corner of her eyes. "Why, thank you, sir."

The reservations were for six thirty, and they found Arnold Cring waiting in the lounge with a martini in his hand. He, too, wore a blazer and tie and turned from the bar with a kind smile. "John!" He held out his hand and the two men shook hands and gripped elbows. "And Miss Harris." Cring turned to Gretchen and held out his hand in a gentler way.

Gretchen took his hand and did her best to act casual. In Cring's world, people made a point of keeping business and private matters separate, and she was determined to shed her provincialism. "It's nice to see you," she said.

Their conciliatory gazes hung for an instant. "It's nice to see you, too."

When their hands parted, the three of them stood for an embarrassed moment. Then John jumped in. "You are going to love this place," he said.

"You've eaten here?" Cring asked.

"I have."

"It's only been open for two weeks."

"Got to support places like this, unless we want to go back to eating at the truck stop."

Cring gave a little salute and touched his swept-back silver hair. "I hear that."

"The chef is out of Denver."

Gretchen knew she had to join in or be left behind. "And what is their specialty?"

"It's nouveau fusion gourmet."

"What?" Gretchen and Cring spoke in unison, then laughed.

John shrugged. "Hell," he said. "I don't know. The specials are great."

Just then a pretty young girl came up to them. Her hair was dark and held severely back to reveal one ear with a row of silver rings. "Are you the Tully party?"

"Saved by the bell," John said.

Gretchen laughed at his boyishness. "The dinner bell," she said. The menus were large and elaborate, and even before the waiter presented the specials, John ordered a bottle of wine and a spinach brochette as an appetizer.

Gretchen puzzled over some of the entrees, but after John and Cring passionately discussed in front of the waiter the virtues of littleneck clams poached in Chardonnay, she felt free to ask about the brussels-sprout ragout and grilled swordfish. She was having great fun even before the bottle of Chenin Blanc arrived.

By the time the entrees and the second bottle of wine appeared, they were talking about the development of Lakota County, and the men were quizzing her about what it had been like twenty years before. Any discomfort that she might have felt dissolved in the earnest and polite discussion of national trends and the role of technology in the homogenization of society. Both men were convinced that a lot of coastal business was being done from McDermot, and a lot more would soon be done via satellite. Both men were engaged and knowledgeable and Gretchen heard them articulating thoughts that she had often had but never expressed. She had never had the nerve to order steamed clams before either, but she did that night. And loved them.

They were steamed in an anise garlic sauce, and even though something in her wanted to eat them all, she shuttled several onto John's plate for two reasons. First, they were offered in trade for a piece of his lamb chops, and second, she did not want to be the only one with garlic on her breath. She even slipped one onto Cring's plate in trade for a chunk of sea bass.

The desserts of the day were crème brûlée and tiramisu. "Both highly overrated," Cring said after the waiter had left. "I'm ordering off the menu. Poached pears and homemade ice cream." As soon as the words were out of his mouth his demeanor changed. "Excuse me," he said. "I'm on call." He was removing his cell phone from his belt as he stood up. John and Gretchen could hear it vibrating in his hand.

When he was gone they looked at each other across the table. "Having a nice time?"

She nodded. "A very nice time." She stretched her hand across the table and touched his fingertips. They were large, well-kept hands with a trace of fine hair barely visible on the backs of the first joints. The half moons under the nails were prominent and shiny. She caressed the fingers. "A very nice time," she said again. But suddenly she was thinking of Steve's rough hands and wondering what she had found exciting about them. She shook her head to expel the thought.

When she looked up to John's questioning eyes she laughed to cover her lapse. "And," she said, "I am full. I'll pass on dessert."

"Well, I'm ordering the Death by Chocolate and two forks." He smiled. "You know, just in case."

"You do that. I'm going to powder my nose. Don't start until I get back." She stood up and smiled. "Just in case."

By then the restaurant was full and Gretchen breezed through the crowded tables with an air of disbelief. Who were these people? Where had so many people like this come from? How could it have happened so fast, without her noticing? Since she was a child, almost everywhere she went in McDermot she had been recognized. In this new restaurant, men and women glanced at her, her dress, perhaps the way she moved, but no one knew the first thing about her. In some way she enjoyed the feeling of anonymity. She allowed herself to stride boldly between the tables, keeping her eyes to the front as if she were not aware of the glances. She steered for the rear of the restaurant, to the rich wainscoting and textured wallpaper that framed the restroom door and the pay telephone. Leaning on the telephone counter but speaking into his own cell phone was Arnold Cring. His broad back startled her, and because he partially blocked her path to the woman's restroom, her playacting crumbled and she was embarrassed.

But she refused to be intimidated by her own shyness and lightly touched Cring on the back as she slid past. Cring was in deep conversation and finished his sentence before he moved forward and out of her way. "No," he said. "I don't think there is anything we could do." He turned and found Gretchen slipping along the opposite wall. Their eyes met and he finished his conversation. "No. I told you. I won't be coming in."

Gretchen entered the ladies' room before he could hang up the phone. She stood inside the door and told herself that she was being silly, that Cring had been on a business call, and it was normal for his demeanor to change.

They had had just the right amount of wine. The night was chilly but not cold, the wind lay still, and the loose-knit shawl was enough to keep Gretchen's shoulders warm. Still, she took the liberty of turning on the car's heater as soon as John started the engine.

"Cold?"

Gretchen shuddered for emphasis. "Just a bit."

John raised his arm up to the top of the car seat. "Come here."

She did not hesitate to snuggle under his arm. "I don't want to be late to pick up Jake."

"I'll drive you out."

Gretchen hesitated. She didn't want to send John home, but she didn't want to show up with wine and garlic on her breath and a new man as a chauffeur. "Maybe I should pick him up alone."

They were already moving, but John looked down at her to see that she was serious. He was disappointed but understood. "I'll drop you off at home," he said.

They rode in silence, not thinking of much, each amazed by the smell of the other. Gretchen moved her face into John's jacket, and he lowered his nose to her hair. When they turned into her driveway, his embrace tightened; and when they came to a stop, he cradled Gretchen's cheek and raised her face to his. Slowly his lips descended to hers and they kissed, first with careful pressure, then with a hunger that surprised them both. They rotated to put as much of their bodies together as possible, and Gretchen let her fingers grip his thick black hair. "Hey, hey. Whoa, whoa," John pulled back and laughed. He sat back and exhaled. "I would love to continue this, but you've got a boy to pick up."

Gretchen laughed too. "And we might be a little old for making out in a car." She leaned and kissed his cheek. "Thanks for a great evening," Gretchen said.

"My pleasure." Then, "There's going to be a lot more."

Gretchen pressed her face close to his. "I hope so. I sort of wish this night wasn't ending."

John exhaled. "Me too."

Now they were both sitting up, facing forward. The car was still running and the lights shown on Gretchen's garage door. "I've got to go," Gretchen said.

John nodded and kissed her once more before she opened the door. He put the car into reverse. "A rain check," he said.

"You've got it." She closed the door and moved quickly to the house and went inside.

She took a deep breath as she leaned with her back against the door. It had been quite a night, and Gretchen wanted to think about John Tully. There was certainly plenty to think about, but she felt antsy and pushed away from the door. Suddenly her mind narrowed on Jake. She needed to change her clothes and get to him. As she hurried, the inexplicable anxiety built, and when she finally backed the Jeep out of the garage and into the dark, her heart was running like a small electric motor. The streets of McDermot were light enough, but once she was out of town, the headlights seemed to be pointed down an endless tunnel and she pushed the accelerator toward the floor.

The deer moved at the edges of the tunnel and poked their

heads into the light. Gretchen knew she should slow down but she couldn't. Not until it was necessary to brake for Arvid's driveway did a deer step fully out onto the roadside. As she passed, the deer looked into the Jeep with wide round eyes and huge ears rotating like antennae. She wondered if Annie had caught a glimpse of those eyes, if she had seen the shadows of the huge ears. The Jeep moved up the driveway and the sound of loose gravel hitting the undercarriage sounded like distant fireworks. As she approached the house, Gretchen's feelings accelerated even as the car was forced to slow down.

The single light burning in the kitchen eased her mind slightly but when she pulled to the front gate and still had not seen any movement in the house, she was seized with dread. She was out of the Jeep before it stopped rolling and onto the porch in three strides. Anyone who saw her would have thought that she had lost her mind. But her senses had not betrayed her. She moved quickly through the house, into every room, and burst out wild-eyed onto the back porch. The sky was filled with a thousand stars but the house was empty.

4

✒ **48** ✒

Now the roadway was thick with deer. They drifted up out of
the ditches and onto the road as if drawn by Gretchen's building
panic. She tried to focus on the road ahead and tried to think.
She wanted to be calm, knew that this was the wrong time to
make a mistake. She willed her mind not to explore the things
that might have happened to her son and Arvid Thurston, to get
herself home in one piece. The gravel sloshed under the tires and
threatened to throw her into the ditch. The road made its usual
turns and twists and the deer continued to creep at the periphery of her vision, but Gretchen kept both hands high on the steering wheel and her eyes straight ahead.

Once on the asphalt and in sight of the pinhole lights of McDermot, Gretchen had to keep herself from speeding. She wanted to
go as fast as the Jeep would carry her, but that would be a mistake. She tried turning on the radio but the sound was murky
and only served to fill the empty space until the lights of town
began to separate into familiar streets. She turned onto Main,
then onto Grand, and finally Pleasant. It was after ten o'clock
now and Gretchen's street was deserted. When she was a block
away she saw a light in her front window and grinned with relief.
But the grin faded when she turned into her driveway and came
to a stop behind Steve Thurston's pickup. In front of the house,
parked along the street, was Bob's battered pickup.

The two men were silhouetted and motionless at her back door.

The light from Bob's cigarette pulsed in the darkness. Steve sat on the porch steps with his shoulders hunched and his hands dumped down between his knees. She told herself that they had brought Jake home. But Steve would not have stayed around, and where was Arvid?

She came to a bucking stop and leaped from the Jeep. She could see well enough to know that something was very wrong. "Is it Jake?" she asked before she stopped moving.

Steve shook his head. "No," he said, "he's asleep inside."

"He's safe?"

"He's safe."

Gretchen was panting and stepped up between the brothers. She looked first at Bob, then at Steve. Neither would meet her eyes. "What?"

"We've been at the hospital," Bob said.

"Arvid?"

"He's dead."

Gretchen reached out for the railing then sat down slowly beside Steve. There were crickets and the sound of distant music. "What was it? What happened?"

"Jake said he went a little nuts. Tried chasing Tully's bull out of the corral with a chunk of firewood."

"Oh, God."

"We told him," Bob said. "We told him to just leave that bastard alone."

"And Jake was there?"

"He did good," Steve said. "Got Dad drug to the shed, then called 911 and me. Bob met us at the hospital. I brought Jake home and put him to bed. He doesn't even know Dad's dead."

"Jake did good," Bob said.

They were silent for a long minute. Then Gretchen sat up straight. "When did he die?"

"Half hour ago." Bob said. "I got here just before you came."

"And when did he get to the hospital?" Her voice was calm and thoughtful.

"About seven thirty." Steve said. "Took him almost three hours to die, and I wasn't even there with him at he end." Steve's voice was at the edge of breaking. "They called a specialist."

Now Gretchen was on her feet and looking up at the sky. She knew what Bob was going to say before he said it. "There wasn't any specialist," he said. "Just an ER doc and a couple of nurses."

"They called a specialist," Steve said. "They said they did. Just before I brought Jake home."

"There was no specialist with him when he died," Bob said. "It was just me and him."

Gretchen's voice was small. "There was no specialist," she said. "There was no specialist because he was having dinner with fancy friends. Baked sea bass. Chenin Blanc. Poached pears and home-made ice cream for dessert."

By the time Gretchen had told them all she knew, Steve Thurston felt sick. His hands fell deeper into the void between his legs, and his stomach ached as if he were about to vomit. He heard Bob speaking to Gretchen, probing her methodically for details until she, too, was drained. When the hollow night fell back on them, Bob took two steps to the front of Steve's truck and tapped it twice on the hood. "Well, there it is. I'm going home and going to bed." He walked out to the street, and after two tries, his pickup started-ed. Gretchen and Steve were left in the dark and alone.

It might have been an excellent time to talk about their lives, but Steve couldn't do it. Without a word he stood up and walked to the door of his own pickup. He wanted to be away from Gretchen. He wanted to be away from everyone. He didn't even want to see her, and so he left his headlights off until he had backed out onto the road and was pointed down the highway, along the river, and west into a clear and starry night.

He thought he might find a quiet bar and drink, but it was only a thought. Instead, he let the pickup drive itself, and as if the truck knew only the way to Steve's job site, he found himself sitting in the driveway of the big new house where he had been working all summer. He got out, hoping that the cold night air would ease the pain in his stomach. He looked up at the stars but felt nothing. It was his intention to sit on the bundle of building material that had been delivered to the side of the house in preparation for the next week's work. But when he got to the pallet he saw that the cottonwood that he had cut into pieces had not yet been cleaned up. Before he knew it, one of the six-foot-long limbs was in his hands. He hefted it as if he were selecting a baseball bat. The first swing took out the huge front window. He swung it hard enough to break the molding along each side, then moved to the other windows on the first floor. He swung and screamed until he was exhausted and the house looked as abandoned and abused as old Rudy Swiegert's place had looked on the night Carl had played his bagpipes. He stood before the house, with the battered cottonwood branch in his hands, and sobbed until the club slid from his grip. He moved away from the house and what he had done, until his back hit the pickup truck.

Once inside the cab he felt safer and spun the tires around in the new driveway. He followed the highway into the night. The river lay to his left, and when the oxbows were just right, the reflected moonlight shimmered like ice, but when the road turned to change the angle, the river went bottomless black and he could have been anywhere on earth. He did not let the pickup gallop; he idled along the road as if piloting an electric golf cart, quietly and seemingly without effort. Perhaps an hour passed before he began to think of his father.

The emotion that struck him was fear. Preposterously, he felt suddenly alone and unprotected. Arvid had not fulfilled the role of guardian for decades, but he had always been there: the older generation, the keeper of all the knowledge a person needed. Weak as he might have been, he had somehow always been the one with final responsibility. From that night forward, everything would be different. Now the ranch was totally gone. There was nothing left of the Thurstons except himself and Bob. He thought of the bar again. He thought of calling Carolina Riggins. But all he could do was drive.

By midnight he was far into the hills where the Pawnee originated. Rough sagebrush country that would soon become Wyoming. Perhaps the land had already become Wyoming. He was like an animal driven from his territory. He felt as if he were floating, unsure of exactly where he was or where he was going. It frightened him to know that now such feelings would become commonplace. Then he knew what the horseless Lakotas had felt as they moved westward, away from what had been their valley and away from Henry McDermot. A long line of burdened women moved along the road ditch. The few remaining horses of the warriors did not see the pickup. Their heads were low; the war paint on their rumps and shoulders was smudged and faint. He slowed the pickup even more as he moved past the column. He tried to look into the eyes of the people, but their faces were blank.

The encounter shook him out of his malaise, and when he came to an asphalt road he rubbed his face and forced himself to figure out where he was. He had traveled a hundred miles without realizing it. If he went north he would hit the highway and could be back at his trailer in an hour and a half. He was too far from home, and suddenly it was important to get back. There was still a brother who had suffered the same loss that he had suffered. A dull worry replaced self-pity in his consciousness and gave him at least a sense of purpose as he drove. By four thirty, when he pulled up in front of his trailer, he was cursing his selfishness for not thinking of Bob. He, after all, was the fragile one.

All the way home Steve had imagined the worst, his brother pacing the floor, sleepless and tormented. But when he came into the trailer Bob was not sitting on the couch watching mindless television as he was prone to do when troubled. Steve moved quickly through the few rooms of the trailer, and to his surprise found his brother asleep in his own bed. Steve stood over his brother for a minute and knew that the rhythmic breathing was genuine. It was the sleep of the just and Steve shook his head with sudden, complete exhaustion. Tomorrow, he thought, would be a new day. It was something that his father had often said.

☜ **49** ☞

Steve felt the tiny morning light outside his eyelids, as if the sun was warning him. He had been dreaming of Carl Lindquist, playing his bagpipes as he walked the hills above the Pawnee. The music came from all directions, and when Carl turned to look at him, his eyes were wild and his bare chest was smeared with blood. The dream had told him what was happening. It had taken his breath away to realize how he had missed the danger in the situation, and now the dream was gone and he was gripped with panic. Even before he opened his eyes, Steve knew his brother's bed was empty and he knew exactly where he had gone.

He burst from the rickety trailer door with his shirt in hand and saw the vacant space where Bob's pickup had rested next to his. If he squinted he could see a trail of blue where the tires left their mark, backing up on the gravel, then doubled until they lined out on the road that led to the Pawnee River valley. It would have been possible to follow those blue lines, but he knew where they were going, and once in his own pickup, Steve sped after his brother faster than his eyes could have ever tracked him.

Even at breakneck speed the morning prairie pulsed with the ripeness of late autumn and the last rush to store its energy for winter. The browns with breathy greens surprised Steve. With the ranch gone, and now his father gone too, it had not occurred to him that things would go on as they always had. The breeze gathered in the tops of the cottonwoods and Steve knew without thinking that it would slip down and strengthen as the day passed. All the landscape was slow in the morning, and in the rocketing pickup there was the mushy feeling of being invisible, as if he would pass through a deer unnoticed if it jumped from the ditch.

Carl's yard was about like he knew it would be, lined by Carl's pickup, Eleanor's car, Bob's pickup, and John Tully's new Dodge. There was only one surprise. Gretchen's Jeep was parked closest to the back porch, and Steve slammed to a halt just behind it. He burst through the door and into the kitchen. A deck of cards was stacked in the center of the table and a pair of cards lay face down in front of the two chairs. He pushed right through the house and found Eleanor and Gretchen sitting at one of the front windows. They were bathed in morning light and held coffee cups suspended in their hands. Their faces were stark and neither bothered to stand as Steve stood over them. Their eyes told him what he needed to know, but as he passed the kitchen table, he flipped over the cards and found a three of spades and the jack of hearts. He was back behind the wheel of his pickup before the screen door slammed.

The meadow pasture gate was open and told him that they had gone that way. The rise above the old Butler corral would be his best bet, and as he bounced past the sorting chute he refused to acknowledge the wave of old Edward Butler standing in the center of the corral with huge roweled spurs and a horsehair rope lithe in his gloved hands. The view from the hilltop was long and eternal but Steve scanned the near distance. Like searching for nervous water on the ocean, he let his eyes rove the contours. Carefully, up one draw and down the next, straining for movement that finally came in the shape of a flowing white dog. He was already moving toward the dog when the hunters came into view. He was calculating how to reach them and knew instantly that the pickup was no good. The draws were too deep, and with the building wind rolling toward him even the horn was useless.

He took the pickup as far as he could before bailing from the door and plunging on racing boots toward the bottom of the first of several draws that undulated perpendicular to his path.

His arms cartwheeled, and it hit him hard that this was not country to be afoot, that cowboy boots belonged in stirrups, and by the time he reached the bottom of that first hill, he was as winded and scared as a man lost in the black woods. It was a new sort of fear that pushed him, gasping for breath, to the top of the hill where he caught a flash of hunter orange disappearing into a thicket, still two draws away, and that flow of white forever coursing in front. Still too far to call out. And what would he say? Stop? All of you stop? Go back? Change the world? He plunged down again, and this time he stumbled, as he was afraid he would. But he did not try to stop himself. He rolled through sage and wheatgrass and snowberry, and the smells of each, crushed beneath his body, filled him with memories and bitterness. At the bottom of the hill his knees found soft ground and he knelt, humbled and panting, until he could move again.

The top of the next hill found him closer but still winded, so that his voice was weak and unheard. But the hunters, clearly four of them, were beginning to spread out in a bowl with its own set of draws and hillocks. There was nothing to do but push ahead. One more dip and then into the basin of the hunters. They would think he was mad, and maybe he was. Maybe he was crazy and always had been. Maybe none of this was happening, and he was still in his wretched trailer, sleeping in his wretched bed.

When he gained the high ground, he was closest to Carl Lindquist, and from his eyes Steve knew that he was not in his own bed and that he was not crazy. The eyes were narrow like he'd never seen them. Behind Carl stood John Tully, and Carl stepped to shield John from having to look at this panting, scraped, and sweating dervish. Tully might well have thought that Carl was shielding him from a jealous and violent man, but neither

Carl Lindquist nor Steve Thurston was so deluded. "Bob," Steve panted.

Only Carl's eyes betrayed the pact he had made early that morning, and when Steve turned to look, he saw Leo's white flag of a tail. It flicked twice at the top of the swell and dove down and out of sight in the depression where Bob and Dr. Cring must surely be hunting. A last and fleeting wild look to Carl and Tully, Steve ran up the hill to look down into the valley he had always suspected might be waiting for him.

Tolstoy had never looked prouder. He stood nearly on tiptoes, his tail elevated and even his chin high with the smell of invisible grouse. Holding the shotgun high, pointing to the sky but with a finger at the ready, Bob looked awkward. Wheezing for breath and trying to shout, a moment of clarity settled on Steve. His brother hadn't held a gun since 1969, but with their father's old Mossberg in his hands, he looked cold and oddly calm. Cring rushed forward to flush the birds and began his swing the instant the first bird rocketed from the grass. In unison the two men swung their guns, but just as Cring's barrel caught up with the fleeing grouse, Bob's barrel swung to the back of Cring's head. Steve found a single word: "No." But his voice was drowned in the roar of the twelve gauge.

When the silence fell, it crashed. Cring kicked once and lay still only ten yards from Bob's feet. They could have been granite statues depicting defeat, or triumph, or chaos, or revenge. Even Leo stood solid, his focus on the remaining birds too strong to be shaken by death. Only Steve moved, but there was no more need to hurry. He walked slowly to his brother, and before he took the shotgun from his hand, he reached his right hand out and patted his shoulder. "It will be okay," he said. "I saw it. It was a hunting accident." But already he felt eyes on his back and heard the sound of the other hunters. Before Steve turned to see that Tully had been at the top of the hill overlooking everything, he looked to Leo, who still stood tall, intent on the remaining birds. Bob's gun was secure in Steve's hand when another bird came up, and instinctively the old Mossberg came to Steve's shoulder and began to swing. The silver sighting bead at the end of the barrel raced to catch up but swung far ahead of the bird without the pulse of the hammer-fall. The bird careened safely over the hill and the silver bead stopped its arc at the center of John Tully's chest.

If there was any sound in that tiny valley Steve Thurston did not hear it. He felt the weight of the gun and savored the curve of the trigger. He let his gaze drift upward from the gunsight until it met Tully's eyes, and what he saw was a profound and silent fear. It was the first time in Steve Thurston's life that he felt such power. Bob and Carl were watching. Leo was still intent on what made him great. Slowly, in ones and twos, the remaining birds flushed and fled. But there was no sound. Just the feeling of power that Steve had longed for. But it was only a touch of power, a taste of champagne. It was not in Steve Thurston to pull the trigger, and when he lowered the gun, Tully sank to his knees. That, at least, Steve Thurston could savor.

☙ 50 ❧

It had been a long time since Erwin Benson had been on foot
among the Pawnee breaks at sundown. He realized, once again,
that it was the shadows that gave the prairie its depth. The early
winter grasses were a mosaic of subtle color that couldn't be seen
from a car passing a mile away. Since he was a kid he'd viewed
this land mostly from paved roads. Up close, with the light like
this, you could see a hundred shades of brown, and green, and
ocher. Erwin Benson was close indeed. Had he been younger
he would have been on his hands and knees with the sheriff's
investigators. But it wasn't necessary to be that close. He could
see the spray of blood from where he leaned with his hands on
his knees, and when he squinted at what the last deputy on the
scene pointed out, the last few seconds of Dr. Arnold Cring's life
were clear. Didn't even need to study those splatters, dried now
to blend with the browner grasses. Easy enough to see what happened here. Harder to understand exactly why.

Benson straightened from where he had been scrutinizing the
scene and looked around to the raucous yellow of the crime-scene
tape. No one had attempted to fashion the outline of a body from
the tape, just an X over a huge incongruous spot of darkest brown
where Cring had bled out. Another X where the oldest Thurston boy had stood. The young one, Steve, the one Benson knew
from years before, rated only an eight-inch orange flag tied to a
bush—was it buffaloberry? He stood right there, Benson thought.

Said he took the gun from his brother. And Tully? Benson turned stiffly to see where Tully had come over the little hill. Must have been quite a sight. Must have seen a lot from that hill. A hill like millions of other hills in the Pawnee River valley.

The deputy had been quiet, simply watching the old prosecutor. It was not his call, but he was curious about what was going on in the old man's mind. The other officers and the state lab investigator had been gone for over an hour. The deputy was there just to make sure the old man made it back to his car, help him get out if he needed it. Benson was almost three times his age. Too old, the deputy had heard some people say, but there was something to admire in the way he walked stiffly about the crime scene in his brown suit with the bow tie still intact.

Benson was standing upright now and arched his back in a stretch. He straightened his rumpled suit coat and took one more careful look at the *X*'s and up the hill to where Tully had stood. "Too bad," he said. "Pretty place. Never be quite the same."

When they started up the slippery hill, Benson reached out and took the deputy's right elbow for support. "He ain't afraid of much," the younger man thought. He put his left hand over Benson's and tightened his biceps.

They'd driven as close to the scene as possible in the patrol car and had to take the same circuitous route back to the river road where Benson had left his Buick. It was rough country, filled with hidden draws, and twice the deputy lost his track and had to back up. Neither man spoke for a half hour and it was nearly dark by the time they got to the road. Even then, sitting in the patrol car with the bumper only a few feet from the Buick's bumper, they sat in silence watching the light retreat to the west-facing slopes.

"You ever fish?" Erwin asked.

"A little, when I was a kid back in Ohio."

"Ever have one of those reels they used to call casting reels?"

"Where you control things with your thumb?"

"It's what I learned on."

"My dad had one," the deputy said. "I tried it a few times. They were a pain in the neck if you didn't keep the thumb pressure just right."

"That's it. Backlash if you didn't apply enough pressure."

"Short cast if you squeezed too hard." Both men smiled remembering those old low-tech reels.

"Did you call the mess the backlash made a bird's nest?" Benson asked.

"Yep."

"Remember how, when you tried to straighten things out you'd have to strip line to the tangle, then straighten that and strip line the other way until you came to the next tangle?" The deputy nodded and Erwin continued. "How, to straighten it out, you almost always had to go deeper than you thought you'd have to go?"

The deputy was beginning to understand and nodded in the last rays of sunlight. They sat silent again and Benson was again impressed with the kid. He knew enough to shut up just before things were clear. "Those old reels weren't worth a shit," Benson said.

"They tell me the real pros still use them." He was a good kid. Smart.

"That's right," Benson said. "Still standard equipment for some applications. Long casts but you got to be willing to clear the bird's nests." Benson put his hand on the door handle but waited a beat before he opened the door and the hard overhead stole the last rim of light from the distant hill.

Erwin Benson was tired, but from years of experience he knew that he would gain strength if he drove slowly and didn't force his mind to think. Once he was moving, the interior of the car warmed with calmness and control and he allowed the present problem to return. He had learned only hours before that Arvid Thurston had died in the night. When the call came in about Arnold Cring, it was impossible not to put two and two together. He'd had Linda call down to the emergency room at the regional hospital, but the doctor who had been on call was gone. From what Linda learned and what Erwin now knew, it looked like Ida Miller had left town about the time Bob Thurston's gun went off.

He'd talked to everyone involved when he'd arrived at the Butler place. He started with Carl Lindquist and knew within seconds that he would get nowhere with his questions. He'd known Carl's family: old Ralf Lindquist and his wife, Sarah. They were both bright and had produced a son who had found a way to hang onto his family ranch by leaving it. No, Carl Lindquist was too smart to bother with. Besides, he'd been over the hill, said he'd only heard the shot. He questioned the Thurston kids too and the whole time had to fight the feeling that they were still the clean-cut athletes they were in high school. Of course they weren't high school kids anymore. All that innocence had begun to diffuse about 1966. It had been a tough time to be a kid. Even tougher if you were a ranch kid.

They were hard to read too. Hunting accidents like what might have happened out there, that day, in that draw, happened every year. It was hard to say, but if the Thurston kids ever had a support system besides each other, it was long gone now. Both of them were as vulnerable as a 1950s black man with a white girlfriend. When what might have happened soaked in among the new citizens of McDermot, with their keen sensitivities, there would be a clamor for the Thurstons' heads. The only insight he gained from his interviews was when he tried to talk with Tully. It was impossible to tell what Tully knew for sure. The starch had seeped out of him and he was barely able to speak. But Benson had seen this reaction before. It would not last long. It was a temporary numbness in a man who, for all Benson's misgivings about his worldview, possessed substance. He would come out of his stupor and be a player. He would be difficult to stop.

Benson kept driving the old roads and thinking until his thoughts settled on Lucy. He could remember her as the beautiful girl she was—the firmness and the color of health. The way she laughed. Her devilish nature. He had been so lucky. Even after they were married they'd driven these roads in the old coupe, drinking moonshine whiskey—a daring act for the times and a secret neither of them had ever divulged to anyone. The thought of Lucy and those late-night forays tickled him, and for the last five miles of his drive he talked and laughed with the bright, wise woman he had loved, as if she sat in the seat beside him.

It was almost nine o'clock when he got back to his office, and he sat in the darkness for another twenty minutes before he called John Tully at home. He was not surprised to hear Gretchen Harris answer the telephone. "It's Erwin Benson," he said, and they sat in silence, neither knowing just what to say, but Erwin couldn't help thinking she and Tully might not be that much different than he and Lucy. There was no way of knowing. In the silence he could feel the pressure on Gretchen building. It was unfair to let her twist, so Benson pushed on. "I imagine John would prefer not to be bothered on this unhappy night, but I'd like to speak to him. Just tell him that I'm in my office."

For a moment he thought she was going to say something about what had happened. Not just that day but all of it, starting sometime before either of them were born. But it was too much, and she didn't know where to begin. "I'll tell him," she said. "I'll tell him you're in your office."

"Thank you." Benson hung up without saying good-bye.

Gretchen turned from the phone and met Tully's eyes. "Erwin Benson," she said. "He would like to see you tonight."

Tully did not seem surprised. He exhaled and stepped to take Gretchen into his arms. She met him and pressed a cheek against his chest. "Before you go," she said, "I've got a silly question."

He took her shoulders and held her out where he could see her face. "How silly?" he asked.

They smiled at each other. "Do you still know people at the University of Nebraska?" He nodded with mock caution. "The president?" she smiled. "Maybe a board member or two?"

It was after ten fifteen when John Tully arrived at Benson's office.

After the initial nods at the doorway, the two men did not speak for several minutes. They walked silently to Benson's office where the old man took his place in the old oak swivel chair behind the massive oak desk; Tully found a seat in one of the worn brown leather chairs across from the prosecutor. That night the dark weight of the office struck Erwin Benson as musty and long out of style. The wood might once have been described as rich, serious, even dignified, but it was still musty. He imagined that Tully would change things if he were elected. Tully would run against him in next year's election, and if he won, a lot of things would change. Prosecutor's offices in other counties, other states, were stainless steel and some sort of blond wood. Perhaps the attorneys at the café were right, perhaps it was time for Lakota County to move into the twenty-first century.

"I assume," Tully began, "that you called me here about what happened this morning."

"Correct. I thought you might have gotten a chance to process things. Time to get over the immediate shock of things."

"That's going to take a while."

"I'm sure, but I thought you might have gained some insight on what happened out there."

"You're asking me to do your job?"

"Not yet. Just asking you, as a citizen and a witness, what you saw. What you think might have happened."

Tully sat up straight in the old brown leather chair and picked at one of the cracks on the arm. Erwin loved those old chairs and was annoyed to hear the tick, tick, tick of Tully's fingernail. But there was nothing he could do to stop Tully. He had to put the annoyance out of his mind, and so he focused on Tully's mouth. Waiting for the words that would come very soon.

Tick, tick, tick, as Tully considered his answer. But Benson understood nothing until the younger man spoke. "I wasn't sure what happened until I talked it over with Gretchen."

Gretchen. Yes, she would have power here. "And?"

"I didn't know about Dr. Cring and Arvid Thurston. If I had, I wouldn't have consented to going out in the field with guns. Lindquist was very careful to introduce Bob Thurston simply as Bob. Dr. Cring had no way of knowing. No one told me what happened to Arvid."

"No one is blaming you for the accident."

"Accident?"

Benson shrugged and the two men stared at each other. "Kind of my call," Benson said. They continued to stare at each other and neither man blinked until Tully's head began to nod.

"Two things," Tully said. "One, I don't think it was an accident. Two, if you don't handle this perfectly, I will beat you badly next fall."

"You don't have a chance of beating me in an election."

"I do have a chance of beating you and I have a better chance of beating you after what happened today." Tully stood slowly and stretched before moving toward the door. Benson did not look up from where his fingers tapped lightly on the dark oak of his desktop. He let Tully nearly reach the door before he spoke. "All right, John, sit your ass back down in that chair and let's talk turkey."

Tully turned back toward Benson and held his chin high. "I can hear what you have to say from here.

Benson nodded. "What I have to say is this: I'm tired. I'm thinking of going fishing."

"Fishing?"

"Permanently. It's possible that I could be convinced to resign my position as prosecutor. I think you'd have a better chance of winning a special election to fill my position. You'd be running unopposed."

Benson pointed to the chair and Tully shrugged and took his seat again. "Exactly what would it take," Tully asked, "to convince you to resign?"

❧ 51 ❧

Arvid's funeral was small and quickly planned. Steve borrowed a backhoe from the construction site and ran the machine while Bob worked the ground. He moved the wrought iron fence and stood between the backhoe's bucket and their mother's grave. The coffin arrived from town in the shiny Cadillac at one o'clock, and the two tall, solemn men from the funeral home stood watching the backhoe work with disapproving expressions on their long faces. Steve watched them from the corner of his eye and hurried with the digging. But eventually the older of the two moved to Bob, and Steve saw that they were talking about their father's coffin. Finally Bob threw up his hands, went to the back of his pickup, and came back dragging two chains. He laid the chains out parallel and four feet apart. The older man nodded and Bob walked to the side of the backhoe and drew his finger across his throat.

It only took a few minutes for the four of them to wrestle the wooden coffin to a position on the chains. "It's not usually done this way," the older man said.

"We'll handle it," Steve said.

"Be sure the chains are tight."

"We'll handle it."

"If they slip off the bucket and the coffin tips . . . "

"Thanks," Steve said and walked toward the backhoe. The man tried to talk to Bob but Bob would not look at him, and finally the two crawled back into the Cadillac and drove back down the hill. They had to pull far to the right to let Carl Lindquist's pick-up pass.

It was another twenty-five minutes until the hole was deep and square enough to suit Steve. Bob and Carl and Eleanor stood beside the coffin in the wind and watched in silence. When the hole was ready Steve raised the levelers on the backhoe and backed around so that Bob and Carl could bring the chain ends up and attach them to the bucket. The coffin was very light and floated in the air like the thousands of cottonwood leaves that had just that day begun to fall. Carl and Bob stood at opposite ends of the grave and motioned to Steve with twitching fingers. Eleanor stood on the far side of the grave and was revealed to Steve only as the coffin disappeared into the hole. When the load was settled, the chains were detached and pulled out with the bucket. The backhoe was parked outside the fence, and when the diesel engine clanked to a stop the sound of the prairie wind suddenly filled the void.

Steve took his place between Bob and Eleanor and opposite from the mound of dirt that would soon cover his father. It wasn't until that moment that they realized that no final words had been prepared. The four of them stood staring into the grave until a gnawing embarrassment made Steve raise his head. When he did, his eyes fell on the eyes of his mother, standing at the head of her own grave. On the grave rested the bleached skull of a horse. Beside his mother stood her own mother and father, Carl's grandparents. A group of tall, blond women, drawn at the eyes, were surrounded by tow-headed children and broad-shouldered men with long, rough hands. Edward Butler leaned on one of the corner posts that supported the graveyard fence. Rudy Swiegert stood slump-shouldered beside two other men in cowboy hats. McDermot himself stood between tall Lakota braves, and horses grazed beyond. Steve nodded to them but felt only a deeper embarrassment for not having something to say for his father.

Then, like an answer to a prayer, Eleanor began to hum. She had completed only two notes when Carl, in a surprising baritone, began to add words. "Amazing grace," he sang.

Somewhere in Steve's mind the words roused and struggled to the surface. "How sweet the sound."

Then, hesitant but strong, came Bob's hollow-log bass. "That saved a wretch like me."

The days had been shortening so it was nearly dark as Steve methodically and carefully pushed the prairie over his father's coffin. The wind had not quieted and it was getting cold, but Bob remained at his post, leaning on a shovel between the graves of his parents. He watched the dirt cascade downward. Because the backhoe cab was six feet off the ground, Steve saw Benson's Buick coming up the hill first. It came slowly, just the way an old man would drive, slowly but steadily, and Steve felt dread as the car approached. When the car was close enough for Bob to hear it, he looked up from the nearly filled-in grave for only an instant. As the car came to a stop, Bob scooped a small shovelful of soil from the grass and added it to the mound in front of him.

Steve did not let Benson's presence hurry him. He let the backhoe bucket smooth the dirt over the grave, then backed away so Bob could move the section of wrought-iron fence back and attach it to the corner post. The Buick pulled up close to that post, and Benson pulled himself out. There in the wind and the long, afternoon sunlight the three met like traders from disparate worlds.

"I'm not even going to ask you what really happened," Benson began. "At this point, it doesn't much matter."

The Thurstons stood hickory-faced. They would let Benson speak his piece and give him no ammunition.

"It hasn't started yet," he said, "but it will. The people of this county are going to start adding things up and then they're going to want to know how Cring came to be dead."

Bob measured his words. "You're saying that you're going to charge somebody with something?"

"I'm not saying that." Benson folded his arms across his chest with his hands tucked tight against the wind. "I'm not prosecuting anyone. Never again." The Thurstons waited for an explanation. "I'm going to resign my job. There's going to be a new prosecutor in Lakota County."

"And he's going to bring charges?"

"He said he wouldn't. But politics is a funny thing. I wouldn't guarantee it. If you two are walking the streets there will be a lot of pressure."

The wind had begun to settle for the evening. The cold from the clear sky was coming down. The last light of the day was flat and pale. Bob and Steve glanced at each other and tried to understand. When they looked back to the old man, Steve spoke for them both. "You're saying we should leave."

"Your presence would just be an irritation."

"You're giving up your job?" Bob asked.

"Hell," Benson said. "It's time."

Steve couldn't imagine Lakota County with a different prosecutor. "What are you going to do?"

Benson moved to his car and slid into the driver's seat. It seemed as though he was not going to answer, but once settled into his seat with the door closed, he spoke to Steve through his open window. "Ever hear of place called Belize?"

"I guess I have."

"Well, it's warm down there," Benson said. "They got an ocean and the ocean's full of big, blue fish." He smiled to think of it. "I'm going to catch some of those goddamned fish." The smile remained on his lips and he started to roll up the window. But with one eye squinted, he rolled the window back down and motioned Steve to come closer. When Steve leaned toward him the old man looked into his eyes. "I always liked you," he said. "Always thought you'd come to something."

"Sorry to disappoint you."

"You haven't disappointed me. You have lots of time. Go away. Find a new place. Do some good."

Steve folded his arms over his chest and didn't speak. But he didn't pull away either. "It's funny how the weight falls on a man from nowhere," Erwin said. He looked at Steve and squinted one eye. "But it isn't that bad. You can handle it." Without another gesture he started the Buick and rolled up the window for good. He made a slow turn to head back down the hill. He left the Thurston brothers alone beside the graveyard of their ancestors to contemplate their last night in the only land they had ever known.

❧ 52 ❧

They spent the hours before midnight going through the old house. There wasn't much to box up. Except for the goose-down coat they had bought for him the Christmas before, their father's old clothes weren't worth saving. They left them in the upstairs closet of what was now John Tully's house. All the tools in the shed were John Tully's, too. They weren't sure about the saddles and bridles, but they couldn't very well take the horses. "We got no land to keep them on," Steve said.

Bob nodded. "Well, there it is." He went back to searching the closets for relics of their past.

Steve could not stand to help and walked outside, across the yard, through the gate, and into the corral where his father had been killed. He looked over the broken corral rail and the overturned oats barrel. All he could do was stand with his hands at his side and his head bowed. Then he felt a pressure at the back of his neck and turned to face the three horses, motionless and staring as if they did not recognize him. But when he spoke their ears relaxed and the horses began to shuffle his way. They encircled him and, one by one, he touched their faces and stroked their chests. His chin quivered and he pressed his forehead against Blacky's neck. "I know I never told you," he said. "I'm not good at it." Tears materialized and began to soak into the horse's hair. "But you were the best." He pushed his face harder into the strong ebony neck. "There was never a horse like you."

In the end they took only a small box of things that had been their mother's, the coat, and a portable welder that Steve had bought at an auction two years before. They left the welder in the back of Bob's pickup and left the pickup in one of Carl Lindquist's sheds. There wasn't much to say to Carl or Eleanor, so they hugged all around and drove silently back to McDermot. It was after two in the morning when they got back to the house trailer.

They sat looking at the trailer for a full minute. "I hate this fucking place," Bob said.

Steve snorted and nodded his head. "Me, too."

"I'm not sleepy. Let's just pack 'er up and hit the road."

They were still sitting in the pickup and staring at the trailer. Steve's head began the tiny nod again. "Suits me," he said.

The phone was ringing when they opened the door but neither of the brothers bothered to pick it up. They found large garbage bags under the sink and filled them with pots and pans, dishes, and silverware. All the time they were wondering if any of it was worth the effort. The phone rang again at a quarter to four, but by then they had moved to their respective bedrooms and were stuffing more garbage bags with clothes. Steve considered leaving the two trophies he had won at high school rodeo but decided he'd take them along. There was no telling where they'd end up. They might mean something to the people who lived wherever they landed.

The garbage bags piled up at the front door along with a pair of floor fans and the old vacuum cleaner that neither of them had used since Gretchen and Jake had begun dropping by to clean. "What about the beds and the furniture?" Bob asked.

"They aren't worth much," Steve said.

"Guess you're right about that."

They stood looking at the mountain of garbage bags. "None of it's worth a shit," Bob said, and Steve had to laugh.

"Well, there it is," he said, and that made Bob laugh.

It was still dark when they started loading the bags into the back of Steve's pickup, but anyone who was paying attention could feel the sun gathering itself behind the eastern ridge. The pickup was backed up to the front door and nothing was so fragile that it couldn't be tossed in. Their belongings filled the pickup, but once it was tarped down the load was only level with the bed rails. They took a last look around inside the trailer and Steve pulled the door shut. "I'd leave the key in the mailbox if we had a key."

A few cars were beginning to move on the streets, and Steve wondered what their headlights looked like from above. The town was waking up, but the Thurston boys wouldn't see it in daylight. The engine started and Steve switched on the lights. It was a good pickup, and he let it warm up for a minute while he waited for a car to pass the end of their driveway. But the car slowed and pulled in beside the pickup. It was a red Jeep, and the brothers watched silently as it came to a stop and Gretchen slid out.

She moved to Steve's open window, put her hands on each side, and leaned to eye level. Nothing came to her for a moment. Then, "You know where you're going?"

Steve shook his head. "I guess, West. Somewhere where they're building houses." He grinned. "You know where you're going?"

"I'm going to be waiting at TCBY when it opens. Going to talk a young lady into going to college." She looked into the back of the pickup. "You got all your stuff?"

"There's some junky furniture inside. Guess the landlord will take it for the rent." He thought for a second. "And there's three old horses out at the place." He looked at his brother. "I guess Jake can have them." Bob nodded and Steve looked back at Gretchen. "Get him to ride them for us."

She nodded. "Will you come back?"

Steve shrugged and looked straight ahead. He shifted the pickup into first gear. "We'll have to see."

Then there was silence and Gretchen took her hands from the car door. "You take care." She stepped back and the pickup began to roll. Steve glanced into the rearview mirror only once. Gretchen stood in the driveway watching after them but as they turned onto the street, she disappeared. The river was ahead of them and so Steve turned the pickup toward the west as soon as he was able. The sun had just cleared the eastern horizon and neither brother wanted to see the long, morning light begin its eternal march across the valley of the Pawnee.

Other Works by Dan O'Brien

Novels

The Indian Agent
The Contract Surgeon
Brendan Prairie
Center of the Nation
Spirit of the Hills

Memoir

Buffalo for the Broken Heart: Restoring Life to a Black Hills Ranch
Equinox: Life, Love, and Birds of Prey
The Rites of Autumn: A Falconer's Journey Across the American West

Short Stories

Eminent Domain

Photography

(with Michael Forsberg) *Great Plains: America's Lingering Wild*

In the Flyover Fiction series

*To order or obtain more
information on these or other
University of Nebraska Press
titles, visit*
www.nebraskapress.unl.edu.